PRAISE FOR J. A. ROST'S
RIVER FALL MYSTERY SERIES

"J. A. Rost's engaging River Falls Mystery Series is an immersive and suspenseful adventure with twists and turns around every corner. Her character development will have you connecting with every high and low in this exciting and relevant story line."

—JIMMY PRUITT, SENIOR CAMPUS PASTOR,
OAK HILLS CHURCH, TX

"The River Falls Mystery Series by J. A. Rost is packed with all the mystery and romance one hopes to get when you sit down to a book of this genre. It tips the scales when you add miracles? They are great reading, not only for those who believe in God, but, also those who are unsure of where they stand in their journey."

—TRACEY ANDERSON & MARK ANTHONY,
KOOL TV, ALEXANDRIA, MN

"With a knack for captivating a reader's interest with the fictional pen, J. A. Rost utilizes the world of make-believe to force one to rethink their own family, peers and community while, at the same time, contemplating the authenticity of one's personal faith and moral fiber. Is Christ's *"Golden Rule"* a command or merely a suggestion?"

—JOHN TAPLIN, PASTOR,
NEW LIFE CHRISTIAN CHURCH, ALEXANDRIA, MN

BOOKS BY J. A. ROST

RIVER FALLS MYSTERY SERIES

Secrets in the High Rise (2017)
No Reasonable Doubt (2018)
Saved by Grace (2019)

J. A. ROST

SAVED BY GRACE

River Falls Mystery Series | Book Three

Copyright ©2018 by J. A. Rost

Printed in the United States of America

All rights reserved. No part of this publication may be reproduced, stored in a retrieval system, or transmitted in any form or by any means—for example, electronic, photocopy, recording—without prior written permission of the publisher. The only exception is brief quotations in printed reviews.

ISBN: 978-0-9991751-3-2

Scripture taken from THE HOLY BIBLE, THE NEW INTERNATIONAL VERSION ® Copyright ©1973, 1978 1984 by International Bible Society. Used by permission of Zondervan. All rights reserved.

Scripture taken from THE HOLY BIBLE, KING JAMES VERSION.

This book is a work of fiction and any resemblance to any person, living or dead, any place, events or occurrences, is purely coincidental. The characters and story lines are created from the author's imagination and are used fictitiously.

Cover River Scene photography by J. A. Rost
Cover Design and Interior Formatting by Crystal L. Barnes.
    www.crystal-barnes.com

ACKNOWLEDGEMENTS

To my daughter, Officer Cindy Rost of the St. Paul, Minnesota Police Department for her help in researching the forensics and legal views of law enforcement in Minnesota.
To my daughter, Jodi Berning, owner of Broadway Floral in Alexandria, Minnesota, for the use of her flower shop as the setting for both No Reasonable Doubt *and* Saved by Grace.
To my two beta readers, Jennifer Petler and Andrea Culpepper, who took time out of their busy schedules to review the book and give their feedback.

DEDICATION

To my grandchildren: Jasmine, Benjamin, Derek, Abbygail and Carter

"Do not forget to entertain strangers, for by so doing some people have entertained angels without knowing it."
—Hebrews 13:2

CHAPTER ONE

A river runs through the small town of River Falls, Minnesota, creating a divide between the residents, tourists, and seasonal cabin owners. There are only a few bridges to connect the two sides of the river in the county.

A few days before Valentine's Day, Azalea Jasmine Rose, owner of Roses N'More Flower Shop, made it her personal mission to deliver a special bouquet to Jennifer Williams, who lived on a gated estate along the river. Her late husband ordered and paid for the bouquet to be delivered to Jennifer for Valentine's Day. He died the day they moved into their new home several months ago.

Azalea wanted to deliver the flowers in person in case Jennifer needed prayer. After her husband's death Jennifer turned into a recluse and seldom ventured out to her job as CEO of The Pearl Candy Company.

She pushed the buzzer on the intercom near the gate. "Roses N'More with a flower delivery for Mrs. Williams."

"The gate is open," announced the Hispanic housekeeper on the other end.

She needed the long drive as she approached the house to calm the butterflies in her stomach. It had been over a month since Elena Wadsworth, Jennifer's personal assistant and Wade Williams' killer, was arrested following her attempt to poison Azalea and Mark D'Angelo, Elena's partner in crime. Mark's death, along with the death of Wade Williams, and the arrest of Elena left the Pearl Candy Company in turmoil.

Jennifer stood at the open front door and waved to Azalea. Both grew up in the small town, but Jennifer's successful candy business left her separated from the average person in town. Azalea, who considered herself an average hard-working business owner, still remained friends with Jennifer even though not on a social level.

"Azalea, how nice to see you. Come on in. How are you doing after your stint in the hospital?" she inquired after Azalea stepped into the large open foyer.

"I've recuperated. No ill effects from the poison. The concern of the people in town amazed me while I was in the hospital and afterwards."

She set the arrangement down on the foyer table and started to unwrap it. Jennifer's eyes widened as she viewed the special order of tropical flowers.

"I brought this out myself because Wade called this in shortly before he died. I forgot we had the instructions in the computer until we printed out the Valentine orders for the week."

"Oh… they're so beautiful." She touched the Bird of Paradise flowers interspersed throughout the bouquet along with the lilies and roses. "Wade's favorite flowers."

Her eyes teared, and she wiped them with a tissue she held in her hand.

"I wanted to make sure you would be okay with the bouquet."

"Yes… oh, yes. Wade always sent me flowers. Didn't make sense to send candy since we own a candy factory." Her attitude changed with a slight lift to her lips. An ill attempt to form a smile.

"I'm glad. I hope things start to get better for you at the factory and at home."

"You've been a good friend, especially when you helped to solve Wade's death."

"Thank you, Jennifer. It's very kind of you to call me a good friend. I still wake up some nights in a cold sweat reliving the nightmare of being poisoned. Time and praying for peace has made it easier for me."

"I wish prayer would help me right now."

Azalea reached out to touch Jennifer's arm. "It will, Jennifer. Remember God does everything in His own timing. You will get peace, but only when He's ready to give it to you. Keep praying, and it will happen."

"I'm so sorry for all the trouble Elena caused you. It's a good thing she's behind bars now. Are you going to testify at her trial?"

"The county attorney already subpoenaed me. After all, she tried to murder me and did succeed with Mark and Wade, plus she attacked Sunny. I'm sure she'll be put away for a long time."

Jennifer's lips tightened in a thin line. "I want to make sure she pays for all the pain she caused. Jealousy is so overrated. There was no reason for her to kill anyone. Wade loved me, and she knew it when she pushed herself on him. His compassion for others led him to do things he knew wasn't right, but he was not a strong person and succumbed to the evil one."

"I'm sorry, Jennifer, I don't want to bring up bad memories for you."

"Yes... you're right. We need to move on with our lives." Her eyes rested on Azalea's ring. "I heard you and Mitch got engaged in the hospital. What a romantic story."

Azalea stretched out her hand to show off her engagement ring. "Yes, it took us awhile, but we finally admitted our feelings for each other. Both our daughters are so happy. Right now, we're looking for a house to fit our larger family once we're married. Steph offered to design and build us one, but I want to live close to the flower shop. Mitch doesn't care. He just wants to get married so we can start our life together."

"Have you set a date?"

"We're waiting for Steph's and Rafe's baby to arrive. I want Steph as my maid of honor, so it'll be this summer or early fall. Plus, it can't interfere with any flower holidays."

"When is Steph expecting?"

"End of July."

She got a smile out of Jennifer. "I bet they're both excited."

Azalea giggled as she remembered both Steph's and Rafe's faces once they found out about the pregnancy. "I believe they're beyond excited."

"Thank you again for bringing the flowers out yourself. If there's anything I can do for you, please don't hesitate to ask. I'm so grateful for everything you've done for me."

"You're welcome. I'll keep it in mind if I should ever need your help. I need to get back. We're swamped today with phone calls and orders. We can't answer the phones fast enough."

Before she left, Jennifer's larger frame engulfed Azalea in a hug. It seemed an unusual act on Jennifer's part as she never was a demonstrative person. Azalea returned the gesture and walked away smiling.

She drove back to town with a sigh of relief to get Jennifer's delivery done. It had weighed on her mind since she first saw the order on the computer. Her cell phone rang. Sheriff DeVries popped up on the caller ID.

I need to change the ID on my phone to read Mitch and not Sheriff DeVries. After all, we're getting married within a few months.

She pulled over to a safe spot on the road and pressed redial.

"Hello, love of my life," came the husky sexy voice over the phone.

"Hello, yourself. I hope you are not in a public place answering the phone like that."

Mitch laughed into the phone. "No, dear heart, I'm in my office. We finished our meeting with the prosecuting attorney for Elena's trial."

"Oh," her voice dropped to a dull thud.

"Are you all right?"

"Yes." She remembered Jennifer's face as she unwrapped the bouquet. "I'm returning from Jennifer Williams after delivering those flowers I told you Wade requested months ago."

A short silence. "Oh… how did it go?"

"Surprisingly well. I don't want to go through it again. I'm glad it's over."

"This weekend after your big Valentine's rush, I made plans for all of us to get away for the weekend. I thought we'd take the girls and go to Arrowwood in Alexandria. We can do some antiquing you like so much, and the girls can swim and take in some horseback riding."

"Oh, Mitch, it sounds wonderful."

"Well, it's your Valentine's gift. I can't give you flowers, but I can give you time away from the shop. I hope your mom and Sunny can take over Friday and Saturday. I reserved connecting rooms at the resort."

"I'll ask them when I return. I'm excited. The last time I left town… um… Steph and I went shopping for her wedding dress at Mall of America."

CHAPTER TWO

The day before Valentine's Day customers, more male than female, stood at the counter and waited their turn to order flowers. Even though a few months back she thought a new competitor would take business away from her, she realized most of those customers would not walk into a flower shop in the first place. They were more box store and grocery store customers. Whereas, she offered quality verses quantity. She wanted to keep Aunt Aggie's and Donna's traditions alive.

Buttercup Schmidt drove in behind her returning from her deliveries for the day. Buttercup's real name, Gertrude Abilene, irritated her, so she kept the nickname her father gave her because of her blond curly hair.

"Did you find everyone home?" inquired Azalea.

"Almost. A few stragglers. I'll try a little later in the day to get those delivered."

"Maybe you should stay here the remainder of the day and let our substitute drivers finish the deliveries. You'll be busy marking the orders complete in the computer."

"You bet, Boss." She hesitated as she put her hands on her

generous hips. "You know I wasn't too happy to know you hired extra driving help for Valentine's Day, but after seeing how fast the deliveries went today, all I can say is thank you... thank you... and thank you. Tom and Willy did a wonderful job. They sure know their way around the county."

Azalea rented several vans from a local car dealer for the holiday and hired her mother's new friend, Tom Bertrum, and his friend, Willy, to make flower deliveries throughout the county. Since they were both retired from the sheriff's department, they knew their way around and could easily find the addresses.

"I'm glad you approve. I didn't want to take away your fun, but with all the orders for today and even more for tomorrow, you'd be a nervous wreck even with one of us helping you."

"Yeah, I know. I do miss the interaction of watching customers' faces when they receive flowers, but glad we're able to do it with more efficiency this year. It was always a mess all those years with Aggie and Donna."

"Glad we're doing something right." Azalea giggled as she removed her coat to help at the front counter.

Her sister, Sunflower Lily Rose, dubbed Sunny, returned to work after several weeks off to recover from a sore jaw that turned her face black and blue. She didn't want the public to see her even though she received newspaper acclaim when she rescued Azalea from the hands of Wade Williams's killer.

Azalea's daughter, Becca, and Mitch's daughter, Natalia, arrived after school. Azalea gave them a few chores to keep them busy: sweeping up the flower scraps and assisting the designers by running for different materials to complete their bouquets.

Sheriff Mitch DeVries drove his squad car around the back of the store at closing time. As he entered the store, she gave him her best welcoming smile. Still dressed in full uniform, including his utility belt, he looked spectacular to Azalea. Both girls ran to him with hugs. Her heart remained full of thanks for Mitch's acceptance of Becca. Even though Becca's father, Jake, stayed in her life, he led more of a social existence and only paid attention to Becca when it suited him.

"I thought I'd take everyone out to eat. Are you girls ready to go?"

Both girls gave him a winsome grin and were ready to put down their brooms.

"You guys go ahead and bring me back a sandwich. We'll be here late tonight."

Mitch's eyes creased and his lips taut, he lowered his voice. "I know you're busy, but I need to talk to you about something important."

Something's up. He wouldn't carry that look unless it was serious.

"Let's step outside." She grabbed her coat and wrapped a scarf around her neck. Even though the weatherman predicted thirties and forties tomorrow, the night air still held its chill.

"Okay, what's up? Something to do with the trial?" She inquired as they stepped outside the door.

"I wish." He took a deep breath as he shook his head and pulled on his ear, a habit he developed since high school. "It would be an easy one to solve. I don't want to spoil your Valentine's Day, but I got word this afternoon Susan is being released from prison."

Azalea's hand flew to her chest. "Your ex-wife! I thought she received a ten-year sentence."

"She's been paroled. I didn't know it was even being considered. Don't know if she'll show up here. I assume she'll go to her parents."

Azalea's eyebrows creased together in a frown. "What does this mean for Natalia?"

"Susan never wanted to see Nat when she moved back to Minneapolis, so I'm not sure what her plans are right now. She hasn't contacted me in years to even ask about Nat."

Azalea crossed her arms and started to pace back and forth. "She could come back and want to be involved in her life again. Have you discussed any of this with Nat?"

"Nooo."

"Tonight might be a good time. Nat should be prepared for the possibility of her mother's return."

"Yep, I know you're right." He ran his fingers through his hair and a few strands stood on end. "The difficulty is coming up with an explanation of why she left. I want to protect her from her no-good mother. If she tries to start a relationship again and screws it up, Nat will be devastated. You're her mother now. It might confuse her with two mothers."

Azalea put her arms around Mitch's neck and smoothed those few strands of hair into place. "Mitch, I can understand a mother wanting a relationship with her daughter. You've not interfered with Jake and Becca's relationship, and I won't interfere with Nat and Susan's relationship—if Nat wants one with her."

"I don't want her near Nat. The judge gave me full custody, so if I don't feel right about it, I'm not going to allow it."

"I believe this is a time when we both need to pray and trust the Lord will lead us through this."

"Yes, you're right. I'm going to talk to Rafe tomorrow and see what his take is on this."

"Please talk to him. I'm sure he's trained in how to handle shattered families. Susan is a broken person, but I do hope she leaves us alone."

"I finally let go and forgave Susan for leaving us and getting back into drugs. Now if she shows up, I'm not quite sure how to handle it."

"After the chaos is over for Valentine's Day, I'd be glad to sit down with you, Nat and Becca. We can talk about it as a family. Of course, you still need to sit down tonight and have a personal conversation with her."

Mitch gathered Azalea in his arms and nestled his head over her shoulder. "I don't know what I'd do without you by my side."

"Well, you don't have any choice. You proposed, and I accepted. You're stuck."

He gave her a disarming smile. "I'm happy to be stuck. I'll talk with Nat tonight, but I agree we should sit down… as a family."

"Let's say a quick prayer and hope it calms your fears." They put their foreheads together and held tight to each other. Azalea began, "Father, when I'm afraid, I'll put my confidence in You. I will trust Your promises. You gave us the spirit of power, love and sound judgment. Help us now to overcome the power of fear. Give us peace of mind and heart we're doing the best for Natalia. Lord, you are our Light and Salvation, protect us from all evil so we may raise our family to love You, and they will not stumble and be afraid. Be with Mitch tonight as he talks to Natalia. Give him the right words to erase any fear she might feel. In Your name we pray."

They both said, "Amen."

CHAPTER THREE

When Azalea mentioned chaos to Mitch, she understated her meaning. Mitch stepped into the back entry by the garage at Roses N'More around noon on Valentine's Day to: first, not being able to find a close parking spot, and second, to see the employees running around like the day after Thanksgiving. No one stood still.

Azalea had two tills set up to accommodate the walk-in traffic. Bernadette, her mother, manned one of them while the other employees took turns using the other. The back room remained open to the outside cold to keep the flowers fresh as the coolers were full.

Buttercup, with a pen behind her ears, one in her hand and a clipboard in the other, frantically organized the arrangements for different areas of town. Her eyes scanned Mitch as he entered. He grinned, and she rolled her eyes.

He held up both hands. "You don't need to say anything. I can see what's going on."

"We're more organized than ever with the extra drivers. I'm delivering last minute orders, but I'm so glad for Tom and Willy this year."

Mitch knew Tom and Willy as retired deputies. Both worked for the city until the city and county combined their law enforcement agencies. Tom and Willy transferred over to the county.

"Aren't you cold back here?" Mitch pointed to her light fleece jacket.

"Not with all the running around. If I get too cold, I go up front to the chaos and am happy to get back here again."

"I'm going to say hi to Azalea and then leave."

"Good luck."

Mitch walked up front toward Azalea's work station. Her nimble fingers finished the final touches to a rose bouquet. She smiled as he kissed her on the cheek.

"How's your first Valentine's Day coming along?"

She rolled her eyes. "Does it look like fun?" Her eyebrows drew together. "I hope I don't run out of roses."

"With all the free publicity your shop got in the paper these past several months, I would think you should do a massive business."

"I hope people come in because of the quality of flowers I sell versus the publicity of finding Wade Williams body."

"I won't keep you, but I wanted to tell you in person I talked to Natalia last evening."

"How'd it go?"

"She doesn't remember much about her mother. I put away all the pictures of her when the divorce became final, so she doesn't even know what she looks like."

"You should show her a picture in case she does show up."

"I'll do it when we can both sit down and talk to her."

Karol, Azalea's oldest employee, picked up a finished arrangement and started toward the back room. Something startled her, and the vase slipped from her hands. As it hit the floor, it shattered. Her voice let out a low shriek.

"What!" Azalea glanced around to see Karol point to the floor by Azalea's station. A muskrat slipped unnoticed into the store and stood close to Azalea's feet. It proceeded to gobble up all the loose rose petals and flower greens around her station. The muskrat seemed oblivious to all the people in the store and kept on its voracious hunt. Azalea backed away from it. "Oh, the poor baby. He must be starving."

"Don't anyone move," said Mitch as he raised his arms. "If it gets scared, it might bite someone. I'll get my gloves from the squad and remove it."

While Karol grabbed a mop to clean the mess from the floor, Azalea kept an eye on the animal. Its long claws kept her from any attempt to touch it. Curious customers stretched their necks and giggled at the sight of the muskrat wolfing down the flowers.

Mitch returned with a pair of heavy gloves and reached down to pick up the animal. It did not put up a fight but kept chewing on the greens. Customers snapped pictures with their phones of the muskrat to put on social media. Azalea gathered a bag full of flower scraps and followed Mitch outside. He carried the muskrat to the back parking lot and set it free. Azalea dumped the bag of scraps on the snow. The animal sniffed at the scraps and continued to eat. She grabbed her phone and took a few pictures.

"This is so cool."

"Well, it's unusual for a muskrat to get near people. He must be desperate for food. It'll be okay for now."

"Thanks, Mitch. I better get back. There are no dull moments around here."

Mitch's laughter rang in the stillness of the parking lot. "Compared to this past year, this problem was a piece of cake."

Azalea returned to the shop and embraced the busyness. Customers still arrived as she attempted to lock the doors for the evening. She decided to stay open an extra hour for the late comers.

"Thank you all for your help today," said Azalea, as she took a quick tally of the day's receipts before they officially cashed out. "We did well. I checked the files from the last few years, and I believe we exceeded our goal."

"Hurray," sounded Buttercup as she entered from the back room. Tom Bertram and his friend, Willy, followed her. She stuck her thumb out and pointed to them. "I can't thank these men enough for their help this year."

"It was a pleasure," replied Tom with a slight blush. "Retirement sucks, and both Willy and I enjoyed ourselves today. It's so nice to walk up to a home and present them with a bouquet of flowers and see the smiles on their faces. After so many years in law enforcement you got used to seeing sadness and anger when you knocked on doors. This was a welcome reprieve."

"Ditto," said Willy. "I'd be glad to do this again whenever you need an extra driver."

"You're hired," proclaimed Azalea.

Tom walked over to Bernadette. She looked exhausted, and he wrapped his arm around her shoulders.

"How about I take you out for supper tonight? You can relax with a nice glass of wine."

Bernadette's mouth dropped open. For a moment she was speechless.

Tom's wife died several years ago, and Bernadette lost her husband over five years ago. They became friends when he strolled into the shop at Christmas to pick up an artificial poinsettia to lay on his wife's grave. She told him she did the same thing every year. He invited her to go the cemetery together, and within a short time span they started to attend different retirement functions together. She invited him for Christmas dinner with the family.

"Why, I'd love to go to dinner with you, Tom. Thank you for your invitation," Bernadette acted very formal. "I need to go home and change."

"I'll pick you up in an hour. I'm sure we'll find some place we can eat without standing in line. I need to drop Willy off, and I'll see you later."

Sunny and Azalea raised their eyebrows toward each other as they watched their mother blush with anticipation. As far as they knew their mother never accepted any invitations from men in the past five years unless it involved a group—except for Tom.

Bernadette's eyes focused on her two daughters who stood gaping at her. A strand of her teased hair dropped out of place and she blew at it with her mouth. "I think I'll rush home and shower. Sunny, would you mind digging in the refrigerator for leftovers?"

"Mom, of course not. You go and enjoy yourself. Tom is a nice man, and I'm sure you'll be safe with him."

"I better be safe. He's a former cop," her voice giddy with excitement.

"You know what I mean. He's a kind man." Sunny wrapped her arms around her mother. "Just don't wear your purple and pink sneakers," she whispered in her ear. "Wear something sexy."

"I don't own anything sexy," her mother whispered back loud enough for Azalea and the remaining employees to hear. "I'll wear one of my church outfits."

"Mom. Sunny. TMI. TMI." Azalea pretended to cover her ears and shake her head while still grinning at the two.

Her quirky mother raised Azalea Jasmine and Sunflower Lily in the flower shop until Chrysanthemum Iris came along. After the birth of their third daughter Bernadette made the decision to retire from full-time work at the flower shop and sold her share to Aunt Aggie's friend, Donna. She helped out during holidays and as a fill-in when needed. When Azalea became the new owner, she started to help almost every day after their full-time designer, Karol, broke her ankle.

"Well, I'm off…if it's okay with you?" She looked toward Azalea.

Azalea raised her arms in the air, "Go for it, Mom."

Even at sixty-five her mother's energy for life encouraged all her children to embrace their time on earth as special.

The last of the customers dribbled in while everyone pitched in to do the final cleanup at the end of the day. Barbara, Lexi and Karol were anxious to go home to their own families. Buttercup finished entering the delivery times into the computer. Azalea and Sunny each took a till and cashed out the day's receipts. The till overflowed with cash and checks.

Maybe I'll finally be in the black for the next couple of months until Mother's Day.

Azalea removed the cash and checks and stuffed them into a bank bag to take home with her. She did not want to leave a large amount of cash in the shop overnight. With no report of robberies in town for a while, she still did not want to tempt anyone. She left the tills open just in case someone did decide to break in.

"Is everyone ready to go?" Azalea asked.

She locked the front door and exited through the back door. The staff parked behind the store, so customers could use the parking lot during the day.

"See everyone tomorrow." She waved to all the employees as they walked to their vehicles.

Sunny pulled her long blonde hair out of the ponytail she tied earlier in the day to keep the hair out of her eyes. She twisted her head and ran her fingers through her hair.

"Got any plans for tonight?" Azalea asked as Sunny entered the passenger side of the vehicle.

"I hoped maybe… oh, well, I guess not."

"What do you mean by I hoped?" She started the car and backed out of the parking lot.

Sunny remained quiet for a moment and then started to pick at the green from the flower foliage under her nails. "I hoped Steve Bishop would maybe ask me for dinner."

"I didn't know you two dated."

"We haven't dated, but I started to like the guy even though he's a fuddy-duddy. I enjoy our conversations. I don't think he has a girlfriend. Maybe he doesn't like women… I don't know."

"I think he's shy when it comes to personal relationships."

"We got off on the wrong foot when we first met, but I've come to respect him and the job he does."

"Maybe he's not the romantic type. Valentine's Day is really for love. If you don't feel love for him right now, it's better he didn't ask you for a date."

"Yeah, perhaps you're right," she released a deep sigh. "Is Becca waiting for you at home?"

"I think so. I haven't had time to talk to her today. Are you sure you want to be alone tonight? You're welcome to come over."

"No thanks. I'll watch a little television to wind down and have a glass… or a bottle of wine."

Azalea glanced at her rear-view mirror and bit her lip. Her hands tightened on the steering wheel. "I think someone is following us."

CHAPTER FOUR

They arrived at Bernadette's. Azalea pulled up behind another car, but did not turn off the engine.

"Mom left the porch light on for you, but it looks like someone is sitting in the car in front of us."

The vehicle following them slowed down and then continued down the street.

"False alarm." She glanced at the vehicle and let out a sigh of relief. For the past several months her mind continued to stay on high alert.

Sunny stepped out and walked to the middle of the street to see where the car turned.

Steve Bishop opened his car door and strolled toward Sunny.

"What's the matter?"

"We thought someone followed us. Azalea's got the cash sales from today in her car, and we got worried when we saw the car tailing us."

"It's gone now."

Azalea rolled down her window as Steve and Sunny walked over. Sunny bent her head to talk to her.

"He turned down the street. Probably a neighbor going the same way."

"Phew! I guess I overreacted."

"No problem, but you better go home right away and stash the cash."

"I should've taken it to the bank and did a night deposit." Azalea hit her hand to her head. "Stupid of me not to think of it."

Sunny straightened up and faced Steve while Azalea hung her head out the window. "Nice you were here," she commented to Steve, at the same time trying to assess why her sister liked him.

They made an odd couple with Steve, not being Mr. Body-perfect but more of a Columbo-type cop, while Sunny stood tall and statuesque with her long blond hair and fair skin. Because of her previous life as a biker and private detective, she covered her tattoos under long sleeves and the jacket she wore on a daily basis.

"I hope you don't mind. I didn't know when you'd be home, so I purchased some takeout from the Chinese restaurant and hoped you'd share it with me."

Sunny turned to give a wink to Azalea. Azalea clasped her lips to keep from giggling, but her eyes sparked with humor.

"I'd be delighted," chimed Sunny as she shook her long mane of hair.

So that's why Sunny took her hair down. She hoped Steve would show up.

The ride home made her a bit sad because she would not see Mitch tonight. However, they would spend the weekend together with the girls. She did not pay attention right away to any other vehicles around her as she passed through town and started to drive out to her neighborhood.

After several minutes she noticed the same car following her again. She dialed Mitch on her cell.

"Hey, what's up?" he answered.

"I'm sure someone is following me." Her voice shook. "I

noticed the same car when I dropped Sunny off at Mom's, and now it's following me again."

"Okay, don't panic. I can hear it in your voice."

"Yeah, right. I'll do the best I can. I believe they're after my bank bag."

"How far are you from home?"

"Just a few blocks."

"Okay, I'm at your house. Drive around the alley to your garage. I don't have the squad, so I'm parked on the street. Whoever it is won't recognize my car."

"All right. I'll be there in a minute."

Her hands started to perspire as she gripped the steering wheel. She rubbed them on her jeans. She drove the car to the back alley and pressed the automatic door opener. She saw the other car turn off its lights and follow her into the alley. As she started to drive into the garage, she saw Mitch with his pistol drawn. He motioned her to continue. He stayed in the shadows close to the large door, so the other car couldn't see him. She sat in the car and was not about to exit until she knew it would be safe.

The two men exited their vehicle and walked toward her car. She noticed one draw a gun from his jacket and the other a knife, and her body froze. They still did not see Mitch. A tall lanky framed man and a short rangy figure stood a few feet behind the car.

"Come on out, lady, and give us your bank bag."

She threw the bank bag under the seat and shifted the car in reverse. The tires screeched as she hit the gas pedal. One of the men did not move fast enough and the car hit him. He flew off to one side and laid on the snowy ground. The other man grabbed the handle on the driver's side and tried to open it, but she made sure it stayed locked. He pounded the window with his pistol. It cracked but did not break.

Mitch, shocked by Azalea's action, responded and jumped out from the garage.

"Drop your gun or I'll shoot," he demanded.

The rangy figure raised his arms while he held the pistol.

"I said drop it."

He glanced toward his buddy, who laid on the ground, to see if he would be able to help him. The man clutched his limb and rocked back and forth. "My leg's broke," he hollered.

With no other choice, he dropped the gun. Mitch ran over to him. "On the ground, to your knees."

The man dropped to his knees, and Mitch handcuffed him. Several squads pulled up on the side street near the alley with sirens blaring.

Azalea drove her car back into the garage and exited. She hurried toward Mitch.

"I'm so glad you were here," she said, shoulders shaking as she hovered close to him.

He wrapped his arm around her shoulders until she quit trembling.

Without ceremony, one deputy grabbed the handcuffed man and put him in one of the squads.

"I think you better call the ambulance for the other one," he snorted. "He had a little accident."

Another deputy walked up to Mitch. "What happened here, Sheriff?"

"Attempted robbery. They followed my fiancé from the flower shop ready to rob her of her bank bag. She called… terrified. I hid out here as she drove in. I wanted to catch them red-handed, but Azalea beat me to it by backing over one of them."

The deputy shook his head and grinned. "Leave it up to the Rose ladies."

Azalea raised her head. "I wasn't about to let them get my hard-earned money."

"I'll let you men handle it from here. I'll come in tomorrow morning and fill out the report."

"Yes, sir."

The ambulance arrived and took the injured man to the emergency room. One of the squads followed to make sure he did not attempt to get away even with a broken leg.

Azalea pushed the garage door button and grabbed the bank bag from under the seat. "There's over ten thousand dollars in checks and cash."

"Azalea, your safety is worth more than a hundred thousand dollars. Don't ever try anything like you did again."

"Yes, dear," she smirked as they walked arm in arm into the house. She could feel the tense cords of muscle on his arm.

The girls heard the door slam and ran down the stairs. Becca threw her arms around Azalea and Mitch. Natalia followed close behind and clung to Mitch.

"Mitch told us to go to my room and lock the door. He said not to open it for anyone but him or you. What happened, Mommy?"

"Someone followed me home and tried to rob me of the money we made today at the store."

"Azalea, you should have…" started Mitch ready to scold her.

"I know… I know," she held up her hands in defeat. "I should have taken the bag to the night depository at the bank. I wanted to get home and didn't think anything would happen. Uff da… was I wrong."

"I'm sure it'll never happen again. Right?"

She sank down in a kitchen chair. "You bet it won't." She glanced at the clock. "It's after nine. What are you doing here?"

"First of all, rescuing you. Second, we brought take-out from the Chinese restaurant to share with you. We knew you would be hungry."

"Ah, you sweet guys. I love all of you so much. Thank you for making this a special day."

"We can reheat everything in the microwave. Girls, would you take care of it for us, please."

"Sure thing."

"Chinese, huh. I saw Steve with a bag of Chinese food for Sunny."

"Yeah, we both had the same idea. It's been a long day for you. I saw you ladies running yourselves ragged for your customers. You deserve a treat."

She licked her lips. "I love Chinese food."

After they filled their plates and ate, Natalia handed out their fortune cookies.

Azalea opened hers and let out a short snort of laughter.

"What does it say, Mom?"

"It says, *Today is your day to make your fortune.*"

CHAPTER FIVE

Their weekend trip to Alexandria ended up a restful getaway for Azalea and Mitch. The girls spent most of their time in the pool while the grownups sat in the hot tub and sipped wine. They wanted to go on a trail ride Saturday morning, but found out the horses did not work during the winter months. They ended up hiking through the woods around the resort. The girls wanted to watch a movie in the afternoon, so Mitch and Azalea drove to Main Street to take in a few antique shops. Azalea also wanted to check out some of the flower shops in town.

Saturday evening Mitch and Azalea sat down with Becca and Natalia.

"I brought several pictures of your mother, Nat. I want you to look at them."

"I don't want to see them, Daddy. She's not my mother anymore."

"I understand how you feel, sweetie, but I want you and Becca to look at them in case she comes to the house or the school to try and see you."

Becca and Natalia picked up several of the pictures, glanced at them, and handed them back to Mitch.

"Why did Nat's mother leave?" Becca's innocent mind questioned.

Mitch hesitated as he glanced at Natalia. *I guess I need to tell Becca and Natalia the truth.*

"What I can tell you is she started on pain killers after she had Natalia, got addicted, and moved to more potent drugs. As a deputy I couldn't have my wife involved in the drug scene. We fought a lot. I took Nat and moved out several times. My parents were still alive, so I stayed with them. Each time she promised to quit the drugs, so I went back. I even purchased a house believing it would keep her busy. Soon after she left town. Any correspondence ended up going through her parents in Minneapolis. We haven't heard from her since she was arrested and sentenced to ten years in prison."

Curiosity got the best of Becca. "How long ago?"

"You are an inquisitive young lady. Six years."

Becca looked at Natalia's somber face. "Nat, you were only four years old when she left."

Azalea wrapped her arms around Natalia. "We love you, Nat, and will always be here for you. In a few months you and Becca will be sisters, and we'll be the family you said you wanted."

"I know." She crossed her arms and scowled. "I hope she never comes back."

Azalea glanced over Natalia's head and mouthed the words "ouch" to Mitch. He started to pull on his ear.

Azalea thought it was time to change the subject. "How about we talk about the wedding? Let's set a date or at least a close date."

"When is Steph having her baby?"

"Middle of July, so I'm thinking sometime in August or September."

"August might be too hot," chimed in Mitch. "That is, if you want my opinion. I'd rather do it this weekend."

Azalea snuggled into Mitch's embrace. "It would be nice to do it right now, but there's a lot of planning to combine two households. We need to sell both houses and find a house which fits us. Remember, we agreed to start our new life together in a different house. With both of us working long hours, it can't be done overnight."

Natalia clapped her hands, "You could get married tomorrow."

"Not gonna happen. Zalia's right. We need to start house hunting. I would like to see us married before school starts in the fall."

Azalea gave Mitch a loving glance. "You know, it's the first time you called me Zalia. It's always been Azalea."

"It slipped out. I hope you don't mind."

"All of us girls have nicknames, but I never liked mine. Coming from your lips it sounds wonderful."

"What do I call you when you and daddy get married?"

"You can call me Azalea or Zalia, but it would mean something extra special if you called me Mom. After all I will be your stepmother."

Natalia lifted her eyes shyly to Azalea, "If it's okay I want to call you Mom like Becca does."

Mitch stepped into The Nest, a cozy, vintage-style restaurant, where many of the locals hung out. Its garish design of bright raspberry-colored walls accented with large-flowered wallpaper on alternating walls gave it the eclectic look rare to any restaurant chains. He glanced around and found Reverend Rafe at a corner table—their favorite spot to meet for coffee.

Molly, the owner, brought Mitch his standard cup of coffee with a pitcher of real cream. Rafe already hugged a mug of coffee.

"Congratulations, Sheriff," offered Molly.

"About what?"

"Your engagement to Azalea Rose, you silly man." She slapped his shoulder.

Mitch's face turned a slight shade of pink. His focus was on his daughter, and since the engagement was six weeks old, he did not think of it as an announcement.

"Thank you, Molly."

"Set the date yet?"

"It's up to this man and his lovely wife as to when their baby will be born. We're waiting so Steph can stand up as Azalea's matron of honor. We hope sometime in July."

She looked at Rafe. "Steph was just in here yesterday. She doesn't even look pregnant yet."

Rafe laughed. "Well, you talk to her about it. She thinks she's a blimp already. I told her she's beautiful no matter how she feels about herself."

"She's a lucky lady. Can I get you guys anything else?"

Rafe shook his head, "We're good."

After Molly went back to the counter, Rafe leaned over and said in a low voice, "She now knows everything about you and me."

"Yeah, I rather figured. Town needs something to gossip about."

"What's going on that's so urgent?"

"It's not urgent, but last week the Corrections Board at the State Prison for Women notified me Susan, my ex-wife, is up for parole. I know you never met her, but I'm concerned she'll show up here in River Falls. I tried to talk to Natalia, but she doesn't want to hear anything about her. She blocks it out of her mind. She says Azalea is her mother. Both of us tried to talk to her several different times, but she puts a deaf ear to what we try and discuss with her."

"It doesn't sound unusual for a child abandoned at an early age to act any different, especially when there's another female role in her life. Now she's got Azalea, and to have someone else come in and upset her tidy little world is not something she'll welcome.

Does she remember what her mother looks like?"

"No, I put pictures of her away in a box soon after she left us. I haven't seen her since. Our divorce was done over the mail. She never bothered to show up in court. I got full custody of Natalia. As far as I know she ended up getting busted for drug possession. Last I heard she went to prison for ten years."

Mitch raked his hands through his hair and started to pull on his ear. "I hoped we'd never see her again. At least not until after Azalea and I are married."

"Tell me a little bit about your ex-wife?"

"She's a con artist. Been spoiled all her life. She brought excitement to a small-town boy fresh from the country. As a cop in Minneapolis I was pulled into her world of parties. Her folks didn't want us to get married, so we eloped. I regretted it ever since. I don't regret Natalia, but I do the marriage."

"How did you ever get her to move to River Falls?"

"It wasn't easy, but I wanted Natalia raised in a small community. However, Susan found people to party with here and started using drugs again. We separated several times, but she promised to quit, and I'd move back home. She wanted to buy a house, and Jake got involved and started to show her different listings. A few months after we purchased a house, she left us."

"Did Azalea ever know her?"

"She said she knew her by sight."

"When did you start dating Azalea?"

"My divorce was final after a year of petitioning the court. Jake and Azalea were already divorced. I knew about Jake's drinking and abuse, but nothing ever went on record."

"Why?"

Mitch shrugged his shoulders. "Small town politics—one of the reasons I ran for sheriff. Jake and I competed in sports in high school, and we built up a respectable animosity toward each other ever since."

Rafe started fishing. "How well did Jake know Susan?"

Mitch hesitated, then bit his lip. "It wouldn't surprise me at all if Susan and Jake were involved since she was so adamant we purchase a home from him. Azalea told me she believed Jake was seeing someone else after they separated. Both Jake and Susan liked to party."

"Do you know this for a fact?"

Mitch shook his head. "No, just hearsay. I didn't want to know."

"Leave it alone and forget about the past. Think about Natalia now."

"Yes, you're right. I've got the most wonderful woman in my life now, and Natalia has someone who loves her as much as I do."

"All I can say is you need to set boundaries. What are your plans if and when she returns?"

"I don't know. All I know is I plan to handle it, but I'll need my friends by my side."

Rafe lifted his coffee mug and saluted. "You got it."

CHAPTER SIX

One Month Later

Mitch stood at the stove and concentrated on the meal he was preparing for Azalea and Becca when the doorbell rang.

"I'll get it, Dad. It's probably Azalea and Becca." Natalia shut her book and started for the door, glad to leave the homework behind.

In the middle of watching everything on the stove it dawned on him.

Couldn't be Azalea. She has a key to my house and wouldn't ring the doorbell.

"Nat, don't answer the door," shouted Mitch, as he threw down the potholders and leaped toward the front entrance.

"Why not?" She held her hand on the door knob.

He held the door shut. "Remember, never open a door unless you know who's there."

She backed away while he put the chain on the door. He put his eye up to the peep hole in the door.

Oh, no. I need to get Natalia out of here for a few minutes.

"Nat, please go and watch the potatoes on the stove so they don't boil over."

"I want to see who's at the door."

Mitch's voice grew stern. "Nat, please do as I say…right now."

"All right." Her lips pouted as she stomped into the kitchen.

Mitch opened the door far enough so he could stick his head out. His ex-wife, Susan, stood outside. His eyes widened at her appearance. She looked radiant as if she just walked out of a fashion magazine with her blonde hair styled and highlighted and her high-end clothes. A wave of nostalgia washed over him. He gasped. He loved this woman many years ago, but yet she betrayed him. In his heart and head, he forgave her, so he could accept the love of Azalea and Jesus Christ. His heart skipped a beat. For a brief moment some of the old feelings came back.

He shook his head.

No, this can't be happening.

"Hi, Mitch. Aren't you going to let me in?" Susan smirked.

"No." He shook his head again. "You're not welcome here." He squeezed through the door, stepped outside and shut it so Natalia did not see her mother.

"What are you doing here, Susan?" he said through tight lips.

Susan gave him an alluring smile and put her hand on Mitch's chest. He removed her hand with a swift push.

"I know we're divorced, and I'm not here to cause trouble. I want to see my daughter. I bet she's a grown-up little lady by now."

"All she remembers is the hurt she went through when you left. We've moved on and don't need you around."

"Please, Mitch." Her eyes wide and sympathetic. "I've changed. I learned my lesson. Prison life created a new me. I'm not the party girl you used to know. I just want to see Natalia." Tears started to form in her eyes.

I'm not sure I can believe those tears. She tried the same trick on me many times before.

"I'm not sure I can trust you… or if you deserve to see Nat." His eyebrows lowered and pinched together.

The forgiving process needs to start with me giving Susan a second chance. Dear Lord, please help me get through this.

"Wait here. I need to prepare Natalia." He re-entered the house and left Susan outside. "Nat, will you come here for a moment."

Her curiosity peaked, Natalia stepped out of the kitchen. "Yes, Daddy, who's outside?"

"I want to talk to you about the person outside." He gulped, not ready for this. "Remember when I mentioned your mother might come back to River Falls and want to see you."

Natalia nodded her head in mute silence. Her body started to tremble. Mitch grabbed her small frame and hugged it. He put her at arm's length and lifted her chin.

"Your mother is outside the door. She wants to see you. Remember we talked about the forgiveness process."

Natalia shook her head. "I don't want to see her."

"Nat, you need to see her one day. Whether it's on the street, in church, at school, or right now at our home. It's safer to let you meet her in our home."

"Okay, Daddy. At least I can see what she looks like."

"That's my girl."

Mitch opened the door and placed his hands on Natalia's shoulders.

"You can come in and meet Natalia. You can't stay. We're expecting guests."

"I just want to see my daughter... even if it's only for a few minutes."

Susan's eyes focused on Natalia, who twisted and moved discreetly behind her dad.

"She has your eyes, Mitch." She bent down and reached for Natalia who was now hiding behind her dad.

"You're a beautiful child. I know I haven't seen you in years, but I've been away."

"You've been in prison," spouted Natalia.

Susan's face turned red as she bit on her lower lip. "Yes, child,

I've been in prison. I hope never to go back there again."

Mitch could hear the potatoes boiling over and searing the stove top. He rushed to shut off the burner and wipe up the water. He tried to keep an eye on Susan and Natalia even though there was a wall between them.

"Let's sit over here on the couch where I can get a better look at you."

With reluctance, Natalia moved to the couch but stayed as far from Susan as possible. Susan tried to touch her hair, and Natalia pushed her hand away.

"Daddy says to never let a stranger touch me."

"You're right." Susan's eyes looked down. "I guess I am a stranger to you."

Mitch walked back in the room.

"Where did you get the money for the new hairdo and fancy clothes?" he started his interrogation but backed off to give her some space.

She answered anyway. "I spent some time with my parents. They made sure I received money to start over. I report every week to a parole officer, but I need to find work. I thought I could try River Falls, so I could see my daughter more often."

"I'm not so sure…"

The front door opened. Azalea and Becca walked in. Azalea held her key in her hand.

"The door was unlocked. It surprised me because you've been so cautious." She glanced at Mitch's set face and knew something was wrong.

Susan turned toward Azalea. Even though her hair color changed, she recognized Susan's facial features from the pictures Mitch showed her. Natalia ran over to Azalea and wrapped her arms around her waist.

Mitch stood with his mouth open, unable to utter a word.

With her arm around Natalia, Azalea walked up to Susan and

stretched out her hand. "Hi, I'm Azalea Rose, and this is my daughter, Becca." She pointed to Becca as she tried to keep a smile on her face to keep things light.

"I'm Susan DeVries... sorry, now it's Johnson." She put an emphasis on DeVries as though she was claiming Mitch and Natalia as hers.

Mitch finally got his voice. "Azalea is my fiancé, and we're getting married in a few months."

"Oh... I didn't know. Mom and Dad never said anything about it to me."

"Why would they? They haven't seen Natalia since before the divorce. Not once did they try to contact us, nor have they recognized Natalia at Christmas or her birthday. I assumed they didn't care."

"I'm sorry if we interrupted your time with Natalia. We can leave so you can have your visit."

"No!" Mitch almost shouted. "Susan came uninvited, and she can leave. If she wants to see Natalia again, she'll need to schedule a time."

I'm following Rafe's advice and setting boundaries upfront.

Susan's face dropped. "I'm sorry I stopped at a bad time. I arrived in town yesterday, and it took everything in me to get enough nerve to knock on your door."

Azalea glanced from Mitch to Natalia, who still clung to her waist. The animosity was evident in Mitch's stance and in Natalia's fear of her mother.

"I'm sure Mitch doesn't want to be inhospitable, but I agree you should call before you come over. Maybe you could pick a neutral place to meet if you want to see Natalia."

A small smile picked up the corners of Susan's mouth. "I would love to see my daughter again...that is...," she turned to look at Mitch, and her eyes pleaded, "if it's agreeable with you, Mitch?"

"In fact, if it's all right with Mitch, why don't you stay for supper? He usually prepares way too much for all of us to eat."

Mitch's eyes grew huge as he digested what Azalea suggested. *My ex-wife and fiancé at the same table. Azalea, only you would suggest such a thing. I wish I could be a better Christian like you.*

"You're welcome to stay," he said begrudgingly. "It'll give you a chance to see Nat a little longer, and it'll also give you a chance to know what a wonderful woman Azalea is, and how great a mother she'll be to Nat."

Susan's eyes lit up. "It'll be a pleasure as long as it's no extra trouble."

"All we need to do is put an extra plate on the table."

"Thank you."

"Why don't you get to know Natalia and Becca while we set the table? I'm assuming everything is ready." She looked to Mitch for confirmation. He nodded.

In the kitchen they talked in low voices. "Why did you invite her for dinner?"

"It was the Christian thing to do. Remember Jesus invited some of the worst people to eat with Him, and they converted to His way of thinking. You should give Natalia at least a chance to learn more about her mother. Maybe they'll find some common ground."

"I don't want her alone with Susan until I find out what she's up to."

Azalea gave him a puzzled frown. "What do you mean…what she's up to?"

"The old Susan didn't do anything without a purpose. When we first married, I could easily fall into her trap. I learned fast from the school of hard knocks."

"Give her a chance. At least you can say you tried."

"We'll see."

In the living room Susan tried to grill Natalia. "What grade are you in now?"

"Fifth."

"Are your grades good?"

"Yes," she hesitated. "I'm in… like… the top ten percentile of my class… it's what my teacher said at the last parent-teacher conference."

Susan pursed her lips and nodded. "Oh, impressive."

"What about you, Becca? What grade are you in?"

"Eighth grade, Ma'am."

"What does your mommy do?"

"She owns a flower store called Roses N'More Floral."

"Is it the one on Broadway?"

Becca nodded.

"Ah… I used to shop there."

"It's different now. Mom put in more unique gift shop items to attract the weekend tourists."

"Yeah, I even helped paint the inside of the store. I get to go there almost every day and help," chimed in Natalia.

"That's good. Do you walk there from school?"

"Sometimes. When it's cold Dad will pick me and Becca up and drop us off. I don't need a sitter much anymore with Azalea around."

"I see a for sale sign out in the front yard. Are you moving?"

"Yeah," Natalia's voice held her first enthusiastic feeling for the evening. "We're buying a house, so we can all live together. Daddy doesn't like this house, and Azalea's too small for all of us."

"Dinner's ready," announced Azalea.

The awkwardness of dinner proved a little too much for Azalea. Even though she tried to play the good hostess, the stress to keep conversation light gave her a headache. Susan offered to help clear the table and do the dishes.

"You are a guest. Mitch and I will handle the dishes."

"I think I'll leave and go back to the motel."

"Which motel?" Mitch inquired in his official sheriff's voice.

"Sunset Inn. If I can find a job, I'll move into an apartment."

"I'll get your coat," offered Azalea, eager to get out of the stressed environment. She walked into the bedroom and rubbed her temples before she picked up Susan's coat. The softness of the material peaked Azalea's curiosity, and she glanced at the label.

"Wow!" she whispered to herself. "This cost at least a thousand dollars."

Mitch stared across the table at Susan. The girls gave each other a sideways glance and picked up their dishes to put them in the dishwasher. They tiptoed into the living room to watch television.

Susan placed her elbows on the table with hands folded under her chin. "You never did like this house, did you, Mitch?"

He ran his fingers around the coffee cup rim. "No... but it's been fine up to now. I'm ready to start a new life."

"Jake, our realtor, thought it would be the perfect house for us." Susan's eyes roamed around the rooms. "You've painted recently."

"Okay, Susan," Mitch leaned across the table. "Cut the small talk. What is your reason for coming back here? It certainly can't be for Natalia. My parents took care of her most of the time when I worked. Who knows where you were. When I wasn't working, you thrust her in my arms."

She looked Mitch straight in the eyes. "I just want you to see I've changed and let me see Natalia. I want to get to know my daughter again."

Azalea walked back into the dining room with Susan's coat and handbag.

"Thank you," said Susan as she slipped into her coat

"Can I call you to set up a time to see Natalia?"

"Let me think about it. Call me at the Law Enforcement Center."

"Bye, girls," Susan waved to them and strutted out the door.

Mitch locked the door and hung the chain in place.

"I checked her pockets and handbag. I didn't see any sign of drugs. I found a pack of cigarettes in her purse but didn't smell smoke on her."

"Zalia, will you ever learn to stop snooping?"

"I guess not," she said with a sheepish grin.

CHAPTER SEVEN

Azalea arrived at the flower shop to find Sunny working on several arrangements on her work station.

"What are you doing here so early?"

Sunny stopped her activity, wrinkled her brow, and let out a gasp of air to blow a strand of hair back in place.

"I thought I would try some new arrangements I found on the internet last evening... while I sat by myself until after eleven."

"By yourself." Azalea's eyes widened. "Did Mom play bingo or go to one of her ladies' gatherings?"

"No," she rolled her eyes. "She went out with Tom Bertrum... again."

Azalea pursed her lips. "Oh."

"They didn't arrive back at the house until close to eleven. She's never up that late. At her age, plus when she helps here, she's always in bed before nine or nine-thirty."

"Well, she is old enough to take care of herself. Now you're starting to worry about her. The shoe is on the other foot. Remember how worried she was when you returned with bruises all over your body? You told her to mind her own business. I bet if you mention this to her, she will tell you the same thing."

"I couldn't stay at the house and face her this morning. I know I'd put my foot in my mouth if I mentioned her late night out. So instead I decided to experiment with a few new designs."

"Let's not mention it unless she says something. I'm surprised she's not here yet." She started to pull the orders for the day and put them on the bulletin board. The backfire of a vehicle sounded. "I hear Buttercup's vehicle in the parking lot."

Karol and Buttercup walked in the back door together. Buttercup's pickup made so much noise she did not realize Karol followed her into the parking lot.

Azalea whispered to her sister. "Was Mom even up when you left?"

Sunny's eyes widened as she grabbed her long strands of hair to tie back in a ponytail. "No. I heard her snoring, so I'm sure she'll be late."

Azalea wished her dark tresses were long enough to pull back. Her hair remained thick and heavy and the strands of hair strayed out of the bands as she worked throughout the day. She wanted to grow her hair out for her wedding, but it continued to hang at an uncomfortable length which made her feel awkward.

The crew gathered in a circle for their morning prayer before they opened the doors.

"Heavenly Father, please guide us today as we go about our daily work. Help us to provide what is needed for those customers who come to us today. Whatever our tasks let us work at it from our souls for the honor and glory of God. Any special requests?"

They all shook their heads. "Okay, let us serve the Lord today. Amen."

"Amen," all replied.

An hour later Bernadette rushed in, face flushed, devoid of her makeup and Carnation Red lipstick.

"Good morning," she cheerfully shouted as she bounced on her toes into the shop.

They all stopped their work and recognized her coat was askew and her gray hair not brushed.

"I know I look a mess, but I overslept. I thought I'd bring everything here and fix myself up."

Azalea bent her head to keep from laughing and refused to make eye contact with her. She never saw her mother without makeup and lipstick in place, much less not having her hair fixed.

Sunny turned around and winked at Azalea. "The way you snored this morning, I thought you'd sleep all day."

Bernadette gave her daughter a stern glare. "I happened to go out last night to the movies. After the movies Tom suggested we go to the bar for a nightcap. It's not a normal thing I do, but I thought why not."

"I hope you enjoyed yourself. You need a night out," Azalea's big goofy grin gave away Sunny tattled on her.

"We enjoyed ourselves." Her eyes caught Azalea's grin. "Azalea wipe the smirk off your face. I need to tell you who we saw last night."

Everyone turned toward Bernadette.

Azalea whipped around to the display floor to make sure there were no customers in the store. "Okay, give."

"I know you told me Mitch's ex, Susan, is back in town. We saw her working at the Corner Bar."

Azalea rolled her eyes. *Oh dear, I hoped she would leave town.*

The room silenced as they waited for Azalea to comment.

The grin faded from her lips. She jabbed a pick and card in a vase of flowers. "I guess there's nothing we can do about it. She's out on parole and needed a job. I suppose she still wants to get visitation with Natalia. Mitch says she's going to have to go to court to get visitation rights." She sighed as she carried the flowers to the delivery table.

"All I can say is, she sure does flirt a lot. Last night she flirted with two deadbeats who were giving out tips like crazy. Tom said they were too strung out on drugs to care."

"In defense of her, it doesn't mean she's back doing drugs."

Karol raised her finger and interjected. "We saw her the other night after my husband picked me up from work." Everyone turned toward her. "I didn't want to say anything, but we saw Jake at the bar flirting with her. The bartender needed to call her away several times to get her to wait on customers."

"What did Jake do?" Azalea grew curious.

"After the bartender gave him a few dirty glances, he looked embarrassed and left as soon as he finished his beer."

That's unusual. I always believed Jake did a little philandering before and after we divorced. It wouldn't surprise me if he was attracted to Susan before she left town... and now she's back.

"I need to give her the benefit of doubt. She's trying to go straight, but working at a bar is not the right job." She turned to Sunny. "You've been friendly with Detective Bishop... right?"

"He's still a little shy."

"Do you think you could do your private eye thing and keep an eye on Susan... or talk to Steve about her? She doesn't know you guys. I'm worried about her having a negative influence on Natalia."

"It wouldn't be hard to keep an eye on her as long I can keep a low profile. I'll talk to Steve and see if he'll be my escort to the bar. I'll be starting to paint the inside one of Steph's and Rafe's rehab projects next week, so I hope you won't need me every day here."

"Just take care. I know the Corner Bar's reputation."

Karol cleared her throat, "I should also mention Callie Weber's also working at the bar. We've seen her several times. She buys a lot of pull tabs, and she was getting pretty chummy with Susan and flirting with the same two men."

"I wonder if she's spending all her wages on pull tabs."

"I don't know Callie," said Sunny, "but I do remember Steph

telling me about what happened at the high rise and her involvement."

"Yeah…Callie was a disgruntled employee and caused Steph a lot of stress. Both she and her husband asked Rafe for help to save their marriage. He gave them names of professional therapists."

"Wasn't she doing drugs while working at the high rise? If so, maybe she's involved again. I'll talk to Steve. The drug task force should know if she's under suspicion. We would both have to wear disguises if she knows who Steve is."

County attorney, Sam Harris, walked into the Law Enforcement Center and asked for Mitch.

Mitch walked out of his office with an outstretched hand. "Hey, Sam, what's up?"

"Could we talk for a moment?"

"Sure, come on back."

Sam seems a little disturbed. I know he's been under a lot of strain lately with the Williams and D'Angelo case.

"Okay, Sam, what's on your mind? I know it's not your normal procedure to drop in without a call beforehand."

"First, I wanted to tell you those two men who tried to rob your fiancé were able to put up bail money. A bondsman stopped in the judge's chambers today and paid their bail. It was set at fifty thousand each, and I can't believe they'll be released. I wanted to give you heads up. I don't want them to skip town before their trial next month."

"I can't believe the judge even set bail for them. They're a flight risk. What's the matter with the judge? He's been a little loose with letting people out on bail in the past few months."

"Yeah, I know. It's why I'm advising you right now. The papers should arrive shortly for their release."

"Thanks for the warning. The big guy still has a walking cast on his leg, so he won't be running too far. Now I need to let Azalea know."

"Do you think there might be some retaliation against her because she hit the guy?"

"Good question. I don't know if either one of them learned their lesson… do not mess with the Rose sisters."

Sam laughed. "Yeah, good one, and as far as I can see…true."

CHAPTER EIGHT

"Azalea," Mitch cleared his throat. "I need to talk to you, and it's rather urgent."

Azalea held the phone on her shoulder as she continued to work. "Mitch, I'm in the middle of getting arrangements prepared for a funeral. Buttercup's standing here waiting for me to finish the last one, so she can deliver it. What's up?"

"I hate to tell you this but the two men who tried to rob you…"

Azalea stopped work and grabbed the phone with her hand, a worried frown on her face. "Okay, what happened?"

"They made bail. Their trial is next month, but they are now free until their hearing."

"You're kidding… right?"

"Nope."

"Do you think they might cause trouble for me?"

"Well, let's hope not. If they do, I can throw them back in jail for harassment. The judge will have to deny them bail if anything happens."

The bell clanged above the front entrance. Stephanie McGowan, Reverend Rafe's wife and Azalea's best friend, rushed in. A long trench coat covered her pregnancy. Steph was busy overseeing the construction of a new apartment complex being constructed by the river and flipping older homes for resale.

Azalea waved a greeting with her spare hand.

"I've got you for protection, so I'll leave everything in your hands. Steph just arrived so I gotta go. Love you." She made a kissing sound into the phone and hung up.

"Hey, Steph. You're looking…or not looking like you're even pregnant."

"Oh, I definitely feel like a blimp. I know the weather's getting nicer, but when I meet with the crew at the site, I don't want to appear big and fat…so I wear this loose-fitting coat."

Azalea laughed. "You don't have to worry about being big yet. Wait until your eighth and ninth month. July will come soon enough, and you won't want to wear a jacket."

"At that point I won't care. I'll be full of joy to welcome my little bundle into the world." She hugged her arms around her growing tummy.

"What's up? I need to get this arrangement finished. Come back and talk to me."

Steph opened her purse and pulled out a certificate. "I am now a licensed real estate agent. I've already talked to several agencies to see if the brokers are willing to let me work with them. They understand I don't want to work full-time but instead flip houses and sell them as my main job."

"Wonderful! I didn't know you took the test. I'm so excited for you."

"Thanks. I kept it a secret in case I didn't pass the exam. With my contract ending this summer on the complex, the extra income will come in handy. I can take the baby with me most of the time."

"You know both girls are willing babysitters."

"They'll make great sitters. Rafe wanted me to check out a few new houses on the market. I think I found one you and Mitch might want."

"Oh, really, where is it?"

"Edge of town, close to the river, and it has a large backyard... from what I could see with the snow. It's a two-story with a wrap-around front porch and nice sized garage."

"Give me the address, and I'll drive by it on my way home. We haven't received any offers yet on either one of our homes. Jake says it's too early. Once the snow melts and yards are cleaned up, then people start to think about moving."

"He's right, but this one just came on the market. It's an estate and I think it'll sell right away. I'd look at purchasing both your homes, but they're in too good a shape to flip. We wouldn't make any money."

Steph jotted the address and handed it to Azalea.

"If we like it, can you write up the offer for us?"

"I sure will. I need to find out first which agency will accept me as an independent agent. I'm staying away from Jake's company. If you like the house, it'll be my first sale."

"Jake has the listing on both our homes, so I don't think he'll mind if we use you as our buying agent."

Azalea could not wait to drive by the house before it got too dark. She wanted to check the mileage to make sure it would not be too far from the shop. River Falls took less than a half hour to get from one end to the other. Crossing the river was another issue, and Azalea did not want to even consider buying on the other side of the river.

The shades were pulled as she drove up, so she couldn't peek in the windows. The house seemed sad, as if it was waiting for a family to bring it back to life. Azalea stopped in front, so she could get a glimpse of the backyard. The wraparound front porch looked inviting, and she imagined sitting in a swing with Mitch on those hot summer evenings... when he wasn't working, of course.

A big enough yard for a dog. Both girls asked if they could get a dog when we got married. I can see them out front or even in the backyard throwing a ball for a...well, whatever, but it definitely would be a rescue dog.

Azalea drove home in a dream-like state as she imagined their lives together. She promised to make supper for everyone.

With Mitch and the girls already at the house, she hurried in and threw her jacket in the closet.

"Mitch, Steph stopped today and told me about this wonderful house just on the market. I drove by, and it's just what we talked about. Can you take off sometime tomorrow to look at the inside?"

"Hold on." He held up his hands. "Do you mind if I look at the outside before I make a commitment?"

"I'm sorry, I got carried away. Can you please go out there tomorrow? If you like it as much as I do, we can make an appointment with Steph to look at it."

"Steph... don't you mean Jake?"

Azalea gave Mitch a mischievous smile. "Nope."

"Okay." He grabbed her around the waist. "What's going on?"

"Steph showed me her new real estate license. She can negotiate for us once she puts her license with a broker."

"You know Jake gave us a good deal when he listed our houses for us. Since he's a broker, he's doing it as a favor."

"I know, but Steph and Rafe are going to need the money more when the baby arrives."

"Okay, but you better talk to him." He led her over to the couch. "Since the girls are upstairs." He leaned in for a passionate kiss. It ended more like making out like teenagers. "I don't know if I can wait too much longer to make you my wife."

Azalea's heart flipped when he said those words, and the butterflies in her stomach gave her a tingle. *This must be love.* She put her hands on his shoulders.

"I daydreamed all the way home about us sitting on the porch watching our girls play with their dog. My heart is so full right now with love for you and the girls, I sometimes wonder if we should just elope."

"Rafe would kill us."

"Yeah, I think Steph would be right behind him along with my mother and sisters." They both laughed as they imagined the outrage from Azalea's family.

"I haven't talked to my brother since before Christmas. He doesn't know about our engagement. I'll call him tonight. I hope he and his family can make it to the wedding."

"It'll be small like Steph and Rafe's wedding. I don't want a lot of falderal."

"I don't either. I'm worried about my deputies. I think they got something up their sleeve for a bachelor party."

"It'll have to pass Rafe's inspection, so I wouldn't worry too much. It'll be fun."

The intercom in Mitch's office buzzed.

"Sheriff, you have a call on line one," Sally, Mitch's secretary, announced.

"Do you know who it is?"

She exhaled. "It's Susan again."

"Aargh," he growled. "I suppose I better talk to her. It's only the umpteenth time she's called."

He picked up the phone and let out a sigh. "Hello, Susan," his voice hollow.

"Mitch, when can I spend some time with Natalia?"

He closed his eyes and counted to five. "Susan, I told you before, you don't have any visitation rights with Natalia. You need to follow the proper legal channels. If you do get visitation, it'll probably be supervised visits at first. I realize you want to see her."

How can I work this out so everyone is satisfied?

He scratched his head and pulled on his ear.

"Let me show you I changed. Can we meet at a restaurant? I'll buy. I want some time with her, so she gets to know me before you get married."

"Susan, I'm not sure…"

I should discuss this with Azalea first.

"Please, Mitch. This is important to me."

"Um," he grimaced, unable to find the right words. "Okay, I guess it won't hurt to meet for a meal. Next week there's a school holiday. Natalia will have a sitter. Maybe we can do lunch."

"Oh, thank you, Mitch. You don't know how much this means to me."

That's one way to get her off my case.

CHAPTER NINE

The trip to the local pizzeria to pick up lunch for her employees proved to be a shocking experience as Azalea walked into the restaurant and expected to grab the pizzas and leave. She heard a familiar laugh and peeked her head around the corner. Mitch and Natalia sat in a back-corner table with Susan.

It was a school holiday, and Natalia was supposed to be with her sitter. A thud hit her heart as she realized Mitch never mentioned this meeting to her. They talked about everything. A stab of jealousy entered her body—a new feeling for her.

Natalia and Susan giggled while Mitch sat and observed. They could not see her through the slats which separated the dining room from the entrance. She was now an outsider looking in.

Should I walk over and say something... like, Mitch, why didn't you tell me you were meeting with Susan today? Or, Mitch, are you keeping secrets from me now? Oh, dear God, I've got the devil in my head making me think all sorts of bad things. In the name of Jesus Christ, take these evil thoughts out of my head.

She paid for the pizzas without conscious movement. Her decision to leave quietly left her with a bitter heart.

Susan is weaving her way into our lives. Am I going to have her around from now on? It doesn't look like it's a temporary situation.

Tears formed on the edge of her eyes, and she wiped them away.

I trust Mitch... I do. I need to believe he will tell me about the lunch.

Mitch stopped by Roses N'More later in the afternoon. He walked over and kissed Azalea on the cheek. She held her posture rigid, gave him a tight smile, and waited for him to explain his earlier lunch.

"I drove by the house on the outskirts of town...the one with the wrap-around porch." He completely missed her cool attitude.

She could not help but snap at him, "You promised to do it the following day. It's been several days."

"I know. I'm sorry. I got busy and forgot about it. With school holiday, more kids are running around town. You know I've worked the last couple nights. I'm taking the next couple days off to spend with Nat and Becca. I thought I would take them to the Science Museum in Minneapolis one day. Can you take some time off to go along?"

Her heart melted. Why couldn't she stay angry with him? He always came up with a reason for her to continue to love him. "It's slow right now. Sure I can. I'll check with Mom to see if she can help out. She only comes in a few days a week now."

"Would you mind calling Steph and see if we can look at the house?

Azalea picked up her cell phone.

"Hi, Azalea. What's up?"

"Mitch found time to drive over to the house you talked about. Can we look at it today? It is empty, right?"

"It is. I'll call the real estate company and set up a showing.

How about right after work?"

Azalea looked at Mitch and raised her eyes in question. He nodded his head. "Should we bring the girls with?"

"Is it okay to bring the girls along?" she asked Steph.

"I don't see why not. No one is living there. It's an estate, and the family is getting ready to have an auction as soon as the weather turns nicer."

"Okay, we'll meet you there."

After she hung up the phone, she explained to Mitch about the estate and also waited for him to say something about his lunch date. Nothing. Not wanting to say anything in front of her staff, she let it go.

"Azalea, what's wrong?" Sunny asked after Mitch left the store.

"Nothing...really."

"Your cool attitude toward Mitch is not normal since you got engaged."

"I know. I got a little bit of the jealousy bug and need to get over it."

Mitch returned to the LEC and found Steve sitting on the far end of Sally's desk. They were in a deep discussion when he sauntered up to them.

"Something going on?" he asked.

Sally gave him an eye roll. "You could say so." She handed him a piece of paper with the resignation of the only female deputy in the department. Margaret was over fifty, and Mitch knew she planned to retire, but not this soon.

"Oh, wow! We need to find someone to replace her. She's at least given us several months' notice."

"Ahem..." Steve cleared his throat. "We kinda discussed a possible scenario if you're willing to listen."

His eyes opened wide as he tilted his head. "Okay, go ahead."

"You know Azalea's sister, Sunny, has her PI experience. The department could send her to the eight-week training course in Alexandria. She already has a bachelor's degree in criminal justice, so all she'd need would be the training."

"How'd you know she'd even be interested? She's busy working for Azalea and Steph."

"I told you we've been casing the Corner Bar lately to make sure Susan is keeping on the straight and narrow. We've talked. She mentioned moving back to the cities and the possibility of a law enforcement job."

"Hum," Mitch rubbed his jaw.

"She'd be a shoo-in after her encounter with Elena Wadsworth. She's a hero. She said the Mayor contacted her and wants to give her a medal."

"I don't know..." Mitch started to turn down the suggestion.

"Give her a chance, Mitch. She's young and in great shape...even with all those tattoos."

"What do you think, Sally?"

"You mean you're actually asking my opinion? I don't have any say in who you hire."

"You've been here long enough to know what's required of a female deputy."

"I think she could handle it." She rolled her eyes towards Steve. "As long as she doesn't get into any more tiffs with Steve."

Steve's face turned red. "That's all over with. I didn't know her when we investigated Wade Williams' death. I thought she was the hippie or druggie type, but she's changed so much since she moved back to River Falls."

"I agree," offered Mitch. "I think she would make a fine deputy. First, we need to know if she's willing to take on the role."

The phone rang in Mitch's office. Sally picked up the extension on her desk.

"Sheriff DeVries office... Yes, he's still here." Her eyes grew large. "Really!" She turned a shocked expression toward Mitch. "I'll tell him right away. Thanks."

"Sheriff, I think you and Steve better go to the front desk. If I told you who's out there, you wouldn't believe me."

Steve and Mitch gave each other a perplexed look and shrugged their shoulders.

"You won't even give us a hint?" Mitch raised his eyebrows at Sally.

"Nope. You got to see this for yourselves."

They meandered to the front desk area and expected some sort of joke to be played on them. A tall elderly man stood with a cane in one hand and an arm on the counter. He turned. It took but a brief moment for Mitch and Steve to recognize the facial features of George Walters, who had been reported missing for over forty years.

CHAPTER TEN

The deputy at the front desk of the LEC leaned forward, "Sheriff, this man claims to be George Walters... *the* George Walters."

"I've never met George Walters, but heard a lot about him through Miss Mattie," explained Mitch.

"Sir, I *am* George Walters. I come to turn myself in. I'm back because I want to clear my name, and I want to see Mattie Turnborn again."

"I'm pleased to meet you, Mr. Walters." Mitch reached for his hand and shook it. "Please, let's go back to a private area where we can talk." He turned to introduce Steve. "This is Detective Bishop, one of my men who's worked on your case."

Mitch and Steve ushered George to the interrogation room.

"Can we get you a cup of coffee or water?"

"Water would be good." Steve left the room to find a bottle of water. Once he returned, they began the interrogation.

The information George gave them matched what Agent Norman Schmidt from the Bureau of Criminal Apprehension (BCA) told them several months ago.

"The BCA tracked you to Canada. We knew where you were

living for the past forty years but made the decision not to extradite you. Our county attorney, Sam Harris, agreed the deaths were an unfortunate accident and not murder. If the four of you involved would have come forward right away and explain what happened, your lives would have ended up quite different."

"Agreed. Back then, returning from the Viet Nam War was enough hell for us. We didn't need any more backlash."

"You are the only one remaining who is capable of telling us what happened that night. We have the written confession from Charles Leddering and one from Donald Hanson, who, incidentally, has been pronounced mentally ill. We want to close the case and would appreciate your statement. If all the confessions coincide, we can call the case closed for good and you can move on with your life."

"I would like to do that, Sir."

"I'll get a recorder. Sally, my secretary, will decipher it. Once you sign it, you'll be free to go."

"Thank you, Sheriff. I want to get this over with, so I can see Mattie."

"You do realize, George, it's been a long time since you've seen her."

"Yes, sir, I do. I've called her phone many times just to hear her voice."

"So, she didn't exaggerate the phone calls. Her sister, Maude, said someone kept calling her and hanging up."

"I didn't want to frighten her. I just wanted to hear her voice. I've led a long lonely existence, afraid to come back… afraid I'd end up in prison for something that was an accident."

"I think you need to take it slow with Miss Mattie. She's not well. I think we need to go through her sister, Maude."

"I want to take care of Mattie. Even after all these years, I still love her. Even if she doesn't want anything to do with me, I still need her forgiveness."

"Steve, please call Maude and ask how Miss Mattie is doing today."

Time does not erase old wounds. The discovery of the skeletal remains and the death of Eddie Barkley last year stuck in Mitch's mind as he entered the high rise. Maude told them Mattie's mental condition remained steady since Christmas. He and Steve accompanied George as they knocked first on Maude's door.

Maude answered the door. Her demeanor remained calm but curious. "For lands sake, it really is George. He looks just like the mock-up drawing, only his hair is shorter." Her eyes turned cold and she shook her fist. "You ought to be ashamed of yourself, George Walters, for running out on Mattie. Do you realize how much she suffered because of you?"

George removed his cap and held it in his hands. "I'm sorry, Maude. I paid for my mistakes with years of loneliness and heartache. I heard about them finding the bodies a short time ago on the internet. It took time for me to face the fact I needed to turn myself in to the law."

"I wanted to make sure it was you before I approached Mattie. You men wait here in my apartment. I'll talk to Mattie."

Mattie lived a few doors down from Maude on the same floor. Five minutes, ten minutes, fifteen minutes went by. The men patiently waited in Maude's apartment. Mitch glanced at his watch more than several times.

I need to pick up Natalia from her after school activities for dinner at Azalea's. What interesting news to tell everyone tonight.

Maude returned with Miss Mattie.

"George, is it really you?" Mattie's eyes squinted as if by doing so she could see him better.

"Yes, Mattie, it's me." He took a few steps forward. "I came back for you."

"Oh, I've waited a long time." Her face lit up in a smile. "The angels told me you'd come back and to just be patient."

George continued his steps toward Mattie, not quite sure if she would accept him. He held out his arms and she flew into them like a child clinging to a teddy bear.

"I want to take care of you, Mattie, if you'll let me."

"Oh, yes, George, oh, yes." Tears rolled down her eyes.

Maude, who stood close to Mitch and Steve, wiped a few tears from her eyes.

"What took you so long?" Mitch whispered.

"Mattie wanted to make herself presentable to George. You know how fussy she is about her appearance. Even though half the time she forgets her pills, her hair and makeup must be impeccable."

Mitch's late arrival with Natalia at Roses N'More was met with a tight-lipped Azalea.

"Did you forget about our appointment to look at the house?" Azalea snarked.

Mitch raised his eyebrows at her remark and wondered if she had a bad day, but knew it was his fault for being late.

"Sorry about the time. We had an interesting afternoon. I'll tell you about it on the way over to the house."

He explained about George Walters and the reunion with Mattie. Tears rose in Azalea's eyes as she realized her snarkiness mirrored her jealousy.

Dear God, forgive me for my attitude today. I need to learn to trust Mitch and not always second guess his intentions.

"Mattie deserves happiness. I hope everything works out for her. We'll need to tell Steph. She's worried Mattie would end up in a memory care facility. Now with her brother, Joe, back in River Falls at the nursing home, her family is complete."

"Yeah, the reunion went well. I hope it stays that way."

Steph stood in the front entrance and waved at them as they drove up the driveway.

"Sorry we're late."

"No problem. I got a chance to give the house a thorough look through. It'll need some work, mostly cosmetic, but it's a gem."

"Mitch will explain to you why we're late. It'll make your day."

"Oh, yeah."

Mitch went through a quick explanation of Mattie and George's reunion.

"Praise the Lord. I'm so happy for Mattie."

"It's exactly the same thing I said," replied Azalea.

"Look around the house and ask me any questions. Here's the info sheet."

Azalea looked at the price. Her eyes just about left her head. "I never asked you about the price of the house." She gave Mitch a bewildered look. "I'm sorry, Mitch, I didn't realize the house would be this expensive. It's worth almost our two houses together."

Mitch took the sheet from Azalea and perused it. "I guess the price is a little high."

"Look at what you're getting?" replied Steph. "You have four bedrooms with a master en suite plus two other bathrooms—one upstairs and the other downstairs, plus a half bath off the kitchen. The kitchen is remodeled. All you need to do is replace some flooring and paint. Other updating can wait."

"Let's take a look and talk about it," suggested Mitch.

"Won't cost anything to look, I guess," sighed Azalea.

Azalea sensed the loneliness of the house. Her gut told her the house needed a loving family. It grew on her as she examined each room.

Mitch noticed the gleam in Azalea's eyes as she moved through the house. She ran her fingers over the woodwork, opened the cabinets in the kitchen and bathrooms, peeked in the closets, and walked down to the basement. He knew she wanted this house. Becca and Natalia already picked out their bedrooms.

"Thank you for showing us the house," said Azalea to Steph.

"No problem. I thought since you both were selling your homes, you'd have enough to purchase this one."

"Yeah, one problem. I've got a mortgage and so does Mitch."

"I've got a solution," informed Mitch. Azalea tilted her head and gave him a quizzical look.

Something else you're keeping from me?

"Girls, why don't you take a look out in the backyard while I talk to Azalea?" Mitch ordered in his professional tone. The girls became somber but obeyed his request.

"What's the matter?"

"I didn't want to bring this up in front of the girls, but we don't need to sell both our houses right away to afford this house. I inherited money from my folks and made some good investments. We can afford this house without selling ours first."

Azalea's eyes grew wide. "You mean you're rich, and you never told me?"

He laughed. "No, I'm not rich. However, there's enough to pay for the house in case ours don't sell right away. That's all."

Mitch always does something to make me love him more every day.

"I do like this house, and so do the girls. If you agree, we should put in an offer."

"Agreed. I do like the house much better than the one I'm living in."

Azalea could not contain her excitement and threw her arms around Mitch.

"We still need to put in an offer," said Steph as shook her head at the two.

The girls ran back into the house. Natalia grabbed Mitch's hand. "There's a tree house out back. Come see," squealed an animated Natalia as she pulled Mitch towards the back door.

"Okay, let's take a look." Mitch turned and nodded to Azalea to follow.

Azalea threw up her hands "Might as well."

After they looked over the backyard and garage, they drove to the real estate office and put in an offer on the property.

"Since this is an estate, all the owners will need to agree on your offer. Even though it's below asking price, it's still a good one," said Steph.

"I do hope they accept the offer. It'll be a perfect beginning for us."

Azalea's giddiness rubbed off on Mitch when he reached out to hold her hand as they signed the papers. He let out a huge breath of relief with the final stroke of the pen and all the tension in his body disappeared. This was a new beginning for them.

CHAPTER ELEVEN

Azalea continued her nervous pacing outside the courtroom. "I'm terrified to testify against Elena Wadsworth. After seeing the evil in her eyes that night, I don't know if I can face her again."

"Sam needs your testimony to wrap up the case. He'll probably call you and Sunny as the last witnesses." Mitch draped his arm around Azalea. Her body tingled at his touch however innocent it appeared.

She turned and smiled. "I know what Sam said, but it's still going to be tough."

"I have no worries," spouted Sunny. "After she tried to break my jaw and almost shot you with my gun, I'm more than willing to testify. She needs to be behind bars for a long time."

"What about her son? Even though he's in a facility for handicapped children, someone has to pay to keep him there."

"Jennifer Williams has made it possible," added Steve.

Azalea's and Sunny's eyes popped. "Wonderful!" both replied at the same moment.

Azalea raised her hand, "Bless her heart."

She hung on to Mitch's arm and leaned her head against his

shoulder. Ready to testify in the same suit he wore for Rafe and Steph's wedding, Azalea looked upon Mitch as her knight in shining armor with his tall stature and dark hair touched with a little gray. There were still a few little chinks in his knighthood status, especially when it came to his ex-wife, Susan.

Sunny stood close to Steve, who just had a new suit tailored to fit—no baggy or wrinkled clothes today. Sunny's eyes remained riveted to the new Steve. He glanced toward her several times and gave a crooked lift to his smile. Even though they were the same height, Sunny's slim figure complimented Steve's stocky build. He pushed the glasses up his nose as he cleared his throat.

"The trial will be closed to the public once the opening arguments are presented, but at least we can listen in on those. The news media won't be able to make a mockery out of the trial until it's over."

The doors to the courtroom opened. The four filed in along with the local and state news media. The news media packed the courtroom; each reporter wanted to get in on the action.

Azalea and Sunny took seats in the back row of the courtroom, while Mitch and Steve sat behind the prosecuting attorney's desk.

Agent Norman Schmidt walked in while the judge was reading the charges against Elena Wadsworth. He recognized Azalea and Sunny and gave them a thumbs up. He moved toward the front to sit alongside Mitch and Steve.

Azalea and Sunny listened as Sam Harris, the prosecuting attorney, gave his opening statement, and continued with other remarks.

"So you, the jurors, will be given an open and shut case with the dying confession of Mark D'Angelo witnessed by Sheriff Mitch DeVries and Detective Steve Bishop and confirmed by his physician, Dr. Sanderson." He pointed with his hand toward Mitch and Steve. His eyes showed relief to see Agent Schmidt. "Also, another eye witness to the capture of Ms. Wadsworth is Agent

Norman Schmidt of the Bureau of Criminal Apprehension."

Sam walked back and forth in front of the jury. "We will also listen to the testimony of Azalea Rose, who the defendant attempted vehicular homicide and later poisoned. Sunflower Rose will also testify as to the physical attack on her, and her later bravery of stopping the potential murder of her sister by the defendant."

He turned his back to the jury and focused his eyes on Elena. "We will ask for murder in the first degree with two life imprisonment terms, plus second-degree attempted murder." Elena's expression remained tight-lipped as her eyes glared at Sam.

The defense attorney attempted to place Elena as the victim of two men who both professed their love for her and in the end deserted her. "Once you see the evidence involved, you, the jurors, will realize all the evidence is circumstantial and hearsay. No one saw her murder Wade Williams, and no one saw her put poison in the wine at Mark D'Angelo's house. We will show Elena Wadsworth to be a victim. We will prove she does not deserve the life sentence term the prosecuting attorney is asking for but ask for leniency for a woman who has endured mental anguish for the past years with constant betrayal."

Sunny and Azalea looked at each other, raised their eyebrows, and shook their heads.

Sunny leaned over and whispered, "I can't believe the jury will fall for the defending attorney's tricks."

"I sure hope not," Azalea returned in a whispered voice. "If the jury believes him, then the justice system is corrupt. People can't just get away with murder by saying they've been in mental anguish. It's disgusting."

The judge pounded his gavel and gave the word to break for lunch.

The five witnesses gathered outside the courtroom when Sam Harris walked up to them. He looked at Mitch and Steve. "I'll call you and Detective Bishop to the stand right after lunch. Agent

Schmidt will follow and then Dr. Sanderson if there's time. I don't think we'll get to you two ladies until tomorrow. Sydney Hines will also testify about the embezzlement. I won't call Jennifer."

"I'm at your disposal," announced Norman, "but I do need to return to Minneapolis as soon as possible. I hope the trial won't take more than a few days."

"It'll depend on the defense attorney. He has access to our gathered evidence which I can present within a few days, but he'll try and bring in psychiatrists and whatever he can find to prove his case."

Mitch and Steve decided to return to the Law Enforcement Center until they were called as witnesses. Azalea and Sunny returned to the flower shop.

"I would like to call Ms. Azalea Rose to the stand," Sam Harris almost shouted. She could hear him from outside the courtroom. The door opened, and the deputy called her name.

Sunny put her hand on Azalea's arm. "Don't be nervous. If it bothers you, don't look in Elena's direction."

Azalea nodded as she picked up her purse, squared her shoulders and walked into the courtroom. Mitch and Steve were allowed to stay in the courtroom. Mitch winked at her as she walked past.

The bailiff swore her in, and she took a seat in the stand next to the judge.

"Ms. Rose, please state your full name."

"A... Azalea Jasmine Rose," she said barely above a whisper.

"Please speak up Ms. Rose so the jury can hear you."

She cleared her throat and raised her voice. "Azalea Jasmine Rose."

She heard a few giggles from the jury box and glanced toward the jurors.

"Okay, Ms. Rose. Would you state how you know the defendant?"

"She was Jennifer Williams' personal assistant. I am the owner of Roses N'More Floral. Jennifer Williams introduced us when she hired me to make artistic arrangements for several parties, plus I worked with her on floral arrangements for Wade Williams' funeral."

"Was it your only relationship with her?"

"Yes."

"You and your sister found Wade Williams' body, correct?"

"Yes, sir."

"Give us a brief description of what you found that day."

"We were scheduled at the Williams' home right after lunch. Wade was to meet us there, but when we entered the house, we couldn't find him. We started setting the arrangements on the first floor. The caterers arrived. We went upstairs to decorate the bedrooms when Sunny, my sister, called me to the master suite. She saw the body on the bed. I called out to see if Mr. Williams was sleeping. There was no answer."

"The sheriff testified earlier there was a bag over his head. Didn't you and your sister see the bag from the door?"

"No, there were pillows piled up in the middle of the bed. All we could see were his feet. I called a little louder and walked in. I noticed the bag over his head with the helium machine beside the bed and the hose inside the bag. I untied the bag; the hose fell to the floor while I felt for a pulse. There was no pulse. I called the sheriff and he sent several deputies out right away to secure the area."

"Did you touch anything else?"

"No, but Sunny made the remark it didn't look right because the bed wasn't messed up. If he laid down in the bed himself to commit suicide, the bed would have been more messed up."

"Motion to strike the last sentence," the defense attorney demanded. "It's a matter of opinion of someone who is not an expert."

"Motion to strike allowed," answered the judge. "The jury will disregard that answer."

Azalea could see the frustration in Sam's eyes as he turned toward her again.

"Okay, what happened next?"

"Sunny kept taking pictures. After she made the statement to me about the bed, she knelt down to look under the bed. I pulled her back because I was worried about preserving the crime scene. She hit her head on the bed frame. Wade's mouth dropped open and melted chocolate candy oozed from his mouth. It grossed us out, and we moved to the hallway to wait for the sheriff and deputies to arrive."

"Now we get to other events which involved you. According to a statement from the sheriff's department, Stephanie McGowan was run off the road by an unknown car."

"Yes, she was making deliveries for me and borrowed my vehicle."

"The sheriff indicated in his previous testimony the car used in the attempted vehicular homicide was found in another county."

"Yes."

"Let the record show the evidence of paint chips found on the recovered vehicle matched the paint on Ms. Rose's vehicle. This was entered into evidence with the testimony of Sheriff DeVries."

"So entered," said the judge. "Please continue with your witness."

"Mrs. McGowan was unable to identify the assailant because he or she wore a ski mask and there were a few smudged fingerprints in the recovered car. How do you know it was Elena Wadsworth driving the vehicle?"

"She told me the night she attacked Mark D'Angelo and me. She thought I would be dead, and she was going to wait there until we died."

"Liar!" screamed Elena from her seat. "Nothing but lies."

The judge pounded his gavel, "Sir, keep your client quiet, or I'll have her removed from the courtroom."

The defense attorney started to whisper in an aggravated tone to Elena. Azalea glanced at her for the first time since she took the stand. She could see Elena scrutinize her with piercing glances from the corner of her eye. Tears ran down Elena's cheeks as the defense attorney reprimanded her.

"Tell us about that night?"

Azalea paused before she spoke. She lived the nightmare over and over again in her mind.

Maybe this one last time will give me the release I need to end the nightmares.

"The BCA suspected Mark D'Angelo had something to do with Wade Williams' murder, but didn't have enough proof. Since Mark acted as if he was interested in me romantically, they asked if I would go undercover to try and gather evidence. They gave me a brooch with a camera and mic to wear. They monitored me from a nearby van. I agreed to make dinner for Mark, so I could get into his house. He opened a new bottle of wine, and we both drank a glass. I wouldn't have drank any if it hadn't been a new bottle. I created an excuse for him to leave and go to the store. I found the key to the basement, and while I was in the basement, I found the hemlock in a backroom. I heard some commotion upstairs. I wasn't sure if it was the furnace making funny noises or footsteps, so I went back up the stairs."

"You heard footsteps."

"I wasn't sure. It sounded like old floors creaking when someone walks on them, but the furnace also made a wailing noise, so I couldn't be positive."

"Okay, you may continue."

"I walked toward the stairs and stumbled. The brooch dropped on the floor behind the stairs. I re-pinned it to my jacket but didn't realize it was broken. I made my way back upstairs and locked the basement door. Mark arrived back from his errand, and we dished up the food and sat down to eat. He poured several glasses of wine for himself while I sipped on mine. It was his third glass when I noticed the bottle was almost empty, but sediment remained in the bottom of the bottle and also in his glass. I looked at my glass and saw the same thing."

"Again, let the record show the bottle of wine and glasses were tested for poison. Test results show the bottle and glasses were laced with wild hemlock."

The judge nodded. "Continue."

"Then what happened?"

"I commented to Mark about something wrong with the wine. He ignored the remark and went to a cabinet to get a toothpick. When he snapped the toothpick in half, a picture came into my mind of the tire tracks at the Williams with a broken toothpick in the snow. I commented about the toothpick. But then he grabbed his stomach and said I poisoned him. I told him 'no way', and right after Elena walked in the back door with a gun. Her eyes were wild, and she was angry at Mark for deceiving her. He said we were just having dinner and that he loved her. She laughed and said it was too late. She already poisoned the wine and would wait until we were both dead, and she'd have all the money."

"Conjecture on the part of the witness. I ask to strike the last part."

"Overruled," the judge tapped his gavel. "The witness is stating what she saw."

With an anguished look the defense attorney sat down.

Tears filled Azalea's eyes. She grabbed a tissue from her pocket and dabbed her eyes.

"It's okay. Please continue when you're ready."

She sniffed. "Elena confessed both her and Mark embezzled money from the company. She said she tried to get rid of me once before when she ran me off the road, but it wasn't me. It was Steph McGowan. Steph was pregnant, and she could have killed both her and her unborn child."

"Motion to strike."

"Overruled." The judge pounded his gavel. The defense attorney shook his head.

"Continue," said Sam.

"She told me she got rid of my sister. I didn't know if she killed her or what." Azalea needed to pause. She took a few deep breaths before she could continue. "I didn't know the brooch was broken and they weren't getting a decent signal. I wanted someone to rescue us. When she walked over to Mark, who was already unconscious, and gave him a push with her foot, I yelled "HELP" as loud as I could and used all my strength to struggle with her over the gun. The gun dropped to the floor, and I collapsed. She reached for the gun when Sunny came in the back door and pointed her Derringer at Elena. She threatened to shoot Elena if she went any closer to the gun on the floor." She covered her hands over her face and her body started to quiver.

"Are you okay, Azalea?" asked Sam. "Do you want to take a break?" She shook her head.

Oh, God, give me the strength to continue.

Her eyes focused on Elena. She could see the animosity shooting darts from her eyes. Elena's face turned red as if were ready to explode.

"Mitch...I mean the sheriff, Detective Bishop and Agent Schmidt rushed in. I told the sheriff Elena poisoned us. It's all I remember until three days later when I regained consciousness."

"Thank you, Azalea." He turned to the defending attorney. "Your witness."

CHAPTER TWELVE

The defense attorney paced back and forth with his thumb and forefinger on his jaw. "Ms. Rose, what were your feelings toward Mark D'Angelo?"

"I had no feelings for Mr. D'Angelo—only a suspicion something wasn't right from our first meeting. I wanted to help in the investigation."

"Don't you think you should have left the investigation to the sheriff's department and not take things on yourself?"

"I've known Jennifer for years and wanted to help."

"You heard my client say you lied. Do you know the penalty for lying under oath?"

"Huh... why would I lie? I never wanted anything to do with Mark D'Angelo. He pursued me."

"Yet you went along with the charade to get evidence against him."

"Well... yes. I didn't want to see him anymore, but the sheriff's department asked me to go undercover."

"Just answer my question. If you didn't want to see him anymore, why did you agree to go undercover?"

"To help solve a crime. It's in my nature to help people."

The attorney picked up a piece of paper. "I have a record of Mr. D'Angelo's phone calls from his cell phone. There's one made to you from his phone around Christmas from Bermuda. If you were not involved romantically with him, why did he call you?"

"That's a good question. All I remember from the conversation is he asked me to dinner once he returned from going home for Christmas. I did not know he was in Bermuda. In fact, I did hear calypso music in the background and thought it strange. The sheriff was at my house when he called, and I held the phone so he could also hear the conversation. If you want it verified, you can ask him."

He threw up his hands. "No more questions."

Sam wanted to meet with all who testified, including Agent Schmidt, so they gathered at the Law Enforcement Center.

"Since you've all testified, it'll be up to the defense attorney to disprove any of the evidence we brought forward. I don't know if he'll put Elena on the stand with her erratic behavior. It may do more damage than good, but we'll need to wait and see what his plans are. He doesn't have much of a line-up for witnesses except for psychiatric evaluations, so this may go fast."

"Will we need to testify again?" asked Azalea.

"If we need to clarify some further evidence or information brought by the defense... yes, you could be recalled. By the way, you and Sunny did a great job today."

"I hope the jury believes our testimony."

"I watched the jurors as I questioned both of you. None of them shook their heads, which is a good sign, but you could see their eyes go back and forth between you ladies and Elena.

"Thank you, Sam," said Mitch. "I know Norman needs to head back to Minneapolis, but he'll return if he's needed for any further testimony."

Sam picked up his briefcase. He had a little jaunt to his step as he left the room.

"Once this trial is over, I sure hope we can move on with our lives. Sunny and I need to head back over to the store."

"Um... Would you mind going by yourself? Steve and I would like to talk with Sunny. We'll make sure she gets a ride back."

Azalea gave them a perplexed look and shrugged her shoulders. Sunny scrunched up her face in confusion.

"Sure. Why don't all of you come over for supper tonight? I'll make homemade mac and cheese and Mitch can grill hamburgers. I'll call Rafe and Steph and see if they can join us. It's such a relief to get this testifying off my mind."

After Azalea left, Sunny turned to Mitch and Steve. "What's up? Did I do something wrong?"

"No," Mitch smiled, "it's nothing like that. Our female officer is retiring within the next few months. She's given us plenty of notice, but I want to know if you'd be interested in applying for the position. We know you have a background in criminal justice, so if you were selected all you'd need would be some extra training."

Steve kept his voice level, "I know we got off on the wrong foot when we first met, but since then I've seen how you changed." He lowered his voice to a gentle tone. "I'd be proud to work with you in this department."

"Oh, wow! I thought about going back to school part-time to update my qualifications and apply in the cities. I enjoyed working as a private investigator but didn't think I was good enough for a law enforcement position." Her eyes made direct contact with Mitch and her voice trembled. "Are you offering me the job?"

"We've seen you in action. With the mayor wanting to give you a medal and your help in the Williams case, I'm sure the commissioners will go with the sheriff's department recommendation to hire you. That is, if you're interested," said

Mitch.

"Interested." Sunny's face bubbled with excitement. "You bet I am."

―――――

Before she drove back to the flower shop, Azalea stopped at the grocery store to pick up a few items for dinner. She started to push her cart toward the checkout when she spotted Susan in the produce aisle. Not in the mood to talk to her Azalea turned her cart around, but Susan caught her action.

"Azalea, how are you?" She pushed her cart close to hers.

Azalea rolled her eyes before she turned around. "I'm fine."

Susan gave her an innocent smile. "I'm happy Mitch is allowing me a little extra time with Natalia. I can get to know my daughter again."

"Oh... I wasn't aware you got visitation already," her voice stilted.

"I haven't, but Mitch lets me see Natalia as long as he's there."

"Well, I'm glad you could work something out before going to court."

"I heard you and Mitch are purchasing a house on the outskirts of town."

"Mitch told you." Azalea stared at her, annoyed at Mitch for mentioning personal things.

"No, Natalia mentioned it."

"Oh." Her body relaxed.

Where is this conversation going?

"With all the money Mitch inherited from his parents, he could afford to buy you a mansion."

"Huh... what are you talking about?"

There was no mistaking the hard note in her voice. "Didn't you know? Mitch inherited a pile of money from his parents when they passed away. There's enough to buy you several houses and still have some left over."

Is she rubbing this in my face? I can't let her find out I didn't know.

She held her voice to a deliberate casualness. "Is that all you're talking about. Yes, I knew he inherited money. He's using some to buy the house, so we can start work on it. When our homes sell, we'll replace the money."

"Well, don't let him downplay it. He's loaded, but he doesn't want others to know it." She turned and walked away leaving Azalea open-mouthed at her comment.

Azalea invited Sunny and Steve, along with Steph and Rafe, to dinner. She tried to smile and laugh along with everyone else, but her heart remained isolated. She found it difficult to join in the merriment.

Sunny took a knife and tapped her glass at the end of the meal before they cleared away the dishes. "I would like to announce that my future brother-in-law asked me to apply for the position of female deputy in the sheriff's department. I thought about it for a minute... or should I say less than thirty seconds... and said YES."

"It's wonderful," Steph clasped her stomach as she rose from her chair and gave Sunny a hug. "I'm so glad for you. However, it means you won't be working for us anymore. That's a bummer."

Sunny beamed. "If the commissioners approve, I will need to go to special training which means four to six weeks away from here." She glanced at Azalea. "Zalia will also need her employees to work more hours."

Azalea, determined not to let her foul mood spoil Sunny's announcement, piped up, "I'm so proud of you, Sunny. I will miss you in the store, but I'm sure you'll make more money working for the county."

"First, there's a bunch of psychological tests and final approval from the commissioners. I don't foresee any problem especially after the Williams investigation. Sunny showed her true spirit and determination," announced Mitch.

Even though they were not drinking alcohol, Steve raised his glass. "I want to give a toast to Sunny and hope she accepts the job after all the falderal she'll need to go through."

Azalea started to clear the dishes. Steph followed her to the sink.

"What's the matter? You've been acting grouchy this evening. You should be relieved your part of the trial is done."

"I know." Azalea, ready to lose her self-control, instead started to rinse the dishes and fill the dishwasher. "It's Susan. I think she's trying to put a wedge between Mitch and me. She does it so discreetly, but I can tell by her innuendos what she's attempting to do. She doesn't fool me, but I think she can still pull the wool over Mitch."

"I don't think so. Mitch is done with her... and her antics. He knows what she's capable of doing. I bet you feel he's falling for her little tricks, but he's not. For goodness sake, he's smarter than that."

"I hope Natalia doesn't get sucked up in her trap, but she's going to try and cause trouble between us until we get married and maybe even afterwards if she sticks around town. There's nothing for her here. I wonder why she came back."

"Azalea, you have God on your side. Don't let the evil in her get to you. You know Satan is out there just to cause trouble, and right now you're falling for it."

"You know what... you're right," she gave a light-hearted laugh. "I know it's temptation. Thank you for listening."

Steph gave a little gasp and her hands went to her stomach.

"You okay."

"Oh, yes, the baby just kicked." A tear trickled down her face. "It's such a wonderful feeling."

"I know. I've been there."

Mitch carried the last of the dishes to the kitchen. "I'll go out and clean the grill off and be right back in." He grabbed his jacket and went outside.

Steph nudged Azalea. "Go out and talk to Mitch. Tell him how you feel. I've been so tired the past week, so we'll show ourselves out."

"Thanks, Steph, for the talk."

She stepped outside and ambled over to where Mitch stood scraping the grill. She stood behind him and put her arms around his chest. "Thank you for offering Sunny the job."

He turned, and she folded herself into his arms. "No problem. She deserves it after all the help she gave us."

"Hum… I need to talk to you about Susan."

"What about Susan?"

"Why didn't you tell me you had lunch with Susan and Natalia a few days ago?"

"I forgot. I should have told you, but with the trial starting, it slipped my mind."

"Mitch, things like that are important to discuss with me. I know you've been handling things alone for many years, but now we're together we need to share. I didn't appreciate finding this out on my own."

"I'm sorry. Please forgive me. I know I need to share more with you, but I'm learning."

"How about sharing information about your fortune. Susan saw me in the grocery store and pushed it in my face that you're loaded. I didn't know anything about it except what you told me when we made an offer on the house."

He chuckled. "Susan said what… that I'm loaded? What a crock. I'll be glad to show you my bank book. All Susan ever knew was I received an inheritance from my parents. My brother and I shared it. It was after our divorce, or she'd probably have tried to get that, too."

Her eyes danced while her body relaxed. "I love you, Mitch. I want you to know I'm not marrying you for your money."

Standing on tiptoe, she touched her lips to his, and he returned the kiss with exquisite tenderness.

CHAPTER THIRTEEN

"Thank you, Tom, for this wonderful night out," said Bernadette as they were seated on the window side of the River Falls Hotel. Patches of snow lay on the ground outside, but the river started to thaw, and streams of water floated around the layers of ice. The light outside made the last remnants of snow sparkle as the sun set.

Tom smiled as he kept his eyes focused on Bernadette. "I didn't know what to do for your birthday, so I thought I'd take you out for an early birthday dinner."

"Well… what a surprise. My birthday isn't until next week."

"I know. I pried the date out of Azalea. She didn't want to tell me your age either. She says a woman never tells her age."

"She's right, but I'm sure you dragged it out of her."

"Well, not really. She mentioned you're old enough to stay out past ten. Whatever she meant by that."

The waitress brought their menus. "What would you like to drink?"

"How about we order a bottle of wine?"

"I don't drink very much. Anything you want to order is fine with me."

"How about champagne?"

Bernadette raised her eyebrows and cupped her hands over her mouth, "Isn't it awful expensive?" she mouthed toward Tom.

"It's your birthday dinner," he whispered and rolled his eyes.

Bernadette blushed and giggled. "You're going to spoil me."

He ordered a bottle of champagne from the menu.

He skimmed over the food menu. "I think I want fish tonight. I'm looking forward to the opening of fishing season again, so I can get out in my boat."

"Sounds good. I haven't had fish in a while, and I haven't been fishing in years. I didn't know you owned a boat."

"Yeah, I purchase a new one once I retired. I want to do a lot of fishing once the lakes thaw."

"Do you do any ice fishing?"

"Some, but I don't own my own house. Sometimes I go with Willy to his little house."

The waitress brought the champagne on ice and popped the cork. She filled their glasses half full. Tom sloshed the drink around in the glass to get rid of the bubbles before he took a sip.

Bernadette took a sip and rubbed her nose. "It tickles."

"Are you ready to order?" the waitress stood and tapped her order pad with her pen.

"Sure." Tom gave her a quizzical look and placed both their orders.

"I would like to propose a toast before you drink your entire glass." He held up his glass. "Happy birthday—a little early—to the sweetest lady I know." They clinked their glasses, and Bernadette downed the champagne in one swallow.

"Sixty-six," Bernadette muttered.

"Sixty-six... what?"

"I'll be sixty-six. I started to collect Social Security when I turned sixty-two because I needed the income after my husband passed away."

"You know, Bernie, we've known each other now since before Christmas. I've enjoyed our visits and time together."

"Me, too. I love knowing my children live close by, but I miss my husband and our talks when he came home from work. I miss doing things for him."

"He's been gone five years now—right?" She nodded. "My Nancy's been gone three years. She fought a good fight after being diagnosed with cancer. The last year took a toll on the whole family—working and taking care of her. The kids no longer lived around here, but they took turns those last few months helping out a few days at a time."

"I feel your sorrow."

A tear left one corner of his eye as he sniffed, "I loved my wife, and I hated to see her go through the pain, but when she died, I sensed relief. I thought… she's now in Heaven where there's no more pain."

"Oh, Tom, I'm so sorry. My husband never suffered. He died of a heart attack at work. I didn't even get a chance to say goodbye. He looked so forward to retirement. At least you got to say goodbye." She started to sniff and reached for a napkin to wipe her eyes.

"They were both good people, but now we're the ones left behind. I know I'm a few years younger than you, but I've grown fond of you. We're not getting any younger. I… I, um… I wonder if you feel the same way."

Bernadette, in her demonstrative way, put her hand over Tom's. "I've enjoyed our time together. Sometimes I feel like a teenager. I believe at our age a few years difference shouldn't matter." She threw her shoulders back and gave him a satisfied grin. "In fact, I'd rather go out with a younger man. It makes me feel younger."

"I'll be sixty in May, but you make me feel like I'm young at heart again."

"I know you're retired, but I didn't want to pry."

He reached in his pocket and drew out a small box. "This is an early birthday gift."

Bernadette stared at the box, too afraid to open it. Her heart pounded while she wondered if it was—an engagement ring.

"Go ahead and open it."

"Oh... Tom." Her hand shook as she reached for the box and flipped it open. A pair of diamond earrings stared back at her. She breathed a sigh of relief, but also a little disappointed. She lifted her head and smiled. "Thank you."

"The sales clerk said diamonds are the birthstone for April."

"They're precious. I've never had a pair of diamond earrings. I'll think of you every time I wear them."

He leaned across the table and planted a kiss on her Carnation Red lips. It surprised Bernadette, and her eyes turned into saucers.

"I...I love you. I'm not sure if you're ready to make a commitment to us, but I know I'm ready even though we've only known each other a few months."

Not expecting this sort of announcement, she reached for the bottle of champagne and poured herself another glass. She gulped it down as fast as she did the first one and hiccupped.

"Tom, my heart beats a little faster when you're around, *(hiccup)* and I smile a lot more when I know I'm meeting you for lunch or you're coming over. *(hiccup)* I... I think it's something we could consider, *(hiccup)* but I want to make sure it's right for both of us. We need our families' blessing."

Tom's face fell, and a frown replaced his smile. "Azalea is marrying Sheriff DeVries, and he gave me the option to retire early. I'm not sure I'll be welcomed into your family. You know I needed to leave the sheriff's department because of my friendship with Don Hanson. He used me as an informant for his drug habit. I knew he drank but didn't know he did illegal drugs. Then he stole those drugs from the evidence room to incriminate Steph McGowan—a room where I was placed in charge. I had two years left for a full retirement pension, so I never got my full retirement, but it was either that or end up with charges against me. I'm doing okay, and I have my savings. I wanted you to know the full story. You know how rumors fly around town. I'm not sure if Mitch will accept the fact we're together."

"Tom, I know you're a good man. I don't care about the rumors. I know the man." Her eyes glowed with affection for this man, and she tilted her lips in a grin. "How about you use your hankie to remove the red lipstick from your mouth before anyone else sees you."

Sunny sat in the commissioners' meeting room at the courthouse as Mitch and Steve Bishop made their recommendation to hire her as the new female deputy. After a grueling week of drug and psychological testing, Sunny passed all their tests. Now they needed the final approval.

"Commissioners, we're in a time crunch as we don't want to be without a female on board in the sheriff's department. If we started to advertise it could take as long as four to six months before someone would be selected. With interviews and travel expenses, plus the drug testing and psychological testing, it gets expensive. We have the opportunity to hire Sunflower Lily Rose. She has a background in criminal justice and worked as a private investigator, plus we've already seen her in action in the apprehension of Wade Williams' and Mark D'Angelo's killer. With a few weeks of additional training, she could be ready for duty as soon as our current female deputy retires."

"Detective Bishop, I see you're here to act as moral support for the sheriff's suggestion. What is your opinion?"

"I've worked with Ms. Rose on the Williams and D'Angelo cases, and I find her very knowledgeable in her ability to investigate. She'll make a fine addition to our department. Because of her age she could be used in some of our undercover investigations."

"Thank you for your opinion. If there aren't any more questions from any of the commissioners, let's take a vote."

The mayor, who held a position on the board spoke. "I want to offer my support for the hiring of Ms. Rose. She'll be an asset to our law enforcement team." The others nodded their approval.

"Let's vote now." They all pushed their buttons and unanimously voted yes.

Sunny's tense muscles relaxed as she closed her eyes and whispered, "Thank you, God."

Steve turned and gave her a smile and thumbs up.

Mitch was not done with his meeting with the commissioners.

"I would like to bring up one more item before we leave you to the remainder of your meeting. I've been working for the past five years over sixty hours a week. I've built up so much vacation time and according to human resources I need to start to use it or lose it. We don't have a second in command, and I am unable to take any length of time off." He started to pull on his ear and a slight blush tinged his skin. "I'm getting married in a few months and want a honeymoon."

"So, what are you suggesting?" asked another commissioner.

"I would like to recommend Detective Steve Bishop as second in command when I'm not around. I've started cutting back on my hours. Our deputies are well trained, and I don't need to be working twenty-four seven. I know I don't need your permission to promote Detective Bishop, but I would like your approval."

"Thank you, Sheriff DeVries, for bringing this to our attention. I don't think any of us knew all the hours you put into your job. You need time away just like anyone else. Are there any questions from any of the other commissioners?"

Yes," the only lady commissioner on the county board who was closing in on seventy asked in a humorous voice. "I would like to know if Detective Bishop is one of the last bachelors on our law enforcement team?"

Steve's face turned beet red, and Sunny could feel her face burn a little.

"Um… I'm unmarried. Maybe…" he turned slightly toward Sunny, "in the future it might change."

"I figured as much," she chuckled. "I give my approval for Detective Bishop to act as second in command when Sheriff DeVries is unable to act." The remainder of the commissioners nodded their agreement. The three of them left the meeting.

"Welcome to the team, Deputy Rose," Mitch saluted Sunny as they stood outside the meeting room.

"Same here," Steve strained his eyes over the rim of his glasses. "We're proud to have you on our team."

"Me, too," Sunny eyes rested on Steve through the curtain of hair that vibrated loose from her twisted plait. She attempted to push her hair back in place.

Steve's eyes rested on her hair wishing he could run his fingers through the mass of hair.

CHAPTER FOURTEEN

"Can you pick up Natalia and Becca after school today? I got called to a meeting out of town and won't make it back in time."

"Uff da," uttered Azalea. "I'll try. We're swamped here right now. Mrs. Koep passed away, and we've been taking orders all day from relatives. I didn't realize she had such a large family."

"Oh, I remember the sweet old lady. Her husband passed away last year. She said she had a visit from an angel. Who can forget that sweet story?"

"Yep, that's the lady. Gotta go. Love you. I'll pick the girls up. Dinner at my house?"

"Sure. I can't wait."

Azalea dreamily hung up her cell phone.

"What can I do different for dinner tonight?" she posed her question to her staff. "I'd like something special."

"I've got a terrific egg bake with hash browns, ham, and lots of cheese," piped up Karol. "My hubby loved it, and he's not an egg bake fan."

"I haven't made an egg bake in ages. It would be something

different for an evening meal. You got the recipe."

"Sure, on my phone. I'll send it to you in a text."

The drive to pick up the girls was hectic as she had to go to two different schools and wait in line along with other parents. She started to look at Facebook on her phone as she waited for Natalia. Something told her to look up. She glanced out the car window and started to scan the area. Susan sat on a bench across the street in the park.

I wonder why she's here? I'll have to mention to Mitch about her hanging around the school.

Two men lingered nearby, close to where Susan sat. Azalea recognized them immediately as the ones who tried to rob her on Valentine's Day. Susan's purse lay next to her, and she could see the men eyeing the purse.

Should I acknowledge Susan and let her know those men are watching her?

The thought flew out of her mind as Natalia ran up to the car and opened the door.

"Hi, Sweetie. Your dad wanted me to pick you girls up today."

"We're not far from your store. Becca could walk over here if we know you're busy and walk together."

"Maybe when the weather's a little nicer it would be okay, but for now we'll pick you both up."

She turned to check on Susan again and found her face pressed up against the car window.

Azalea jumped. *How'd she get here so quick?*

She rolled down the car window. Susan's syrupy smile made Azalea want to wipe it off her face.

That smile is so fake.

"Hello, Susan, did you want something?" Azalea gave her a similar sugary smile.

"I knew Mitch was out of town today, and I don't work until later. I…um…I thought maybe I could spend some time with

Natalia."

Azalea pressed her lips together in a grimace. She opened and closed her mouth and struggled to find the right words.

Dear Lord, help me with this.

"Hmmm... I'm not sure Mitch would approve."

The smile dropped from her face as she stuck her head in the window. "Natalia, would you like your mommy to visit with you for a while?"

Natalia gulped. Her eyes turned to Azalea for help. Not quite sure what Natalia's thoughts were for a visit, she needed a quick answer without sounding offensive.

"Sorry, you caught me off guard. I need to pick up Becca and go back to work. You're welcome to come to store and visit with Natalia for a few minutes, but they need to do their homework. I don't dare let you stay too long without Mitch's okay."

"It's good enough for me," said Susan. "I'll be along in a few minutes." She walked back to the park bench.

Azalea drove off, but her eyes caught a momentary glance in her rear-view window of Susan's lips moving as if she was talking to the robbers who stood about six feet behind her, or otherwise she stood there and talked to herself.

Strange.

Mitch and Azalea enjoyed a glass of wine after dinner in her living room. The girls were at the table playing a board game. They sat in front of the TV with Azalea snuggled into his chest, but neither paid attention to the show.

"Do you mind if I turn it on the local cable news channel?"

"Go ahead."

He punched in the channel and Elena Wadsworth's picture popped up on the screen. The reporter read from her script, "The verdict just in late this afternoon. Elena Wadsworth found guilty for the murders of millionaire entrepreneur, Wade Williams, of the Pearl Candy Company, and Mark D'Angelo, the head accountant for the same company."

Pictures of Wade and Mark showed on the screen. "She will receive two life sentences and an additional ten-year sentence for the attempted murder of Azalea Rose, owner of Roses N'More Flower Shop in River Falls."

"Did you know this, Mitch?"

"No. Neither Sam Harris or Steve called me."

Mitch's phone rang, and Steve's number slid across his screen. "Did you hear the news on television?"

"Yeah, what happened to Sam notifying us?"

A beep sounded on his phone. "That's Sam calling me now. Talk to you later." He switched over to Sam's call.

"What's going on, Sam? Why didn't you call and tell us the verdict came in?"

"Sorry about the miscommunication. The verdict came in so late I didn't think it would make the news this fast. Usually the press doesn't do much with convictions, but since this was a high-profile case, I guess they were short of news for the evening. When I called, your secretary said you went to a meeting out of town, so I planned to call you tomorrow morning."

"Okay. We know now. I'll tell Azalea. Will you let Agent Schmidt know at the BCA…if he doesn't already know?"

"Sure, Mitch. Thanks for understanding."

"No problem. Touch base with me tomorrow with the details." He pushed the disconnect button.

Azalea sat upright on the edge of the couch, her eyes wide with curiosity. "So it's over?"

"Yes, just like the reporter said."

"I'm glad it's over…but sad for Elena at the same time…and for her son."

She snuggled back into Mitch's arm.

"Mitch, I wanted to tell you about Susan waiting outside the school today when I picked up Natalia. She wanted to take her for a visit."

"What! You didn't let her." He sat up and turned abruptly toward her.

"No, I refused, but I made her an offer to come to the shop. I could see in Natalia's eyes she seemed confused and didn't know if she should say yes or no to her mother's visit. I told Susan she could stay only for a few minutes… and she left after fifteen minutes."

"Susan's never been at the school before now. It's an interesting change of events. I still haven't heard anything from court. She said she petitioned for visitation. I'll need to check the courthouse records."

She turned her head to look him direct in the eyes. "How did Susan know you were gone for the day? It's curious when I didn't even know you went out of town until you called me."

"Um…I may have mentioned it to her when she called. She calls almost every day and wants to know what's going on with Nat."

"Oh…that reminds me. Susan gave Natalia a gift today—a cell phone. My personal opinion is I don't approve of children her age having access to their own personal cell phone. Nat didn't show it to me until after Susan left."

"I'll take a look at it when we go back home. I don't want to make a big fuss in front of Becca, but I agree. She doesn't need a cell phone at her age. She's always around someone who has one."

"I know she's her mother, but to go from almost ignoring your child since the day she was born to acting overly protective to someone she barely knows seems a little strange. Cell phones are not cheap, and who's paying the cell phone bill?"

"You never know about Susan. I will talk to her." He hesitated. "Um… I'm having her watched as much as I can without taking any of our deputies away from their regular duties."

"I saw those two men who tried to rob me hanging out at the park across from the school. They stood behind Susan, and I thought for sure they were going to steal her purse. By the time I looked back Susan was at the car window wanting to see Nat. Her purse hung on her shoulder."

"Their court date is set for May. As long as they stay clean, I can't do anything about where they hang out, but I don't like them at the school either. I'll have patrols drive by when school's out for the day. It should deter them."

"But it looked suspicious. As I drove away, I could see Susan back by the park bench. Her lips moved as if she carried on a conversation with them."

"Are you starting to investigate again? What about your promise?"

"Yes… I know." She held up her hands. "I promise not to snoop or do any more investigating… but I still can worry about what she's up to."

CHAPTER FIFTEEN

"Do you miss Sunny around the house at night?" Azalea inquired of her mother as they worked together to fill orders.

Karol returned to work full time, but her foot still bothered her, so Azalea sent her home early.

"The house did seem empty at first. It's only been a week, but Tom has filled up the void," she blushed. "I didn't realize having your daughter in the house cramped a person's social life."

Azalea put her hand on her hips and chuckled. "Mom, you haven't had much of a social life since Dad passed away except for your family and volunteering at church. Ahh…so Tom's been over more often since Sunny left? Is there something we should know about?" she teased.

"Well…not reeeallly," Bernadette continued to blush. "He would like to make it more of a relationship, but he's worried Mitch won't accept him as a potential step father-in-law because of the catastrophe with Donald Hanson."

"Oh…it's gone that far already?"

Buttercup walked in from the back room. "What's gone that

far?"

"Mom's been seeing more of Tom Bertrum since Sunny's at training."

"Good for you, Bernadette. You need a man in your life again."

"Mom invited Tom over along with the family for her birthday celebration."

"Ooh…I sense romance in the air."

A veil of amusement passed over Azalea. "Both Mitch and I wondered the way he hung around you if he was ready to propose."

"Propose what?" Bernadette pursed her lips as her eyes scooted in different directions.

"Mom, now you're being silly. Propose marriage, of course."

"He's hasn't mentioned marriage…yet…but we both care for each other."

"Sunny'll be back in a month. You won't have privacy anymore. Maybe we should make it a double wedding this summer."

Bernadette pushed her hand in the air, "Pshaw. I'm not in a hurry. It's your day."

The bell tingled, and Susan entered the store. Azalea saw the storm in her eyes as she headed right toward her.

She shook her finger in Azalea's face. "How dare you tell Mitch you don't think Natalia should have her own cell phone? I gave it to her as a gift, and you have no business interfering. She's not your daughter."

Azalea stood with her mouth agape. "Huh."

"You heard me," her face red with anger. She continued to shake her finger, and it quickly turned into a fist.

Trying to defuse the situation, Azalea's eyes darted around the room to make sure no customers were in the shop. "Let's go to the back room and talk about this."

She turned and walked away and hoped Susan would follow. Her hand reached for her cell phone in her pocket just in case things turned ugly.

When they were in the back room, Azalea spun around. Maintaining an even low tone, she put her hands on her hips, so she wouldn't be accused of hitting Susan.

"How dare you come in here and accuse me of interfering in your daughter's life. If you disagree with how I parent, you need to take it up with Mitch. I love Natalia and treat her no different than I would Becca. Very few children her age are allowed to own a cell phone. Becca first got a phone for Christmas from her dad, and she's older than Nat. Mitch took it away because he found a tracking device on it. Did you think Mitch was that stupid not to check the phone out? He wants to talk to you about it. I don't know what you want from me, but I've done nothing but love Natalia."

Azalea could see the animosity in Susan's eyes, which she quickly deflected and lowered her eyes. "I...I want to be able to stay in touch with her. I already talked to Mitch...or rather he yelled at me and said no more gifts unless he approved of them first."

"And who was going to pay the bill? Kids can run up all sorts of charges by downloading different apps. Did you think Mitch would pay for it?"

"Well...he's got the money. I paid for the phone and the first month."

"Look, Susan, I've tried to be nice to you. You served your time, and you deserve a break to get on with your life. The things you are doing right now will only irritate Mitch and upset Natalia's life. She's confused enough with the role you're wanting to play in her life."

"I don't need your holier than thou attitude." The angry retort hardened her features and the years in prison showed on her face.

"Why don't you talk to Reverend Rafe? He's counseled broken families before and can maybe help you transition to where both you and Mitch can be comfortable."

"I have every intention of getting my daughter back and...and

Mitch. He loved me once, and I know he still feels something for me."

The statement struck Azalea in the face, and cold reality sunk in.

I could still lose Mitch and Natalia. Oh, God, give me the strength to deal with her.

A sudden calm overwhelmed her and gave her a spiritual peace. "Susan, I know Mitch. He's not the same man you knew years ago. He's accepted God as his savior, and he's committed himself to me and Becca. Please don't make things more difficult for yourself."

"We'll see about that," she spat. She turned to pounce out of the room and her arm hit a Spathiphyllum foiled and bowed for delivery at a funeral. It crashed to the floor.

What an apropos way to end our conversation—knocking over a peace lily.

Susan stamped her foot on the concrete floor, "What the…" and swooped out the door.

"Mitch, we need to talk," prompted Azalea that evening. "It's about Susan."

"I gave her a good talking to this afternoon about the phone. How dare she give Natalia a phone with a tracking device—not that it's a bad idea for a child to have one, but I didn't like the way she did it—without my permission."

"I understand where you're coming from, but what concerns me is her attitude toward me. She came in the shop today… angry. She thought I had something to do with taking the phone away from Nat. She interrupted my day with shouts and threats. I'll pray for her healing from being in prison, but I don't want her in my shop anymore. When you see her, please relay the message."

"I think things are coming to a head pretty soon. I've checked at the courthouse, and she's not filed any papers to get visitation with

Nat."

"She said… oh, I can't say it." She closed her eyes and swallowed her fears.

"What did she say?"

"It's best left unsaid."

"Zalia, it'll haunt you until you let it out."

She squeezed her eyes shut and recalled the words Susan uttered that left her destroyed.

Between clenched teeth, "She said she has every intention of getting custody of Natalia and getting you back. She said she knows you still have feelings for her."

Mitch's arms wrapped around her, "Oh, darling, please don't worry about what she said. She's just blowing off at the mouth. There is no truth to what she says. There's no way she's going to get custody of Nat. Not with her history. As for getting me back, you-know-what will freeze over before that happens."

"I asked her to talk to Rafe. She refused. All I can do is pray for her deliverance."

"We'll both pray."

Yes, I know it'll be within God's timing, but I hope it'll be soon. You do realize what she said could come true."

"What do you mean?"

"She could get custody of Nat if something happened to you." She put her hands over her face. "I don't even want to think about it."

CHAPTER SIXTEEN

"Mom," Becca shouted as she and Natalia entered the shop, both out of breath. Mitch sauntered in after the girls raced to see who would get to the door first.

"What's up? You girls seem so excited."

"We're studying spring flowers and trees in school," offered Natalia. "My teacher wants us to gather as many examples as we can and bring them to school so we can…like…name them and put them on a board."

"You mean samples, don't you?"

"Yeah, that's right… samples."

"Is it okay, Mom, if I go with Natalia after school tomorrow to help her gather different *samples*?"

"I could pick them up after school and drive them around," offered Mitch.

"Ah, Dad, can't we go by ourselves? Becca's school is only a few blocks away." Natalia pleaded with her eyes. "We could meet after school and…like…walk around the parks and neighborhoods to see what we can find."

Mitch rolled his eyes and glanced at Azalea to see her reaction.

"I think Becca's old enough to be an escort for you," he rubbed Natalia's head, "and keep you out of trouble."

"That's what I'm worried about. They'd get lost going up and down the streets."

"Chill, Mom. I got my phone in the backpack. I can always call when we think we got enough *samples*."

"Stop by here when you're done, and I'll give you some flowers for your class. We have spring tulips and hyacinth you can take to school. Irises might be in bloom around town, too. It's almost May and the weather's been warm enough. Make sure to ask permission before you take anything from anyone's yard."

"Yes, Mom, we know." Becca rolled her eyes. "We're not stupid."

"Nana will have some in her yard. I'm sure she'll let you pick a few. You better start on your homework."

"You sure this is all right with you," whispered Mitch after the girls went to the corner to start on their homework.

"I hope so. Becca knows her way around town and most of the streets are in alphabetical order, so it'll be hard for them to get lost."

Mitch's phone rang. "It's Jake."

"I wonder what he wants," voiced Azalea. They glanced at each other with the same thought. "Maybe an offer."

"Hi, Jake. What's up?"

"Yeah."

"Sounds great. Can you tell me the details over the phone?"

"Ahha... yep... sounds good to me."

"Okay, I'll talk to Azalea." He shoved his phone back in his pocket.

"Well, what?" Her eyes surveyed him with anticipation.

His lips turned into slow grin which widened into a huge grin. "We got an offer on my house."

"How exciting. Is it a good one?"

"Yep. A cash deal... closing in a month. Good thing we have

the big house to fall back on or I'd have to move in with you," he continued to grin.

She put down her knife and wrapped her arms around his neck. "Not such a bad idea. Then I'd have you to myself all night long."

"Me, too. This waiting to get married is killing me."

"I never did ask you if you snore."

"Snore... I don't think so. Natalia's never said anything to me. I'm just head over heels in love with you, and I never thought about our sleeping habits. How about you? Do you snore?"

She blushed and bit her lip. "I do a little sometimes... but only when I'm really tired."

"Oh, this may not be good. We'll need to make sure you never get tired." His lips were warm and sweet as they descended on hers.

"Okay, you guys knock it off. You're in a public place," snickered Buttercup, as she entered from the back room.

They backed out of their embrace, each with a guilty smile on their faces.

"Why don't you guys just elope? I can see you want to be together."

"And deprive you of throwing rice at us? No way," admonished Mitch.

"A couple more months. Steph's in her seventh month of pregnancy." Azalea looked reproachful at Mitch. "I just had a thought."

"Oh, spare me!" Mitch threw a hand to his forehead in a mocking gesture.

Azalea ignored him. "My grandparents had their wedding day on July twenty-fifth." She looked on her phone. "It's a Saturday. How about it? It'll be extra special to me. Steph and Rafe should have their baby by then. If they don't, I'll have a maid of honor with a big tummy."

"The sooner the better for me."

"We need to start work on the house right away if yours is sold. What contractors have you talked to about the remodeling?"

"Let me make a few calls to see who's available right away. You'll need to start selecting flooring and wall paint."

Azalea blushed. "I've already looked around and found what I like... with your approval, of course."

"Sounds great. Show me some samples. I'll go over to Jake's office and sign the papers. I'll stop by for the girls when I'm done."

───※❊※───

The girls decided to walk to the city park after school. It was a little farther than the one across from their school, but too many others from Natalia's class were combing the area around the school for flowering bushes and trees.

"Nat, will you hurry up," shouted Becca as she was a half block ahead and at the entrance to the park. "There's no one here, so we can get first pick." She waved for Natalia to hurry. Becca's longer legs made it easier for her to race ahead.

Natalia carried a small trash bag to hold their treasured finds along with her school backpack. Out of breath, she stopped in front of Becca.

"Can we sit down? I'm tired of carrying all this junk."

"Sure. Mom packed extra snacks for us. Becca stretched as she pulled off her backpack and set it next to her. She reached inside for a sandwich bag of red licorice. They sat down on the bench closest to the parking lot.

"Yum," mumbled Natalia, as she scarfed down several pieces.

"I'm thirsty. Let's find the restrooms and see if the water is running. We can get a drink."

A dirty white van drove into the parking lot near the girls. Becca and Natalia ignored the van as they ventured to the drinking fountain and picked a few blossoming flowers off several trees. They returned to the park bench, and Natalia shoved the twigs into the bag.

"I think I have enough to get credit," she sighed as she twisted the bag shut.

They heard the van's motor start up and back toward them. The shadow of the van blocked their view to the parking lot. A tall man wearing a ski mask opened the side door of the van and jumped out. He moved with a limp toward them. A shorter man in a similar ski mask came from the other side of the vehicle.

Becca held up her hand to shield her eyes from the sun as she looked up. Natalia moved closer to her.

Becca reached for Natalia's hand as the men came closer, and she could see their eyes through the ski masks. The tall man's bloodshot eyes shot darts into her, and her heart raced with fear. "Come on, Nat. We gotta go." She started toward the street.

Natalia pulled away and reached back to pick up her homework assignment.

"You the sheriff's kid?" the tall man barked.

Neither girl answered. Natalia grabbed onto Becca's arm. A panicked look crossed their faces.

Becca knew she did not like the tall man, and the short one driving scared her even more. She reached back and grabbed Natalia's hand again to run—if they had to. Her backpack laid on the bench between her and the shorter man who had come up behind them. Her phone was in the backpack.

Mom said if a stranger scared me to start screaming.

"Pleeeease leave us alone," she stood her stance as she tried to be brave.

"I think we got two for one here," the short man sneered as he let out a raucous laugh.

Becca bit her lip as her eyes glanced from one man to the other. If they ran now maybe they could outrun them.

"Run, Nat!" she shouted.

Both girls took off running, but the men were too fast for them.

The shorter man snatched Natalia and covered her screams with his hand as he carried her to van. Her feet dangled as she tried to kick him in the shins.

The taller man tackled Becca, and landed on top of her. He tried to cover her mouth with his hand, and she bit down hard and drew blood. He cried out, "Ouch! You little…" and his knuckles hit her face. She felt her neck jerk and a wave of dizziness overwhelmed her.

He grabbed Becca, dragged her to the van, and roughly pushed her in. She screamed, "HELP!" but no one was in the park to hear her cry.

The shorter man had already tied Natalia's hands together and pushed a sock in her mouth to keep her from screaming. Becca tried to fight the taller man and kicked his sore leg.

"Ow!" he yelled in pain as he grabbed his leg. "You little bit…"

"Get her tied up so we can get otta here," the short man demanded.

"Quit tellin' me what ta do," the tall man hollered back.

Becca's hands were tied with cable ties and a similar sock shoved in her mouth. It tasted of dirt and grime. She bit the inside of her mouth when he hit her earlier and the blood continued to ooze into the sock.

The girls squeezed their eyes shut as the van screeched out of the parking lot. Becca tried kicking on the door and let out a primal scream through the sock in her mouth. Natalia retaliated and kicked the seats in front. The tall man turned and hit her legs with a cane he had in the front seat.

"Get back," he growled.

She crawled closer to Becca and started to whimper and moan.

Becca, sitting further back in the vehicle could not see. *No windows. I can't see where we're going.* The seats were too high in the front to see over them.

Becca looked at Natalia. Tears streamed from Natalia's eyes.

Terror laced her face as she lay on her side. *Where are they taking us? What's going to happen to us?*

CHAPTER SEVENTEEN

Azalea called Becca's phone again for the umpteenth time and still no answer. The time to lock the store for the day pressed closer and closer.

Worried, she called Mitch. "Have you heard from the girls? They should have called you or me by now to pick them up."

"No. Did you call your mom? Maybe they stopped there."

"You would think Becca would answer her phone even if she went to Mom's. I'll call her. Let me know if you hear anything."

"Okay."

Azalea's fingers shook as she dialed her mother. "Mom, did the girls stop by this afternoon to pick some of your spring flowers and apple blossoms?"

"No, I came home right after I left the store and haven't seen them."

"Okay, if they stop, tell Becca to call me right away."

"Will do."

Now she was worried. She redialed Mitch. "Mom says she hasn't seen the girls."

"Okay, I'll get in my squad and start driving around. I'm sure they probably went to one of the parks and are playing on the playground equipment."

"Thanks. I'm worried. I always know where Becca is."

"Well, don't worry. I'm sure they're fine."

Mitch hung up the phone. All sorts of thoughts ran through his mind. Being sheriff wasn't the easiest job, and he knew plenty of things could happen to two unaccompanied girls even in a small town like River Falls.

He drove to the school and walked across the street to the park. There were a few children hanging out there on the playground equipment.

"You kids know Becca Lederman and Natalia DeVries?"

"Yeah," one of the boys answered. "Natalia's in my class. I saw her leave earlier with another girl."

"Did you see which direction they went?"

He pointed down the street. "I think I heard the older girl mention going to some of the other parks."

"Okay, thanks."

Mitch started to check several other parks close by but did not see any sign of the girls. He got on his phone and asked dispatch to have the officers on duty keep an eye out for Becca and Natalia. He drove to the city park.

He arrived at the park and noticed two backpacks and a plastic bag on the bench nearest the parking area. He walked over and unzipped the backpack.

This belongs to Becca. Here's her cell phone.

He opened the plastic bag, and his face froze as he recognized the flowering buds the girls collected. His frantic eyes scanned the area. No girls. He started to run around the perimeter of the park and checked the bathrooms. No girls. On his way back he saw a hair twist lying on the ground. He picked it up and saw a few strands of brown hair clinging to it.

Oh, no!

His face contorted and turned ashen. The hairs on his arms stood on end as he realized the girls were missing. He examined the area looking for some other clue. He saw fresh tire tracks dug into the gravel parking lot, as if someone sped away in a hurry.

Oh, my god, how am I going to explain this to Azalea? My baby. Where's my baby?

He could hear a tiny voice inside him. *Get your act together. You're the sheriff. Act like one.*

He took a deep breath to calm his shaking limbs and dialed dispatch again.

"Put out an Amber Alert on two missing girls. Becca Lederman is thirteen-years old, brown hair, brown eyes, a little over five feet tall, and..." he stopped to catch his breath as his heart beat faster, "and Natalia DeVries, ten-years-old, blond hair, dark blue eyes, four feet ten inches tall. Both girls wearing blue jeans and sweatshirts. Contact Detective Bishop and have him meet me at the city park ASAP."

Detective Steve Bishop arrived within minutes of the dispatcher's call to his phone. Mitch waited by the entrance to the park. He did not want Steve to drive in and disturb any possible evidence.

"Are you sure the girls are missing?" his first words sounded addle-headed coming from a detective, but his brain swirled with unbelief that something happened to the girls.

"Why would Becca leave her backpack and her phone? There's no other explanation other than they've been abducted. For what reason—I don't know. It's been several hours since school let out, and they were seen walking toward the park from school." He pointed to the spot in the parking lot. "It looks like someone took off in a hurry by the tracks in the gravel."

"I'll get our evidence team here right away." He grabbed his phone from his jacket pocket and scrolled his list of contacts.

Mitch dialed dispatch and shouted into the phone, "Did you put out the Amber Alert?"

"Yes, sir. We put it as soon as you called. It went throughout the state. Do you have any idea what type of vehicle to look for? Any more information would help."

"No," his shoulders slumped. "I arrived too late. I found Becca's backpack and phone and evidence they've been abducted."

"I'm so sorry, sir. We'll keep the Amber Alert going. They've got all the roads blocked leading out of the county. The surrounding counties are assisting with calling out all law enforcement."

"Please keep on it, we're out here right now gathering what evidence we can find."

Steve's eyes scanned the ground close to the bench and walked in circles going out a little more in each circle.

"Mitch, come here!" shouted Steve a short distance away.

Mitch ran over to where Steve stood.

"See, the drag marks on the ground. The ground is still soft from the snow melting, and it looks like someone dragged another person along the grass. See the indentation of the tips of the shoes."

"I sure do. One of them must have tried to run away and was tackled."

"The grass is laid down over here." He pointed to a spot not far away. "It looks like she was tackled to the ground and halfway dragged to the vehicle. Let's follow the drag marks."

The drags marks led them close to where the vehicle dug its tires into the gravel.

Mitch ran his fingers through his hair as he walked back and forth along the drag path. He walked to where the alleged struggle took place and waited for the evidence team to arrive. Darkness would soon be upon them, and he wanted to get the most out of the daylight hours.

I need to call Azalea, but don't know how to tell her.

He knelt down, and his eyes bored into the area where the

alleged struggle took place. On several blades of grass he found a blood stain.

"Bishop, get over here," he shouted. "Blood stain. Mark this area for the evidence team."

Steve ran to his vehicle, retrieved several small flags, and brought several baggies back with him.

"Give me your knife. We'll dig out this area with the blood and have it analyzed."

He handed Steve his knife. Mitch's memory flooded with a picture of Becca shyly giving the gift to him at Christmas. The tears seeped from his eyes. Steve pulled on a pair of gloves and dug out the blood-stained clump of grass.

The few deputies Mitch and Steve trained in evidence collection arrived. Steve barked orders for them to take pictures of the scene and scour the park especially around the abduction site. With his team on the job, he took the time to call Azalea.

It's past closing time, but I'm sure she's still there.

She answered the phone after the first ring.

"Mitch, did you find them?"

"No," he pulled on his ear. "Now, Azalea, will you sit down while I talk to you over the phone."

"Oh my... Mitch, what happened?" She leaned against the counter for support as her heart dropped in her chest.

"We found Becca's backpack and her phone in the city park. It appears both girls have been abducted."

"What! You're kidding me, right?"

"No, Dear, listen to me. I'm at the city park right now. We've put out an Amber Alert throughout the state. All the roads leading out of the county are blocked and the counties surrounding us have their entire patrols out."

"I'll be right there." She did not take time to say goodbye. She dropped the phone on the counter and covered her face with her hands as she screamed. "Oh, my God, why did this happen to Becca

and Nat? Why? Why? Why?"
   No answer came.

CHAPTER EIGHTEEN

Becca and Natalia rode scrunched in the back of the windowless van not knowing which direction or where the two men would take them. Tired of fighting and kicking at the door and the front seats, they settled down and huddled together.

The minutes felt like hours. Becca tried to memorize whether they were on an asphalt road or gravel road. She knew she needed to keep her cool to help them escape at some point. The van slowed down and turned. Soon it stopped.

The tall man with the limp got out. Becca could hear the crunch of gravel as he walked away. A short time later he returned and opened the back of the van. They could see his eyes leer at them even through the face mask.

"Well, now my pretties, we're going to cover your eyes so you can't give away our hideout."

Becca struggled by throwing her head around and moaning through the sock in her mouth as he tied the handkerchief around her eyes. "You might as well give up. We're stronger than you, and I'll give you another hit in the head if you don't hold still."

The thought of being struck made Becca stop and hold still. She did not see how Natalia reacted, but she heard her muffled cries.

The driver strode around and grabbed Natalia by her arms and led her into their hideout. The tall man kept a firm grip on Becca's arm as he pulled her along behind Natalia.

Becca smelled burnt wood and stale fried bacon as they entered and wrinkled her nose in distaste.

The girls were led through another door where the two men cut the cable ties around their wrists. Becca and Natalia rubbed their hands, glad to be free from the restraints. However, it did not last long as the short man pushed them toward two chairs and tied their wrists to the sides of the chairs. Their eyes remained covered.

He pulled the socks from their mouths. The girls could hear water running in the next room. The tall man's footsteps were uneven as he walked back into the room. He carried a glass of water and a bottle of Rohypnol.

"Here, girlie, open your mouth and take this pill."

Becca held her lips tight and refused to open her mouth. The short man grabbed her head and tilted it back. He pinched her nose shut, so she had no choice but to open her mouth to breathe. The tall man shoved a pill in her mouth and poured water down her throat to force her to swallow. He did the same to Natalia. Soon they slumped in their chairs.

The tall man removed the wraps from their eyes as they slept.

"I wonder how long we'll need to keep these girlies as hostages?" He threw the handkerchiefs down on the kitchen table.

"I don't know, Mac. The boss says to hold up here until we can get money out of the sheriff and his girlfriend. The boss says they'll pay to get their kids back."

"We got plenty of pills to keep 'em quiet."

"I don't like messin' with the sheriff and his family. Mc thinks we made a big mistake taking his kid. I hope the boss gets the money here fast so we can get otta here. I think I'll go to Mexico."

"Yeah, I'm with you. Don't care for the cold."

Mac's cell phone rang. "Yeah," he answered.

"Yeah, boss, we got 'em. They're knocked out right now."

"Yeah, Rodney held their heads while I shoved the pills in 'em just like you said to do. They won't wake up for a while. We'll keep 'em quiet. Don't you worry none."

"It was the boss."

"I figured that, Dummy," said the short one called Rodney.

"Don't call me Dummy. I ain't stupid."

"I know you ain't stupid, but you were dumb enough to get run over by the flower lady when we tried to rob her."

"Don't remind me. She'll pay dearly for my gimpy leg," said Mac.

"Your leg'll get better. You just took the walking cast off too soon. It takes time to heal."

"How would you know?"

"I was a medic in the Army. It's how I got hooked on drugs."

"Now that's pretty stupid if you ask me."

Azalea broke the speed limit as she drove, tears streaming down her face, to the park. Mitch was talking with other deputies when she drove up. He turned abruptly and ran toward her. The first thing she saw was Becca's and Natalia's backpacks lying on the park bench. She ran to Becca's first, picked it up, and hugged it to her body as moans of helplessness overwhelmed her. When Mitch reached her they threw their arms around each other.

"I wish I never would have let them go by themselves," he half whispered in her ear as it pained him to admit an error in judgement.

"Becca wouldn't go with anyone she didn't know and either would Nat. River Falls is too small a town for something like this to happen."

"Yeah, I said the same thing about the remains found at the high rise and the Williams' murder."

"What happened to our small peaceful town?" She sniffed and wiped her nose with back of her hand. Mitch handed her the hankie from his pocket. The tears had dried on her face, but she used it to wipe the smeared mascara from around her eyes.

Mitch had no answer but to shake his head. "We'll find them. Don't worry."

"I know you'll do everything in your power to bring our girls back. I've got faith in you and in God. I don't believe He would let anything bad happen to the girls."

One of the deputies who stood guard to the entrance of the park walked up to them.

"Sir, dispatch has the head of the Sheriff's Posse on the phone. He wants to know if their group can help in any way."

"Yes, tell them to meet here and they can take different roads out of town and scour all the backroads for any sign of strangers. If they see anyone or anything odd, call it in to dispatch. Don't take any chances in approaching anyone without armed deputies."

"Yes, sir." He ran back to the squad to deliver the message.

Steve Bishop approached Azalea and Mitch.

"I'm so sorry about this, Azalea. We're doing everything we can. Right now our evidence team is scouring the area for any clues. We believe there was a struggle."

"A… struggle," whispered Azalea. Her eyes shot up to meet Mitch's. "You didn't say anything about a struggle." Her body went cold, and she started to shiver.

"We don't know yet. Azalea, you need to let us handle this. You can stay here, but I don't want you in the way of any of our team gathering evidence."

Steve held out a baggie holding a ponytail holder with little plastic rabbits. "Do you recognize this?"

Azalea reached for the bag. "I put this in Becca's ponytail when she left for school. Who found it?"

"Mitch found it where we believe a scuffle occurred." He held out his hand for the return of the bag. "It's evidence right now." She nodded.

Her hand went to her forehead. "I never called any of my family. They need to know. They can help in the search."

"We'll get the whole town out if we have to," said Mitch. "I love both those girls, and I'll do everything in my power to find them. I'll even call the governor and get the National Guard out here to scour the county… if they're still in the county."

"Mitch, I'll send several deputies from house to house to see if anyone noticed anything or even if they have security cameras. It's too bad we don't have security cameras to cover at least the parking area of the parks in town."

Mitch's mouth twisted in pain. "You know the city council and county board are so tight. Until something bad happens they won't portion out a dime. I agree. We need better security at these parks, especially where kids play."

Azalea rocked back and forth on her heels. School let out over three hours ago and the sun started to set in the sky.

I need to call my family.

Her cell phone rang. Call from Chrys scrolled across her screen.

"Zalia, we had an Amber Alert on our phones. The description of the missing girls sounded like Becca and Natalia. Is everything okay with them?"

Azalea broke down and sobbed into the phone. "No… the girls… they were abducted. I'm at the city park right now."

"We're on our way. I'll call Mom and Sunny. They need to know. I'll call Jake for you."

"Thanks, Chrys. I forgot about calling Jake."

After she hung up, she stared at the sky as it darkened. The deputies searched now with flashlights.

Dear God, please send your angels to watch over Becca and Natalia.

CHAPTER NINETEEN

The Sheriff's Posse arrived and gathered around Mitch while Azalea stood by his side. He gave them instructions to search in pairs and travel all the roads. "If any of you see anything suspicious call the dispatch office. Don't try to be heroes," he added knowing some of his posse members were former military.

Mitch ran his fingers through his hair in frustration. "I can't stand here and do nothing. I need to be out looking for my kids."

"Mitch, someone needs to be in charge," Azalea tried to comfort him. "You are the best man for the job."

Several cars came to screeching halt, stopped by the deputy who blocked the entrance to the park with his squad car. Chrys and her husband, Taylor, jumped out with their two boys and waved their hands at Azalea.

"Azalea. Mitch. Can we pass the line?"

Mitch waved them over. Bernadette followed with Tom Bertrum behind her.

Bernadette threw her arms around her daughter as they comforted each other. Chrys joined the two, and they looked like a football huddle.

"What do you know so far?" inquired Chrys.

"There's not much to tell," Azalea began. "I'd been trying to call Becca after school, and she never answered her phone. I called Mitch... worried. He went out in search of them. He found their backpacks with Becca's phone still in hers." Her face held a conflict of emotions ready to burst into tears again at the any moment. Chrys put her arm around Azalea.

"Take it slow. You need to stay strong for the girls."

"Yes, I know. My mind is going through all possible scenarios."

"Don't think about them. You don't know."

"I can't stop. Mitch says all the roads are blocked going out of the county. The nearby counties are all on alert. The Sheriff's Posse is out searching. I don't know what more they can do. There's so many woods and hunting grounds in the area. Whoever took them could be hiding almost anywhere."

"I called Steph and Rafe. They're on their way."

"Thank you, Chrys. I can't think straight right now. All I want is my girls back."

"I left a message on Sunny's phone. Jake didn't answer, so I left a message for him."

Steve walked up to them holding his cell phone. "Just got a call from Sunny. I informed her what happened. She's on her way back from training. Shouldn't take her too long to get here. Her entire class volunteered if we need to form a search party."

Chrys reached out and touched Steve's arm. "Thank you, Steve. Do you think the girls are still in the county?"

He shook his head. "I don't know. Depends on what time they were abducted. School ended at three thirty and if they walked to the park, it had to be after four thirty before something happened. It's now dark, and they had a good two hours to go into hiding. The entire state is on Amber Alert especially the surrounding counties. If we don't find them tonight, we'll start searching the woods and stop at every house." He put his hands on Azalea's shoulders.

"We'll do everything in our power to find them—hopefully, tonight yet, and throw those rats in jail."

Azalea covered Steve's hand with her own. "I know you will." She tried a limp smile but failed miserably.

Azalea watched Mitch shout out commands to his deputies. She remained grateful for his take charge attitude. She kept out of his way. When his phone rang, she sprinted to his side.

"Sheriff DeVries here," he spoke matter-of-fact into the phone.

"Yes, Governor. We are working as fast as we can with all our deputies in the county, plus members of our Sheriff's Posse are volunteering."

Wow! The Governor calling.

"Yes, if we don't find them tonight, we'll see what we have for volunteers in the morning. If there aren't enough, I'd appreciate your offer to call out the local National Guard."

Another pause. Azalea could see his mouth quiver. "Yes, Governor, one of the girls is my daughter and the other belongs to my fiancé." Another pause. "We don't know why they were kidnapped. We have no idea if it was for revenge or not."

She walked over to Mitch and wrapped her arms around his waist above his utility belt as he continued to talk.

"Thank you, Governor. I'll keep you informed."

"Yes, I know you'll be available twenty-four seven. I appreciate your offer to help. Good bye."

Reverend Rafe and Steph arrived, and Mitch motioned them through the yellow tape. Inquisitive neighbors milled around the tape line.

Steve walked up to the crowd gathering. "Anyone have any video footage that could be helpful in locating any vehicles seen in the park this afternoon." Many shook their heads. It seemed like a dead end with no video footage.

One of the crowd spoke up. "Sir, I know a neighbor two houses down has a few cameras on his property as he's only home on weekends. He might have some video. One of his cameras faces the street toward the park. But he won't be back for a few days."

"Any way to get hold of him?" Steve's voice was close to desperation.

"I can try his cell phone. I have it in case of emergency."

"I think this is an emergency."

"I'll see if I can reach him."

"Let me know when you do."

Steve walked back to his evidence gathering team while Mitch and Azalea reached out for comfort from Rafe and Steph.

"I'm so sorry, Zalia. We heard the Amber Alert, but had no idea it was the girls."

"Can I say a short prayer since all the family is here right now?" offered Rafe.

"I think we all could use a little encouragement," admitted Mitch.

Azalea motioned for her family to gather together. Chrys, Taylor, the boys, Bernadette, and Tom Bertrum along with Azalea and Mitch gathered in a circle with Rafe and Steph. Azalea motioned for Steve to join them. She never knew if Steve believed in the power of prayer, but she invited him to join them. He wriggled in among the family as Rafe prayed.

"Father, I come to you in the name of Jesus, knowing You are my Refuge and High Tower. You are our refuge and stronghold in these times of trouble. We cry for Your help, Lord. Hear us as we stand out here tonight in desperation to find Becca and Natalia. Only You know where they are, Lord. Please keep Your angels watching for them and keep them safe. Help our law enforcement find the clues to quickly discover where they were taken and return them to their family who loves them. We know both Becca and Natalia believe in You, Lord, and You will not forsake them. Amen."

Everyone mumbled, "Amen."

"What can we do to help?" asked Rafe.

Azalea shook her head. "I don't know at this point. I'm sticking close to Mitch as he's running the operation."

Steph raised her eyes to Mitch. "I'm so sorry, Mitch. We want to help. Can we drive around? Anything."

"Actually," Mitch pulled on his ear as his nostrils flared, "you could stay at Azalea's house in case any calls come in asking for ransom money. We're jumping to conclusions here. I know how stubborn she is and won't leave my side. She'll want to be in on every aspect of the search."

"You don't have to talk as if I'm not here," she hissed. Tired and stressed she regretted the comment immediately. Her eyes lowered to the ground.

"Do you mind, Azalea, if we stay at your house?" Steph's eyes questioned.

"I'm sorry. I don't mind at all. I know I won't get any sleep tonight."

Steph's eyes, filled with sympathy, looked at Rafe, who nodded. "We'll stay at your place. I still have your key."

"Thanks. I'll probably stop by a little later."

"What about the rest of your family?"

"There's not much they do can do right now," said Mitch. "I have every available law enforcement person out there, plus the surrounding counties are doing the same. Nothing can get by us on the roads. It's night time, and we can't do much now except patrol the roads and stop all the vehicles since we have no idea what type of vehicle was used. The governor offered to send a National Guard helicopter, but still at night we won't see much."

"The evidence gathering team will be done soon. It's too dark to do much more," announced Detective Bishop as he walked up to the group. "We'll finish yellow taping the area and put a patrol on duty overnight. I'll be out here as soon as it's daylight to try and gather more evidence."

"Detective Bishop," came a voice from the crowd of bystanders. He walked over to the man. "I have the owner of the house with the cameras on the phone. Could you please explain to him the urgency of the situation?"

Steve jerked the phone from his hand and in an exasperated voice, "Detective Bishop, here. I understand you have cameras on your property which might help us find a vehicle that kidnapped two young girls this afternoon."

"I won't be back at my house until the end of the week," sounded the voice over the phone.

"Sir, I don't need to tell you how urgent it is we get the video. We're not sure it'll show anything, but any help we can get from you would be appreciated."

"I'm out of state and even if I leave tonight, which I'm too tired to drive, it would take over a day to travel back home."

"Sir, this is an extreme emergency. I will get a court order in the morning to confiscate your cameras if you're not going to be cooperative."

"It's not that I'm not cooperative. All my backup equipment for the cameras are in the house, so it won't do you much good. I'll leave early morning and drive as fast as I can to get back. Just so you know, I'll be losing a lot of business coming back early."

"But you also may save two little girls lives. You decide which is more important."

Steve hung the phone up. "What a jerk!"

"That's why I was hesitant to call him. He's never been a good neighbor with all the cameras around his house. We, as his neighbors, feel like he's spying on us while he's gone."

"I hope he arrives tomorrow like he promised. I pray there's something on those cameras."

CHAPTER TWENTY

Becca opened her eyes and saw a murky blackness all around her. She struggled to move her hands and feet, but they remained tied to the chair. Becca stretched her neck back and forth. Her jaw hurt from the struggle, and it pained her to move it too much. With the only light coming from under the door, it took a few minutes for her eyes to adjust.

Becca strained to focus as she continued to twist her head. The room was sparsely furnished with a small bed and nightstand. A window covered with a blind broke the emptiness of the walls. The sound of a tree branch snapping against the glass startled her, and she jerked upright in the chair.

"Pssst, Nat, are you awake?"

No answer. Becca's eyes focused enough to see Nat tied in a chair close to her. Her head thrust forward.

What did they give us to knock us out? I hope Nat's okay.

Becca heard a door slam and then voices.

"Here's a few groceries I picked up at Walmart. Whole town's in an uproar," he snickered.

"TV dinners again. I'm getting' sick of this junk."

"It'll get us by until the boss tells us different."

Natalia let out a low groan and threw her head back.

"Nat, wake up."

"Wh… What… Where are we?" Natalia's head nodded with a heaviness.

Becca whispered, "I don't know, but don't talk very loud. The men who took us are in the next room, and they might hear we're awake."

"I'm scared, Becca. I want my daddy."

"Shhh… they'll hear you. They haven't hurt us yet. I don't know what they want with us, but my mom says to have faith and God will protect us."

Natalia started to whimper and sniff. "I wanna go home."

"Shhh…"

The door opened. The men wore the same ski masks.

"Hush up in here or we'll have to stuff your mouths again to keep you quiet," growled Mac as he limped into the room.

"I have to go to the bathroom," sniffed Natalia.

"So do I," seconded Becca.

"Oh… all right… I'll untie one at a time, and you can use the can." He shut the door and soon came back with a knife.

He cut the ties loose from Natalia and grabbed her by the arm.

"Don't try any funny stuff or you won't get any special privileges again."

"What ya doin?" growled Rodney, as he finished pulling on his ski mask. "At least let me know before bringin' 'em out here."

"You watch the other one while this one uses the facilities."

"Yeah, sure."

Natalia was back in a few minutes. Mac took out some new cable ties and tied her to the chair.

"Your turn." He cut Becca's bands. She moved her wrists back and forth and rubbed them while he cut the bands from her legs.

Mac led her to the bathroom and shut her in the room. She

looked around for an avenue of escape. There was a small window above the toilet. She tried to push it open, but the lock was stuck tight with several nails pounded into the sides so it could not be opened.

Defeated, she did her business and washed her hands. She opened the door to a sneering Mac.

"Thought you might try to escape. We're no dummies, ya know."

He grabbed her arm and pulled her reluctant body back to the chair and tied her up.

Rodney walked into the room with a bottle of water and pills. He repeated the same process—pinched their noses shut, shoved a pill in their mouth and squirted water so they would swallow. Within ten minutes the girls were out again.

Mitch stretched and yawned behind his desk. He noticed Azalea nodding off on the chair across from his desk. There was no comfortable place to relax at the LEC. It certainly wasn't designed for comfort.

"I think you need to go home."

"I don't want to leave just in case they find the girls."

"I understand. I don't want to leave either, but we need to try and get some sleep so we can start the search in the morning. Several nearby counties are sending over reinforcements, so our deputies can get some sleep. We won't be any good to anyone without some sleep... even if it's just a few hours."

"Um... I suppose you're right."

"I'll follow you home. I'll spend the night on the couch, and we can start our search again early. Steve will let us know if they find anything."

Azalea dragged her tired body from the chair. "Okay, if I do fall asleep, I want you to wake me at the crack of dawn so we can start searching again."

"Promise," he assured her, feeling her fear and grief.

Mitch followed her home and parked his car in the back alley next to the garage. He flipped his cell phone to vibrate earlier in the evening. Susan called several times, and he let it go to voicemail. The phone vibrated again, and Susan's name ran across the screen.

I'll call her in the morning. Hope to have some answers by then.

Rafe's eyes jolted opened when Mitch and Azalea entered through the back door. He motioned with his finger to his lips and pointed to a sleeping Steph. Rafe's eyes followed them as they sat down exhausted.

"Any word?" His voice anxious. Steph stirred.

"No. Not a thing. Azalea needs to get some sleep, so I think I'll crash on the couch. You guys can go home and get some sleep."

Rafe shook his head. "I don't think it's a good idea. What if the kidnapper tries to contact you at your house?"

Mitch's tired eyes looked at Rafe and then to Azalea.

"Mitch, I think Rafe is right. You need to go home… just in case."

"I'll stay with Azalea," offered a yawning Steph. "She shouldn't be alone. I can sleep in Becca's room."

"Thank you, Steph," said Azalea. "I appreciate you staying."

Rafe put his hand on Mitch's shoulder. "I'll go home with you. No one should be alone tonight."

Mitch only nodded. He needed to keep his emotions in check.

"Let's go. I want to get up early when the reinforcements arrive."

Rafe kissed Steph on the cheek as he pulled her up off the couch. "You take care of Junior, and I'll see you in the morning."

Steph gave him a sleepy smile. "Love you, too."

"Don't worry about Steph. I'll find a nightgown big enough for her."

"Ha. Ha," snickered Steph as she started for the stairs.

Mitch rolled his eyes. His stomach growled. "Sorry, I guess we forgot about eating tonight."

"I think I'm a bit hungry, too." Azalea rubbed her stomach. "How about I make us some sandwiches before we go to bed?"

"I'll help," said Steph.

While in the kitchen, Azalea opened cabinets and the refrigerator several times absentminded of what she was doing.

"Let me make the sandwiches," offered Steph as she noticed Azalea's preoccupation.

Azalea leaned against the counter. "I can hope and pray whoever took the girls are at least feeding them. Both of them have huge appetites."

"They're growing girls."

"Sure are."

"We have no control over what happens. Like Rafe says, everything is in God's hands."

"I know. I just want to know whose hands they are in now. I'd like to strangle and punch something to get rid of my frustration."

Steph reached her arm around Azalea. "Lean on us. We're here for you. You have your family and look how the town turned out when you were in a coma in the hospital. You have friends here, and they all love you."

"Thanks, Steph. It means a lot, but it doesn't help the empty feeling that's in my heart right now."

Steph put the food on plates. "Sandwiches are ready."

The tenseness in the room created an atmosphere of depression as they ate in silence. Mitch rose to leave after scarfing down the sandwich and coffee. Rafe grabbed his jacket to follow.

Azalea walked Mitch to the door and clung to him as he kissed her goodnight.

"I'll see you first thing in the morning. Remember, I love you. We will find the girls. I believe God has given them his protection." He rubbed his ear. "I have to believe it or I'll lose my newly found faith altogether."

"It's all we got right now, Mitch… our faith."

CHAPTER TWENTY-ONE

The harsh sound of the doorbell the following morning woke Mitch out of a sound sleep.

"Darn… Rafe let me sleep too late." He sniffed the scent of fresh coffee, and the smell of fried bacon hit his hunger sensor.

He slipped into his uniform having showered before crawling into bed at four in the morning. It was seven a.m., and he needed to be at the office to coordinate search activities. The few hours of sleep refreshed him, but he knew he couldn't keep going forever on a few hours of sleep.

Rafe answered the door before he made it downstairs. "Mitch, Susan is here to see you," he hollered up the stairs.

Susan, oh, I forgot all about calling Susan back. I bet she's mad.

He made a quick entrance to the front door as he buttoned his shirt and stood in his stocking feet.

"I'm so sorry, Susan. I didn't want to burden you last night."

"Yeah… whatever," she pounced in through the door. "She's my daughter, too, you know. You should have called me. I found out at the bar last night. Several of the Posse stopped by for coffee in between their search. I tried to reach you. We kept coffee going until we closed. Any word on the girls?"

"Not a thing. We're waiting on a neighbor who had a camera close to the park to arrive back today. There might be a video of the abduction. We can get information on the vehicle used and maybe info on the kidnapper."

She handed Mitch a piece of paper. "This was on your doorstep under this rock this morning." She held up a four-inch diameter rock. "You know if you would have left Natalia keep the cell phone, you could have tracked her."

"Drop it, Susan." Mitch growled.

"Mitch…"

He opened the note printed on a cheap piece of computer paper. "What!"

We have your daughter and her friend. They are safe— for now. We demand a payment of $500,000 for their safe return. You have 24 hours to secure the money. We'll contact you later for directions for the drop."

His mouth dropped open as he continued to stare at the print. Rafe leaned over his shoulder to read the note.

"Where do they think you're supposed to get that kind of money in twenty-four hours?" asked Rafe.

Mitch ran his fingers through his hair and pulled on his ear. "I cleaned out most of my savings to buy the new house."

"Mitch, you have this much money?" questioned Susan.

Mitch drew his eyebrows together. "You knew about the inheritance from my parents. I received it several weeks before our divorce was final. You tried to get money out of me then."

Susan opened her mouth, shut it, and shook her head. "Yeah, I know. I would have asked for a better settlement before I signed the final papers if I knew you would come into that kind of money."

His lips tensed into a thin line. "Susan, our daughter's been kidnapped, and all you can think of was the divorce settlement."

"I didn't want the divorce, Mitch. You insisted on staying here, and I couldn't stand living in a small town."

Rafe looked embarrassed as he witnessed what should be a private matter. "I'll leave and check on Steph and Azalea. You two need to work out your differences for the sake of the girls."

Mitch raised his hand. "Don't leave." He didn't want to be left alone with Susan. Rafe ignored his plea to stay.

"I'll check back with you a little later to see what Steph and I can do to help."

Mitch nodded as Rafe walked out the door. Susan shut the door behind him.

"Mitch, about the divorce."

His eyes bore into hers. "Susan, you did everything you could to avoid taking care of Natalia. You partied and embarrassed me within the community. Then you started doing drugs and…and just left. No word… nothing for ages. Your parents wouldn't even acknowledge Natalia. They're her grandparents." He shook his head. "Now you tell me you didn't want the divorce. Do you think I'm that stupid?"

She reached up and tried to wrap her arms around Mitch.

"Mitch, I still love you and want to be with both you and Natalia. This kidnapping is literally destroying me inside." She clung to his neck pulling him down toward her looking for sympathy.

Mitch put his hands on her shoulders and held her at arm's length. "Don't, Susan. We're done and over with. You don't even have court permission to see Natalia. I've been following Azalea's advice and allowing you to see her, so she gets to know her mother. Now you're pulling this 'I didn't want the divorce thing'. It's not going to work."

"You can't marry Azalea. I see the look in your eyes when we're together. You still have feelings for me. I know it."

"No, Susan, I don't." He dropped his arms from her shoulders.

"I feel sorry you missed out on all these years of your daughter growing up…but that's all."

"You have the money. Are you going to pay off the kidnappers?"

"I don't know. All the training I've had says to never pay a kidnapper."

"I want my daughter safe. Please…please pay the ransom."

At the approximate same time Susan visited Mitch, the doorbell at Azalea's home rang nonstop. Steph and Azalea were up and getting ready to leave for the Law Enforcement Center to meet Mitch and Rafe.

Jake pushed the door open as Steph stepped aside to let him in. He walked toward Azalea, his body tense. "How dare you not contact me yourself about Becca's abduction," he screamed point blank in Azalea's face as he shook her by the shoulders.

Steph held on to the doorknob while her mouth opened in surprise at his violent reaction.

"I…I was too upset. Chrys said she called you." She backed out of his hold and put her hands on her hips. "By the way, where were you? You never showed up at the abduction site or at the LEC."

Jake dropped his hands to his side. His face turned a slight shade of red. "I…I was in St. Paul on a business appointment and decided to stay overnight. I turned my phone off and went to bed early."

"Why are you berating me for not calling you?"

"As Becca's mother, I expect you to keep me informed of anything to do with her…not have someone else call me."

"You don't keep regular visits with Becca, but that's beside the point right now. We need to find Becca and Natalia." She shook her finger at Jake. "I hope you informed your mother."

"Yes…after I found out more information from Detective

Bishop at the LEC. Where's your fiancé right now? He wasn't at the station when I stopped there."

Azalea frowned and looked perplexed.

Steph stepped forward. "We are on our way there right now. Both Rafe and Mitch are supposed to meet us there. Now it's daylight and an all-out search will begin. I hope you'll join us."

"You bet I will."

Steph opened the door and stepped outside. She turned to Azalea. "That's funny. Rafe just drove up without Mitch. I'll see what's going on."

"Jake, I need to leave. Mitch said the volunteers would start walking the roads and into the woods early today."

"I'm going home to change into jeans, and I'll be there. She's my daughter, too."

"Yes, Jake. I know she's your daughter. Maybe now you'll realize she's a special girl."

He swore under his breath and merely nodded his head. He turned, walked back to his car, and hit the hood with his fist.

Steph waved her arms toward Jake to come back. "Rafe said Susan stopped by Mitch's house this morning. She found a note on the front porch under a rock requesting a ransom for the two girls."

"What!" shouted Jake. "A ransom! How much?"

"Half a million dollars."

He ran his fingers through his hair releasing some of the long hair tied back in a band. "No one has that kind of money around here."

"Mitch has," whispered Azalea. "I need to get over to Mitch's right away." She gave a wide-eyed look to Steph. "I'll meet you later."

Azalea ran back into the house, grabbed her car keys, and headed out the back door.

"Mitch, please listen to me. You need to pay the ransom. What if something would happen to Natalia? You'd never forgive yourself."

"Susan, this requires some thought. No matter what, I love Natalia with all my heart. I also love Becca as my own daughter. I would do anything to get them home. If I knew paying the ransom would get them back, I'd do it in a heartbeat. Money means nothing to me." He looked up toward the sky. "I have put my trust in the Lord that he'll protect the girls."

Susan's eyes grew large as she scrutinized Mitch's statement. "Trust in the Lord. Phooey! That's nonsense, Mitch. If you got the money, pay the ransom. You said money didn't mean anything to you. Pay it and hope they release the girls."

"They... what do you mean by 'they'? How do you know it was more than one person?"

"Ahh...it makes sense. If it was only one person, one of the girls would have escaped."

Susan's phone rang. She looked at the number. "It's my parents. I need to tell them what's going on." She turned away from Mitch.

Mitch allowed her privacy as he walked into the kitchen and scarfed down cold eggs and bacon.

At least the coffee is still hot.

He poured more hot coffee into a mug as Susan finished the conversation with her parents.

"Mom and Dad are driving up from the cities. They'll be here later this afternoon."

"Good. You can entertain them while I'm out looking for our daughter."

Susan stamped her foot. "Mitch, I mean what I said earlier. I want to be with both you and Natalia. I know my parents are willing to forgive you for the divorce."

"Forgive me for the divorce." His nostrils flared. His voice rose, "Susan, you make this sound like I'm the bad guy here. You ran off and deserted us. What don't you and your parents understand?"

He opened the door to show her out and stepped into the cool morning air. She looked over his shoulder and saw Azalea's car down the street. Susan reached up and grabbed Mitch around the neck. The gesture surprised him, and he almost lost his balance on the porch. He reached out and clutched her around the waist. She quickly leaned in and kissed him on the lips. The kiss stunned him for a moment until he could get his bearings.

He heard a squeal of tires, looked toward the street, and saw Azalea drive by.

His eyes flared with anger. "You deliberately did that." He pushed her away from him.

She gave a sly smile. "I knew you still had feelings for me."

CHAPTER TWENTY-TWO

After seeing Mitch in an embrace with his ex-wife, Azalea's eyes blurred. She gunned the engine and drove past his house.

How could he do this to me now? I need his support. Why would he let Susan get this close to him again? Is he falling for her?

She drove around the block and stopped for a minute before she returned to Mitch's house.

I need to get an explanation of what I just saw. I owe it to him. Watch your temper, Azalea. A little voice in her head kept repeating those words over and over again. *Don't jump to conclusions. Let him explain before you say anything.*

She pulled up in front of the house. Susan's car was gone, and the lights were out in the house. Azalea sped down the road toward the Law Enforcement Center.

Her knuckles turned white as she clutched the steering wheel. Anger built up inside her as she pulled into the parking lot at the LEC. Before she exited the car, she took several cleansing breaths to calm herself.

As she sat in her vehicle, she watched people arrive in carloads and gather at the far end of parking lot in a makeshift tent. The press started to arrive. Several large television vans from the Twin Cities parked in front of the LEC filming the outside of the building.

I need to focus on Becca and Nat... not what I saw on Mitch's front porch.

She put her head on the steering wheel. *Dear Lord, please be with me today. Help me to focus my attention on finding the girls and not my own personal life.*

Without removing his jacket, Mitch sat in his office with Steve Bishop. When Sally saw Azalea enter, she rose from her desk and placed her arms around Azalea. Azalea stood with her arms to her side.

"I'm so sorry to hear about Becca and Nat. I'm praying they're found soon and unharmed."

She gave her a wan smile, but her eyes could not focus on Sally at that particular moment. Her attention was on Mitch. "So am I. So am I."

Sally dropped her arms and held Azalea at arm's length. "The sheriff arrived a few minutes ago and is getting briefed on the night's activities."

"Ah... huh?" Azalea appeared in a zombie-like state.

"Azalea, get yourself together. You're no good to your kids this way."

She nodded her head, "I know. Thanks, Sally," and bee-lined toward his office releasing herself from Sally's grip. Sally followed her to Mitch's office but remained in the doorway behind Azalea.

She stuck her head in the doorway. "Any news?"

Steve shook his head. "No sign. All vehicles were checked at the county line. All the surrounding counties are doing the same. The only conclusion is the girls are still within the county. But *where* is the next question?"

Mitch pulled on his ear. "We need to canvas the entire county. Who are you putting in charge of the volunteers?" His hands started to fiddle with the papers on his desk. A brief look of anguish showed in his eyes. Before Steve even answered, Mitch sighed. "Steve, you've been up all night and need to go and get some sleep."

"I'll go after we organize the volunteers. Tom Bertrum asked to help with the search parties and organize the groups. I also took a call from the governor, and he's going to call up the local National Guard unit to help in the search if we don't find them today."

"I'm going to call the governor this morning and ask for a helicopter to canvas the county. Maybe something could be seen easier from the air."

A frown framed Azalea's face. "I'm worried all this activity might make the kidnappers nervous, and they might harm the girls. I heard you got a ransom note."

Mitch's face crimsoned as he thought about what Azalea witnessed earlier. He cleared his throat and pulled on his ear again. "You aren't the first person today to mention kidnappers in the plural. We don't know how many are involved? It could be one person… or it could be several or more."

Mitch and Steve made eye contact as if there was a clue in her last statement. Azalea saw the movement and did a double take.

She cocked her head and squeezed her eyes into slits. "Isn't it obvious? If there was just one, Becca would have fought like a maniac. You've seen her with her cousins. She can take on both of those boys in a wrestling match. She'd fight like crazy to get away."

"Yes, I believe it's what she did by the evidence we found in the park. Everyone has referred to the abduction in the plural sense. I agree with the assessment… but somehow people are already referring to kidnappers… and not kidnapper." His fist hit the top of the desk in one loud swoop. "I wish we had more evidence."

"Everything's been rushed to the lab for analysis," said Steve. "We hope to have the blood type soon. We're a small town and don't have the facilities of the larger departments.

"What about the ransom note?" Azalea asked testily.

"Yes… the note. Susan stopped by and said there was a note left on the front porch. It asked for a ransom of five hundred thousand dollars. But… again… it didn't say how they would contact us or how to get the money to them."

"I agree with your analysis earlier, Mitch," offered Steve. "These might be amateurs we're dealing with. I don't think you should pay the ransom quite yet. We may get lucky and find the girls. If you pay the ransom right away, we won't have much of a chance to catch the kidnappers."

"Really, Mitch! You don't want to pay the ransom." Azalea's eyes widened with fear as she imagined what could happen if the ransom wasn't paid. "I'll ask Jake for money and anyone else who'll give me money. I don't have it. I'm in debt already with the shop. I don't own anything but my inventory, and the bank still owns my house." Her hands shook as she rolled them into fists.

Mitch came from around his desk and put his arms around her. She leaned into his firm chest and could feel the hardness of his bullet-proof vest. She wished she could put her hand on his chest and see if he actually had a heart.

He clenched his jaw not knowing how to comfort Azalea. "We planned to close on the house this next week. I can use that money if we have to. All our training and experience tell us never give in to kidnappers. Our hope is to find the girls first. I'll call my investment broker and have him cash in whatever is needed."

Steve rubbed the back of his neck to ease the tension he had built up overnight. He shook his head. "Mitch, I'm against doing this right now. Sure, get the money ready if you can get your hands on it in short order, but don't let on you're willing to deal with them. Call the Bureau of Criminal Apprehension this morning. Don't just take my advice. Get other opinions before you go jumping into the fire."

Mitch relaxed his shoulders. "Yeah, you're right. I'll call the

BCA."

Steve rubbed his chin and narrowed his eyes. "Food for thought..." All eyes turned toward Steve. "Whoever kidnapped the girls knew you could get the money fast. They must have known about the house closing, plus you had more money in savings. Who would have access to that information?"

"The same thought entered my mind. I've been mulling it around in my brain. I'll get a list ready of who would know anything."

Sally stepped farther in the room. "Give me your list, Sheriff, and I'll start working on it."

"I'll have it ready a little later on this morning. I need to talk to Azalea for a few minutes. I'll be right out. If you want to start mapping out parts of the county and dividing it among the volunteers. They should all be here around nine o'clock."

"I already have the maps printed out, Detective. I'll get them for you." Steve and Sally meandered over to her desk. She handed him the maps, and he went out to the tent set up by the Sheriff's Posse and members of Reverend Rafe's church.

"I'm sorry this upset you, Azalea, but Steve is right. I'd give anything to get the girls back, but I want them back safe." His face scrunched up as he balled his one hand into a fist and pounded it into his other hand. "I want to get my hands on those scumbags who took the girls and throw them in jail."

"All I can do is continue to pray. I'm not much good at anything else right now. At least we know they're kidnappers and not some child molesters. At least, it's what I hope."

"Oh, darling, don't even think that way."

She looked at Mitch with her lips in a thin line. *"Darling.* After what I witnessed this morning, I'm not sure if I am your *darling."*

Mitch snickered. "Don't let Susan bother you. She deliberately set you up, so you would see that little play. It shocked me as much as it did you. I'm sorry you witnessed it. She played it to the full hilt claiming she wants to get back together and be a wife and mother again. I don't buy it one single bit."

"She's the one who told me you had lots of money and kept the information from me. It shocked me to know you kept something that important from me."

"Please, Azalea, don't get angry. We need to focus on the girls. We can discuss this later. Right now, I need to get hold of my investment broker and call the BCA. Why don't you help Steve set up the volunteer routes? You know the county as well as I do."

CHAPTER TWENTY-THREE

Azalea stepped out into the crisp morning air and wrapped her arms around her body. Her only thought—the girls. Were they warm? Did they eat? What kind of suffering did they have to endure?

Their backpacks along with their jackets lay in Mitch's office. Every time she stepped into his private area, seeing those items tore at her heart. Mitch never mentioned his feelings when he looked at them, but Azalea could see the agony in his eyes and the way his body slumped before he sat down.

She glanced at the volunteers forming at the temporary tent. Her eyes grew large as she caught a glimpse of Callie Weber standing among the volunteers waiting for their assignments. Azalea realized she was staring point blank at her. Callie saw her gaze, lowered her eyes, and turned her back away from her penetrating eyes.

What is she doing here?

Mitch stepped out of the Law Enforcement Center.

Azalea pointed. "I noticed Callie Weber in the group of volunteers."

"Yes, what of it? We need all the help we can get... even if they can help for a few hours… and even if it's Callie Weber."

Azalea lowered her eyes. "I'm sorry, Mitch. I know it's no way for me to act. I realize Steph and Rafe forgave Callie for her part in Steph being held hostage at the high rise, but that woman…" she paused. "There's something about her I can't put a finger on, but I don't think she's trustworthy."

She walked briskly over to the tent. Almost everyone held a steaming cup of coffee to warm their hands. Sandwiches, cookies and bottles of water lay on a nearby table for the volunteers to help themselves. Jake stood by the large coffee urn and handed an empty cup to Azalea.

Azalea poured herself a cup "Um… strong and black. Where did all this come from?" She waved her hand over the table.

"Don't you know? Jennifer Williams arranged all of this."

"I remember Jennifer saying if ever I needed anything, just let her know. This must be it."

She helped Steve hand out the highlighted maps and keep track of which area the volunteers were to cover. Steve and Mitch formed groups to walk the many acres of woods and along the river banks. The sheriff needed to rely on his Posse, plus all the other volunteers, who could take the day off to help in the search.

Steve, exhausted, went home to catch a few hours of much needed sleep, and left Tom Bertrum in charge.

Mitch made sure he put Callie with a Sheriff's Posse volunteer. Susan showed up a little later, and Mitch partnered her with another Posse volunteer.

Sunflower and her classmates from the Law Enforcement Program arrived around noon to relieve the volunteers, who returned for lunch and appeared exhausted from all the walking. Azalea tried to thank each person as she handed them a map. She kept wiping her eyes to keep from crying. Some gave her a hug before they started on their journey. By mid-afternoon a good portion of the county was covered by groups of volunteers.

The day seemed to drag on as Azalea paced back and forth and checked the time on her phone every ten minutes. Every once in a while, she could hear the National Guard helicopter fly over.

Steve returned later in the afternoon at the LEC after what he called a brief nap.

The reporters wanted up-to-date information from the sheriff's office. Mitch spoke several times to them. "No further information was available" came out of his mouth. Each time he stepped out the concern in his eyes grew more worrisome and lines formed around his mouth as the frustration of no news kept coming back. During this time Mitch's attitude changed toward the reporters. They could help spread the word and get others throughout the state to help in the search.

Mid-afternoon a car arrived at the LEC. A man exited with video equipment. He introduced himself as Charles Maxwell, the neighbor close to the park.

"Ah… Mr. Maxwell, I'm Sheriff DeVries. Thank you for driving back early."

"I haven't had a chance to review the videos, so I'm not sure if any of this will help."

"All we can do is try," said Mitch. "Sally, call Detective Bishop and see if he's available to come to the video room."

"Sure thing."

"Let me ask you a question, Mr. Maxwell. No one else has cameras around the park. Why did you set them up in your yard?"

"I work out of town most of the week. I've had some damage to my yard with kids wrecking my grass and some of my landscaping. I'm a computer junkie so I thought I'd set up my own surveillance to see who was doing the damage."

"Are any cameras facing the park?"

"Partially. I focused on any kids coming from the park through the parking lot, so any vehicles going in and coming out would be on this particular camera. It's a wide-angle lens." He punched through several buttons to get the machine to replay. "What day and time are you looking for?"

"Yesterday, late afternoon."

Steve walked in the video room, wearing his long coat. His removed his River Falls Sheriff's Department cap (RFSD) and whatever hair remained on his head brought out the static cling. Mitch smirked to himself. "Detective Bishop, this is Mr. Maxwell, the neighbor with the video cameras in his yard."

"Mr. Maxwell, thank you for your help." They shook hands. "I apologize for being abrupt with you on the phone yesterday, but the kidnapping was my top priority."

"I understand. I don't have any children, but if I can help in any way, I'm more than willing."

"Let's see what you got."

He punched several more buttons and the men watched as the video played on the computer screen. "I can watch the cameras on my computer as long as I can get internet, but I thought you might want to burn a CD if you see what you're lookin' for."

"It's too bad we can't see the entire parking lot," mentioned Mitch.

"There're the girls. You can see what time they got to the park." The corner of the screen read four fifteen.

They watched as the girls floated in and out of the camera's range gathering branches. They could see Natalia placing the branches in her bag. Both girls sat down on the park bench to eat a snack. A white van without side and back windows drove into the parking lot. All eyes in the room focused on the van.

"Any way to see the license plate?" Steve squinted his eyes leaning in closer to the screen.

"Let's watch to see what happens first."

Two men jumped out of the van with ski masks over their faces. Becca grabbed Natalia's hand and started to run. Natalia turned around to pick up her bag and the shorter man grabbed her around her arms. She started kicking him as he hauled her to the van. Mitch could imagine Natalia screaming, but there was no voice recording. Becca ran, and the second man chased her. The rest was out of the camera's view.

Mitch held his breath and waited for the return of the other man. The van opened in the back, and they could see the taller man drag Becca into the van. The wheels spun and spit out gravel as they drove out of the parking lot and out of camera range.

"Oh, my," Mitch covered his hand over his mouth. "We finally have something to go on. Steve, get this copied and sent to all the law enforcement agencies. We'll pass this on to the reporters. Let's try and see if we can get a license plate number."

"Yes, Boss. I'll get right on it."

"Thank you so much, Mr. Maxwell." Mitch shook his hand. "You don't know how much this helps us."

"I never thought these cameras would save someone's life. I did it as a hobby. I'm happy to help."

Mitch smiled as he exited the video room. He sprinted to his office and called Azalea on her cell phone. She had been in the parking lot all day helping with the volunteers.

"We got pictures of the vehicle used to abduct the girls."

"What! Really! Can I see?"

"Steve is burning a CD, so we can pass it around and email it throughout the state to all the other law enforcement agencies."

"I'll be right there." Azalea hurried up the steps and into Mitch's office. She threw herself in his arms, and he held her in a tight embrace.

"It's a start, Zalia. God has given us a start in searching for the girls."

He took her to the video room where she could view the actual abduction. Tears formed in her eyes as she watched the men take her two girls and throw them into the van.

"It's horrible, Mitch. Just horrible." She turned her face into his shoulder.

Sally knocked on the door. Mitch and Azalea jumped apart.

"Sorry to bother you, Sheriff, but your ex is out here and wants an update."

"Great." Mitch rolled his eyes. "Come with me?"

"Yes," Azalea grabbed his hand. "Let's face her together."

Susan's eyes took in the pair and her eyes glared at Azalea as her lips formed a thin line. Her arms crossed her heaving chest.

"I just returned from walking the woods. Your secretary says you found more evidence."

Mitch glanced toward Sally's desk and glowered at her. She lowered her eyes and pretended to focus on her desk.

"We got video of the van which was used in the abduction."

"Really!" A brittle smile twirled on her lips. "That means you'll find the girls soon."

"We're getting the video ready right now to send out to all law enforcement agencies and to the reporters. We'll find the van."

"My parents are here. They'd like to talk to you."

"I don't have anything to say to them, Susan. They've ignored us all these years."

Azalea looked up at Mitch, her eyes rounded, and touched his arm. "Mitch, it's time for forgiveness."

"But…"

"Please, Mitch. Make peace with them."

"Okay. Come with me?"

"You go. They're Natalia's family, too."

Susan took Mitch's arm. "They're outside at the bottom of the steps." She turned around and gave Azalea a satisfied grin as her hips brushed against Mitch's gun holster.

CHAPTER TWENTY-FOUR

"The boss just called. We gotta get rid of the van. Some camera picked up the van at the park."

"Where can we dump it?" probed Rodney.

"First, take a pail of water and wash down the inside and outside. Anything we would have touched. Don't want any fingerprints on it."

"It's stolen anyway. I wonder if it's been reported missing yet?"

"Just take care of it. Tonight, we'll drive it into the river. I'll call the boss. We'll need another. It's vital to get to town… I need food and beer."

"Check on the girls. I haven't heard nothin' out of them all morning."

The house, used as a hunting shack, lay hidden behind a grove of trees; and the barn, which smelled of mice and other varmints, now housed the stolen van. No one knew the men used the shack as their hideaway most of the winter. They burned wood for heat in the fireplace, the stove was bottle gas, and they were careful in using the electric in case the owners got wise when they received their electric bill.

Rodney washed away any evidence. A small amount of blood stained the rug in the back. He scrubbed and scrubbed. He figured any other evidence would wash away once they drove the van into the water.

As darkness fell, they drove the vehicle as far as they could away from town and yet close to the river. Another deserted cabin became the dropping point where the van could be pushed into the water to float downstream.

"Tee hee hee. They'll never know where it came from," chuckled Mac.

"We did good." Rodney reached and patted his buddy on the back.

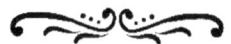

Several volunteers found the van the following day as it floated up against a sandbar. The call came in to the LEC early morning. Mitch and Steve drove to the site, called a wrecker, and alerted their evidence gathering team.

Azalea already left the volunteer tent to check on her staff at the flower shop. They gathered around her with hugs and prayers for her and Mitch.

"Thanks, ladies. I appreciate it." Her heart filled with joy to see the support of everyone she met on the street and now at the shop. "Mom, how are things going here?"

"We're keeping busy. Most of the people coming in want to show their support, so they end up buying flowers. Have you been to the park lately?"

"No. I couldn't bear to go out there and imagine the girls' fear when those kidnappers grabbed them."

"Well, flowers are flying out of the shop. Customers started dropping in and picking up a few flowers at a time and taking them to the park to show their support for you and Mitch... sort of a memorial."

"A memorial. Oh, Mom, I don't want to even think about the

girls not returning to us."

Tears flooded her eyes, and she could not hold them back anymore. "I tried to be brave—to show Mitch I'm strong... but I'm not. I want my girls back." A deep desolate moaning sounded from deep within her. She put her hands over her face and wept. Her mother wrapped her in an embrace. She wiped her eyes on the sleeve of her shirt.

Bernadette handed her a box of tissue. "Honey, you're strong. It's been two days now. Mitch is working day and night getting very little sleep. You need sleep, too."

"I know, but neither one of us will give up. I couldn't stand it anymore at the LEC. I needed to get away from the reporters... even though they've been wonderful in getting the word out. I needed to cry and holler and scream, but I didn't dare do it in front of others."

"You need some down time."

"Yes, I think I'll go to the church and pray. Maybe I'll find some comfort by sitting in church. I've always felt close to God in our church."

As Azalea walked into the River Falls Christian Church, members of several prayer teams looked up from their small groups.

"Why don't you join us?" they offered.

"Thank you for your kindness, but right now I'm looking for peace and solitude, so I can talk to God on my own."

"We're praying for others as well, but our hearts are with the girls."

Azalea nodded with a slight tip of her head, mouthed the words *thank you*, and went to sit in the family's favorite pew. She ran her fingers over the scar marks and remembered when Becca took a pen out of her purse and drew a stick figure on the back on the pew. She could still see the excitement on Natalia's face when she and Mitch came to the church together for the first time.

Why, God, why did you let this happen to the girls? So many things happened this past year—bad and good. Steph returned to River Falls turned out a good thing; discovering the buried remains of Rafe's relatives, good and not so good; Sunflower returned to us, good; finding Wade Williams' body, not so good; me getting poisoned, not so good; Mark D'Angelo dying from poison, not so good. So much to absorb in a year.

"Satan has his demons out there to pull you away from God."

"What? How did you…?" Azalea turned and looked up into Reverend Rafe's dark chocolate eyes. His eyes bored deep into hers.

"Know what you were thinking," he finished the sentence for her.

"Yeah, that's what I thought."

"Satan tests the strength of your beliefs many times. It so happens he's been giving all of us the run around, but God knows what's in our hearts. As long as you continue to hold strong God will come through."

"I believe, Rafe, but the hollow pit of my stomach is still aching for the girls."

"I know. Mitch is looking for you. He called me. Did you shut off your cell phone?"

"No, just turned it on silent. I wanted no distractions while I talked to God."

The doors to the church slammed and Mitch entered. His eyes searched the church and settled on Azalea and Rafe.

"There you are. We found the van in the river. We got some fingerprints we're testing and some blood samples off the floor."

"Blood samples," echoed Azalea.

"Yep. We believe they're the same as what we found at the park. It's not Becca's or Natalia's."

"Phew! Thank heavens for small favors."

Becca could hear movement in the next room. The bedroom door opened. She pretended to sleep. She did not want the men to put their hands on her again and force her to swallow those pills. They made her feel groggy. The dose they gave Nat zonked her out, and she wasn't waking up. Out of the slits in her half-opened eyes she could see Rodney peer in the door and shut it again.

"Ain't waking up yet. I think those pills are too strong for the girls."

"Don't worry about it," sneered Mac, as his eyes squinted out the window blinds. "It won't be for much longer. There's several people walking up the driveway wearing orange vests. Looks like one of those Sheriff's Posse guys and... look who else is out there." Mac slipped the ski mask on top of his head rolled up as a cap and walked out to meet them. He did not want the Sheriff Posse guy too near the house.

Becca heard Mac and gave Natalia a kick with her foot. Natalia's eyes, heavy from slumber, opened into slits.

"I heard someone's coming up the driveway," she whispered. "Pretend to sleep if they come in the room."

Natalia nodded and closed her eyes.

Rodney, with the ski mask over his face, entered the room with duct tape. "Sorry, girlies, but I need to shut you up for a while." He ripped the tape from the roll and placed a piece over each of their mouths. Both girls pretended grogginess.

He stepped out of the room, and the girls heard him leave the cabin. Becca dragged her feet and jerked the chair toward the door to see if she could open it. Even though her hands were tied to the chair she used her chin to turn the knob. It popped open and she used her head to open the door further.

Rodney and Mac forgot to close the blinds. The dirty window distorted a clear view, but Becca could still see the interaction. The two men stood outside talking to one of the Sheriff's Posse and... Natalia's mother.

She tried to scream, but nothing came out but mumbling. She shook her head and screamed again as loud as she could, but no one turned to look toward the cabin. Her voice was not strong enough to catch attention. Since her hands and feet were tied to the chair, she could not kick or knock anything over to get their attention.

She laid her head against the door casing and tears rolled down her eyes.

No one's going to find us. They can't hear my screams.

CHAPTER TWENTY-FIVE

"What ya doin' out here?" asked the Sheriff's Posse volunteer.

"We're gettin' the shack ready for the summer," replied Mac, as he pretended to be the owner. "My buddy and I are doin' some repairs right now."

"Oh, okay." His head moved around as he viewed the shabbiness of the buildings. "Sure looks like you need some work done to this place."

"Yeah, we know," answered Rodney. "We're workin' on it."

"Where's your vehicle?"

Mac stammered and jabbed his foot into the ground. He looked at Susan first, then turned to the volunteer, "It's in town getting' fixed. The check engine light came on, so we drove it into town. We got a ride back."

Susan interrupted, "We're looking for two young girls who disappeared several days ago. There's been an Amber Alert out for them. We're one of the volunteer parties searching the area."

"We know nothing about an Amber Alert," lied Mac.

"It's big news throughout the county and state," said the

volunteer. "Did you see any strange vehicles or unusual activity in the area?"

"No, sir, we didn't. We stick pretty much to ourselves."

"How long have you been here?" the volunteer asked.

"Almost a week now."

He handed Mac a piece of paper with a phone number. "If you see anything out of the ordinary, please call this number. It's the sheriff's kid and his fiancé's daughter who are missing."

"Sure will, Sir." Mac saluted and turned back to the shack. Rodney followed but turned around to make sure Susan and Sheriff's Posse volunteer left the premises.

"Phew! That was close." He wiped his forehead with his sleeve.

"Yeah, I sure hope the boss gets us another vehicle, so we can get outta here soon."

―――――

As the two men walked back to the shack, Becca shut the door using her head and bounced her chair back close to the original position. She now knew she was able to maneuver her chair around in the room even though she remained tied.

With her mouth taped she could only mutter monosyllables, but Natalia got the idea when Becca closed her eyes to pretend to sleep. Rodney opened the door to the bedroom.

"You girls need to use the bathroom?"

Becca fluttered her eyelids and faked being groggy. She shook her head since her mouth was taped. He walked over and ripped the tape from her mouth.

"Ouch!" she cried but was glad to be free from the restraint.

He ripped the tape from Natalia, but she remained silent even though a red stain showed around her mouth. Then her voice took over. "You wait 'til my dad finds you. You'll be sorry. You'll be in jail the rest of your lives."

"Hush, Nat," begged Becca. She did not want to irritate the men any further. *They might do something more drastic than just hit them.*

"You listen to your friend, girlie. You're the one liable to get hurt. Any more mouth from you, and I'll put this tape back on."

Natalia pulled her lips into a tight line and glared at him. He gave a cynical laugh as he walked away and closed the door.

"The little brat is askin' for trouble," Rodney spouted through the door.

Mac ignored his remark as he tipped his head back to get the last drop of beer from the can. "Hope the boss gets a new ride to us today. We have no food left and just coffee to drink. Urp." He belched as he crumpled the can and threw it toward the pail they used for trash. He missed, and it made a tinny sound as it hit the floor.

"Pick it up. I ain't cleanin' up after ya," growled Rodney.

"Just shut up and mind yer own business," Mac snarled back. He limped over and picked up the crushed can. Mac took it back to the chair and tried to make a basket again. He missed again. "Grrrr... sittin' around like this is makin' me stir crazy."

"You ain't a kiddin' no one. Soon as we get our share of the ransom, I'm outta here."

Becca whispered to Natalia, "Heard your mom's voice outside earlier. I'm sorry I couldn't scream loud enough."

Natalia sniffed and whispered back, "I wanna go home."

"I heard the man say they asked for a ransom for us."

"What's a ransom?"

"Money the parents pay to get their kid back when they're kidnapped."

"Does your dad and mom have enough money to pay a... ransom?"

"Depends on how much they're asking."

"Hey, quiet in there," Rodney shouted through the door.

"Oh...oh...I didn't think they could hear us," murmured Becca.

Natalia's stomach growled. "My tummy hurts. I'm so

hun…gry," she sighed and hung her head.

"Me, too, but we better be quiet."

Neither Rodney nor Mac had offered them food since they arrived. All they did was force a pill down their throats and give them a little water. Becca heard them say there was no food left. So there would be no food for them either.

They remained silent, but Becca kept her eyes searching the room for some plan of escape. Becca lost count of the days… if it were days and not hours they had been held captive.

Becca knew her body was getting weaker without food and water. If her stomach hurt, she could imagine the emptiness Natalia felt. Her stomach lurched at the thought of food and her mouth started to salivate. Her eyes rolled around as she experienced lightheadedness.

A few hours later the roar of a car engine could be heard coming down the long driveway. The girls heard the screech of chairs moving.

"Ah ha, we got wheels," shouted Mac, as he looked out the window. He limped out of the cabin. Rodney followed and slammed the outside door.

The girls could hear a female's voice. Becca looked at Natalia and whispered.

"Do you recognize the voice?"

"Sounds like my mom's voice but deeper." Natalia shook her head. "I don't know… could be my mom… or not."

"I thought I recognized your mom's voice earlier with the search party, but she was shouting. I could be wrong. I didn't get to see her clearly… just heard a lady's voice."

The men returned to the cabin along with the woman.

She kept her voice low, and the girls only heard her mumbling. "I'll leave a note tonight with the drop point for the cash. They'll find it early morning. You'll need to follow my instructions to the letter if we're going to get out of this and get away."

She pulled a map out and laid it on the table. "I know the money's ready to go." She pointed to a spot on the map. "Here's a place near the woods where they can't set an ambush. It's close to the falls. We'd notice it right away if they try to set a trap."

"We're not familiar with the area," said Mac.

"I'll drive you by there, so you know where the pickup will take place. I will be on a hill over here," she pointed to another spot, "watching while you grab the cash. You'll need to position yourselves there early in the morning. I set the drop for noon. They won't have time once they find the note to set a trap, because you'll already be in place to watch."

"Right."

"Where do we meet afterwards?"

"Let's meet back here. You'll need to release the girls somewhere far from here. Make sure they stay tied up and tape over their mouths. Drop them on a side road somewhere, and then get out of town fast."

"Let's drive to town and get some food. You can show us the pickup site on the way."

"Yeah, we need food. Nothin' to eat here," complained Rodney.

"You'll need to drop me off outside of town, so we won't be seen together."

"I'll check on the girls. I better tape their mouths shut so they can't scream or holler while we're gone."

The light from the cabin flashed into the bedroom as he opened the door. The girls instinctively closed their eyes to the brightness. Even though it was still daylight, the blinds and shade from the trees darkened the room.

Through the slits of her eyes Becca saw the woman's long dark hair as she kept her back to the door. Rodney tore off pieces of duct tape and put it over their mouths. Becca's and Natalia's eyes focused on the woman as Rodney started to shut the door. She turned and flipped her hair to get it out of her face, and they got a quick view of her profile. Becca recognized her and was sure Natalia did, too.

CHAPTER TWENTY-SIX

The girls heard the car's engine whine down the road away from the cabin. As the sound evaporated, Becca started to wiggle and hop in her chair.

Her hands tied behind her back and each foot tied to one of the chair legs with zip ties, she used the dexterity in her hands to twist back and forth and slip her hands free.

She ripped the tape from her mouth.

"Ouch," she emitted a meow sound as it pulled a scab off her dry lips. "Are you okay, Nat?"

Natalia could only nod and attempt a mumble. Becca reached down and tried to break the ties around her ankles.

"I can't get my feet loose," she cried. Frustrated, her eyes scanned the room for anything she could use to cut. No luck. Becca used her hands to hold the bottom of the chair seat and hop, hop, hop to the bedroom door.

She turned the handle. It opened. "They didn't lock the door," She looked back at Natalia, who still sat tied to the chair, her eyes wide with fear. "It's okay. I heard them all leave."

With the door open she hopped into the main part of the small cabin. She moved her chair side to side toward the kitchen area. "There's got to be a knife or something sharp," she mumbled to herself.

She spied a knife by the stove. It took a few minutes to maneuver the chair to get to the counter. She grabbed it and cut her bonds.

"I'm free," she shouted in a whispered tone and raised her arms in triumph.

Becca ran back to the bedroom, cut the ties from Natalia's hands, and ripped the tape off her mouth.

"Becca, I'm so afraid," she blubbered, as she rubbed her sore lips.

"Don't worry," Becca gave her a hug.

"Where are we?"

"I'm not sure. It looks like a hunter's cabin near the river. All I care about is how do we get back home."

"I can hear the river."

"Yes, I hear it, too, but we could be miles from town. I've listened for traffic and don't hear anything, so we're out in the sticks somewhere." Her thirteen-year-old mind tried her best to maintain support for ten-year-old Natalia.

After she cut Natalia's ties around her feet, they tiptoed to the front door and found it locked from the outside with a chain. There was no way they could squeeze their bodies through the small gap. Becca tried each window, but to no avail. They were old and painted shut.

They headed back to the bedroom. "We need to break a window, so stand back."

She picked up one of the chairs that held them in bondage and with all her might and pent up anger broke the bedroom window. They used the blankets from the bed to remove the broken glass. Becca folded the blanket and put in on the ledge.

"You climb out first," she instructed Natalia as she stuck her head out the window. "It'll be a short drop to the ground."

"Ooh," Natalia paused and backed away, "I'm afraid."

"It'll be okay," Becca reassured her. "There's just trees out there. We need to get out before they come back. Hurry!"

Natalia's body trembled as she neared the window. Becca pushed the chair close to the ledge. "See it'll be easy to jump out."

Natalia climbed on the chair and over the blanket. Becca heard a thud as she hit the ground.

"Hurry, Becca," she whispered. "Your turn."

Becca grabbed the knife she used to cut their bonds—just in case. Her body squeezed a little tighter through the window. Plop. Freedom—for now.

"Run, Nat... run." She shouted in a frenzied whisper. "We need to get as far away as possible."

They ran fast and hard. The adrenalin in their bodies, even though weak from inactivity and lack of food, gave them the incentive to run from their captives.

After a short distance Natalia stopped and bent over as she held her side.

"My side hurts. I can't run anymore."

"We'll stop...but only for a minute. We can't go near the road in case they come back."

Natalia's thin body shivered from the cool air even though they worked up a sweat as they ran.

"I'm better," her teeth chattered.

"Let's go." Becca grabbed Natalia's hand and pulled her along.

"I'm...scared," she whined in between breathing hard and moving fast.

"There ain't such a word as scared," Becca kept them on the run.

The trees and branches scratched their bare arms as they thrashed through the woods.

"When they come back...and find us gone. What'll they do?"

They'll start to hunt for us. Why do you think…I want to keep moving?"

Becca stopped for a moment to catch her breath.

"Mom says to pray when we're scared." Becca clasped Natalia's hands. "Dear Lord, we've escaped. Thank you for the rescue. Please help us now to get home safely."

"Amen," added Natalia.

"I think we're far enough away. If they come to look for us it'll take them awhile. We need to find a crossing. We've been alongside the river since we left. The woods are so thick. I can hear the river but can't see it."

"I'm not a good swimmer, Becca."

"You'll need to do your best. They might do awful things to us if they find us." She held up the knife. "I got this, but not sure it'll do much good. They're much stronger."

"I know… I'll do my best," her face showed determination as she knew Becca was right.

They continued their trek through the trees until they found a deer path and followed it. Becca continued to drag Natalia along even though her own body suffered from exhaustion. Becca knew the path could lead them to the river.

"My dad once took me hiking…through these woods, and he told me…deer would find the easiest route…to water…and to cross the river."

They reached the edge of the river bank. The current flowed strong because of the spring rains, but she still did not know how deep, or if they could swim across the water. Becca knew it would be their one chance to escape.

"I'm sure we're on the opposite side of the river from town," she guessed by the way the sun set, but did not want to frighten Natalia any further. "We need to swim across before it gets dark."

"Can we rest a few minutes before…?" She pointed her head toward the river bank.

"Yes, sit for a few minutes. We'll need all our strength to cross. I don't know how deep it is. Hang on to my hand until we end up swimming."

Natalia nodded and closed her eyes.

"Don't fall asleep on me, Nat."

"I'm not. I'm praying for a safe crossing."

"Oh, Nat, you know Jesus will watch out for us. I'm glad you thought to pray again."

Becca closed her eyes and mumbled, "Lord, send your angels to help us get across the river to safety." She turned her attention to Natalia. "We better go before it gets dark. The sun is setting, and we need to see where we're crossing."

"Okay." Natalia reluctantly stood and grabbed for Becca.

The first few steps into the river made them shiver. "I know it's cold," said Becca, "but we'll get used to it." Becca clutched the knife tight in her fist as she held on to Natalia with the other.

They could see logs and tree branches floating at a slow pace toward them. It was a narrower crossing than any other part of the river.

She wanted to instill courage into Natalia. "If the deer can do it, so can we."

About a third of the way across, the river dipped into a drop off, and the current pulled them apart. Becca tried to clutch Natalia's hand tighter but could not hang on. In her attempt to help Natalia the knife slipped from her hand.

"Swim!" She shouted. "You can do it, Nat. I can't hang on to you anymore."

Becca could see Natalia nod her head as they started to swim and dog paddle their way across the river.

"So…cold," Natalia's voice shook as her teeth chattered. "Can't make it."

Becca could feel the cold seep into her bones. Even though the stronger swimmer, she began to stiffen from the cold water. Natalia would not make it unless she could reach her.

Becca turned and saw Natalia go under the water and pop up again, but she wasn't able to stay on top of the water. Her arms flailed as the current started to drag her away. Becca's adrenalin kicked in, and she could feel warmth again in her arms and legs as she swam toward Natalia. She grabbed Natalia around the neck with one arm and started for shore.

As she continued to swim with Natalia acting as dead weight, her body started to give out again. With one arm to maneuver, she pushed with her legs through the water like a frog. They were still many feet from the shoreline.

I got to make it. I can't let Nat down.

CHAPTER TWENTY-SEVEN

"Here... grab on to the tree limb," a voice sounded out of nowhere. The water splashed in Becca's eyes as she noticed a log floating out toward her. Her cold hand reached out and grabbed a short limb. The log sloshed through the water as Becca's body moved closer to shore. She continued her desperate hold on Natalia until her feet could feel solid ground close to the river bank.

A hand reached out to Becca and pulled her closer to the shore. A woman stood knee deep in the water and dragged Natalia to solid ground. The girls lay along the river bank shivering and coughing up the cold river water. Their teeth chattered so fast that neither spoke.

Astonished by the rescue, Becca's eyes focused on their rescuer. Dressed in a long flowing skirt and a sheepskin jacket, she looked like someone from another century. Her hair was long and curly, almost to the middle of her back. The woman's calm demeanor and kind smile allowed Becca to relax her vigilance of protecting Natalia.

"O blessed Jesus, we need to get you both into some warm

clothes and heat," her melodious voice sounded like Heaven to the girls.

Becca touched her body to see if she was still alive and not in Heaven. She realized the lady was real, and she still lived.

The woman helped both girls crawl up to the solid ground of the river bank. Becca and Natalia continued to shiver, too spent to fight anymore. Everything came alive to them as every little sound made them realize how they narrowly escaped drowning. As their eyes focused on the woods around them, they heard the birds chirping, the chipmunks and squirrels chattering, and the leaves rustling in the wind as if to say they were rejoicing with Becca and Natalia.

"Come to my cabin. The fireplace is lit, and you can warm up. We'll get you back home."

She wrapped an arm around each girl and led them through the woods to a small cabin. The woman opened the door, and the girls' eyes danced to see the roaring fire. They turned their eyes to the woman, who smiled and pointed with an open hand to the fireplace. They hesitated, but the warm cabin and fire drew them in. Their extremities were still numb from the cold water but started to thaw as they moved closer to the fire.

The woman removed her boots and dumped the water in the kitchen sink. Barefooted she walked into the bedroom where she changed her wet skirt and tied her hair back with a ribbon. She returned with two blankets.

"I'm sorry I don't have a dryer for your clothes. Here are two blankets you can wrap around yourselves. By the way, my name is Grace. What are your names?" Her voice possessed a lulling, hypnotic appeal, and the girls relaxed.

Becca pointed to herself, "My name is Becca, and this is Natalia. We've been kidnapped and escaped. Do you have a telephone, so we can call our parents?"

Grace showed no surprise on her face. "No, I'm sorry. No phone. I journey here for the peace and quiet of the woods and don't carry any electronic devices with me."

"Oh… how are we going to get home?" Becca's face turned ashen.

"We'll worry about it later. Let's get you young ladies dry. I made a pot of vegetable soup for supper. There's enough for all of us. I hope you're hungry and will join me."

Their eyes lit up at the sound of food.

"We haven't had anything to eat for a long time," said Becca as she licked her lips in anticipation. Natalia nodded and looked with longing toward the small kitchen.

"You girls go in the bedroom and change out of those wet clothes. When you return, I'll have the soup ready." She bent over to light the stove.

They hurried out of their wet clothes and brought them out wondering how they would hang them by the fireplace. Grace found a portable clothes hanger and set it near the fire. She hummed a soothing melody and her smile never left her face as she helped the girls hang their clothes over the wooden racks.

"I've fallen in the river fishing a few times, so I made sure to bring my own drying rack with me."

Natalia giggled.

"You think it's funny," Grace smiled.

"Yes, ma'am. We're so glad you helped us out of the water."

"It was a lucky coincidence that I took a walk before supper. I love walking the deer trails and along the river."

"Lucky for us," offered Becca.

"Yes… well, let's eat."

Grace set bowls of soup in front of the girls, along with glasses of milk, and crusty French bread. They ate everything down to the last crumb.

"Why don't you girls go sit in the two rocking chairs by the fireplace and curl up until your clothes are dry."

Becca's curiosity peaked and wondered why Grace stayed in the cabin by herself. She did not notice a vehicle outside when they arrived at the cabin. How would they get home?

Grace hummed to herself as she started to clean up the dishes. Becca recognized the song *Amazing Grace*. "It's one of my mom's favorite songs. When they sing it in church, she always sings it on the way home."

"It's one of my favorites, too." Grace started to sing.

Becca and Natalia listened. They understood the melody but not the words.

"What language are you singing? It sounded beautiful."

"It was Hebrew. I learned the words as a child."

Becca glanced at Natalia. Her eyes closed earlier, and she slept. "Ummm…sounds…wonderful," echoed Becca as she relaxed and closed her eyes.

Grace crept into the bedroom and returned with several more blankets and covered the girls.

"Good night, my children." She kissed each one on the forehead. "You'll find your way home in the morning."

༺༻

Becca woke to find herself wrapped in another blanket tucked around her. The fireplace went out during the night, but the cabin remained warm. She looked around for Natalia and found her on the floor instead of the rocking chair.

Realization hit her that they were free, and she jumped out of the chair disturbing Natalia's sleep. She grabbed the blanket wrapped around her body and moved around the room in a searching motion as she looked for something she could use as a weapon. Even though Grace was kind to them last night, she was not quite sure she could trust anyone again.

A soft light lit the small kitchen area, and her eyes focused on a note lying the table. Becca reached for it out of the fold of the blanket.

Becca and Natalia:
I left some breakfast for you – muffins and orange juice. You can find your way home by following the driveway to the main gravel road. Stay in the woods as you travel along the road until you see someone you recognize.
Grace

Becca dropped the note and ran to the bedroom. It was empty. The bed was made and no suitcases or clothes in the closet. She walked back to the main room and saw their clothes still hanging by the fireplace.

"Nat, we gotta to get dressed and get out of here."

"Umm…yeah, sure," a sleepy voice sounded from under the blankets.

Becca yanked her clothes from the drying rack and went to the bedroom to get dressed. She first used the bathroom facilities and looked with longing at the small shower. She decided instead to use a wash cloth in the cabinet to clean her face.

Natalia, with blankets wrapped around her, came stumbling into the bedroom as Becca finished dressing.

"Hurry, Nat, we need to find River Falls."

───※◯※───

Jake Leddering rushed into the Law Enforcement Center while the front desk was changing shifts.

"Is the Sheriff in yet?" his voice frantic as he held a piece of paper in his hand.

"Not yet, but he should be soon," replied one of the deputies.

Jake paced the floor as he waited. He did not wait long as Mitch arrived within minutes. Jake rushed to face him and push the note into his hands.

"What's this?" asked Mitch.

"It's a ransom note I found on my front door this morning addressed to you. It's asking for the money to be delivered at noon outside of town to a spot near the falls. See the map they drew on the note."

"I wonder why they didn't get the note to me. I'm the one the kidnappers wanted the money from. This is strange they would involve you at this point in their tawdry game."

"What are you going to do about it?"

"Looking at this map, there is no way we can get deputies to surround the drop site. It's a narrow path to this spot and someone watching from above can see if there's any interference."

"What about the money? Did you get the money? Do I need to try and get a loan at the bank to cover anything?" Jake grabbed hold of Mitch's jacket in a threatening gesture. "I want my daughter back!" he hissed.

Mitch chalked it up to a scared father… just like him.

"The money's being prepared, but we talked about this before. We want to do everything possible before we give in to these hoodlums. I don't want to risk Becca's or Natalia's lives, but I need to follow police procedure. The note states they'll release the girls within twenty-four hours once the money's been delivered and in their grubby little hands. It doesn't give me any reassurance at all."

Jake plunked down in a chair in the waiting area and covered his face with his hands. "I don't know what I'd do if anything happened to Becca."

Mitch put his hand on Jake's shoulder. "Detective Bishop is outside setting up new parameters to be searched today. Why don't you volunteer for one of the search parties? Volunteers from the local National Guard will also be here as well as anyone else who can help."

"I guess so. It's all I can do right now."

"I'll keep this note and run it for fingerprints. We got your fingerprints on file… right?"

"Yeah, I had a DUI a few years back, and they took my prints."

"Okay."

Jake walked out the building shaking his head and mumbling to himself.

Mitch looked down at the ransom note again while he walked back to his office. "This is getting stranger by the minute. Why would they deliver this to Jake Leddering?"

He sat at his desk and tried to decipher the note for clues.

CHAPTER TWENTY-EIGHT

Azalea arrived at the LEC ready to begin her day helping with the search parties. Glancing toward the tent she spied Jake in the crowd wearing his typical long blond hair tied in a ponytail. Their eyes made contact, but he pulled his glance away. She walked toward the tent and her ex-husband.

"Jake, are you here to help?"

"Of course, why wouldn't I be here?"

"You never offered to put up any of the ransom money."

"I don't have much in the bank. I've made some bad investments in the stock market."

"Yeah, as if I believe that statement." She shook her finger. "You're leaving everything up to Mitch even though I know you're in a better financial situation than I am."

"Go and talk to your boyfriend about the new ransom note," he snarked.

"Fiancé," she retorted and walked away.

Entering the LEC she walked briskly to Mitch's office and gave Sally a quick wave as she passed her desk.

She squared her shoulders and offered a humorless smile.

"Good morning."

Mitch glanced up and returned her smile even though it did not reach his eyes, then his face sobered. "Morning, dear. We got another ransom note."

"Yeah, I heard from Jake. He's outside signing up for the search party."

She walked behind his desk and fixated her eyes on the note. She made an attempt not to cry, but tears still formed around her eyes and her mouth quivered. "Our poor girls. I wish I could do more."

"You're doing what needs to be done. You haven't worked at the flower shop since the abduction, and I'm sure you're not getting much sleep at night."

"How can you tell?"

"Dark circles under your eyes…and you look tired."

She threw her arms in the air and flapped them down her sides. "It's so frustrating. I'm praying every spare minute. Rafe keeps checking on me. He should be concentrating on Steph, but both of them have put their lives on hold for us."

He stood and wrapped his arms around Azalea. "I know. It's amazing how many people put aside their daily routine to help us find the girls."

She leaned into him to inhale his scent. Her heart hammered under her ribs knowing they loved each other. She placed both her hands on each side of his face and pulled him down for a heart-pounding kiss.

"What a way to begin a morning. I can't wait to do this every day," he chuckled.

"I want you to know… no matter what happens I know you did your best, and I will always love you."

Pain in his eyes reflected for a brief second, but Azalea noticed.

"I'm doing everything humanly possible."

She backed away and wiped her eyes. "Mitch, don't you think

it's weird Jake received the note and not you. Do you think Jake could be involved in the abduction?"

"I don't believe he would jeopardize his daughter's life for money."

She shook her finger. "You don't know Jake. He's selfish, conceited, and money hungry. I wouldn't put it past him." She put up her hands in a listen-to-me gesture. "I know he tries to be good, but sometimes he has no conscience."

"In the same gesture, Susan found the first note on my steps. We should include her in all the suspects if you want to include Jake."

"Okay, I get what you're saying." She raised her eyebrows. "Why would a parent kidnap their own child? I'm going to the tent to see what I can do to help today."

"I'll be out in a few minutes after I get this note to our evidence team."

After she left the office, Mitch looked at the note again and pulled on his ear as his nostrils flared with anger. His lips turned into a thin line, and he realized Azalea had a point.

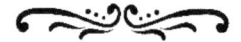

Becca and Natalia gulped down the breakfast Grace left for them. Their hunger pains satisfied, they decided to start their trek back home. Becca placed Grace's note in her pocket.

They stepped outside into the cool morning air and shivered. With no jackets to wear, they returned to the cabin and wrapped the blankets around themselves. They started down the driveway.

Natalia's voice choked with fear when they stopped at the end. "Wh…which way?"

Becca could only guess. "Grace never said. The river is behind us. I think we might be on the town side, so we need to be careful. Those men will be looking for us. Grace is right. We need to stay off the roads."

"Still which way—left or right?"

"Let's go…" she put her finger in the air, "left."

"O…kay."

They started their journey through the woods with the view of the road in sight. They made slow progress through the thick brush with the blankets wrapped around them. Becca stopped to rest when Natalia started to complain.

A state of numb dread ran through their minds as they feared being caught by the kidnappers. If they did not recognize a vehicle they hid in the brush until it passed. Becca did not want to make a mistake.

"Steph, will you stop fidgeting around with your seat belt," said Rafe as he drove down the back roads which angled back and forth around the river.

Every once in a while, they ran across people from the different search parties with walkie-talkies and would stop to inquire if they heard anything yet.

"I can't get this seat belt to fit around my body anymore. I've got less than three months left. Don't know what I'm going to do when it won't reach around me."

Rafe laughed. "Don't worry. I'll fix something up for you. You may need to move to the back seat."

"Ha. Ha. Very funny," Steph retorted. "You're driving slow enough so I shouldn't even need to wear a seat belt. Why can't we get out and walk the woods like the other search parties?"

Rafe rolled his eyes. "And have you go into early labor because you stumbled over something. No thanks. I want our little girl kept safe."

"Little girl. How do you know it's a girl?"

"I don't. I just think of the baby as a she. I'll love whatever God gives us."

Steph smiled back. "I know you will. Your heart is always open."

"Keep your eyes peeled for any activity along the roadside."

"Yes, sir." Steph saluted and watched the passenger side of the road.

"We're getting close to the next county. The trees and brush are so dense along the roadside, it's hard to see into the woods."

"I think you're right. Those in the search parties will be walking through the thick of it. Sure hope the wood ticks aren't out yet."

Steph shuttered. She pulled out the county map Steve Bishop gave her. "We're coming to a bend up here. Our little tyke is pushing on my bladder. Would you stop?"

"Sure."

As they negotiated the tight bend in the road, Rafe and Steph were surprised to see a bright light less than a quarter mile up the road.

"Looks like someone's shining a light." Their eyes gravitated up. They waited to observe a helicopter or airplane flying over. Nothing but blue sky.

"Can you hold on, dear? I want to follow the light."

"I can do anything as long you stop after you find out where the light is coming from."

"Deal." Rafe continued, but stopped before driving into the spot on the road where the light shined the brightest. The brightness hovered over the middle of the road almost blinding them. He stopped the car and got out. Steph clumsily exited the car stretching her back.

"Strange," Rafe squinted his eyes into the light. "My eyes even hurt."

"Sure is strange," echoed Steph.

"Reverend Rafe. Steph," sounded from the depth of the woods to their left.

Their eyes navigated toward the woods. Becca waved a blanket in the air while Natalia ran stumbling toward them.

Rafe's jaw dropped open, and Steph's knees buckled from the overpowering surprise of finding the girls. She grabbed the hood of the car to steady herself.

After the initial shock he returned his eyes to the light, but it disappeared. "Thank you, Lord." He sprung forward to help the girls the last few feet to the road.

Steph ran over to them and wrapped her arms around both at the same time. "I'm so happy to see both of you." They clung to her as they rocked back and forth.

Tears formed in Steph's eyes as she held them. "We were so worried. How did you get away?"

"It's a long story, but we escaped and were helped by a woman walking along the river while we tried to swim across it."

"You swam the river!" Steph's eyes searched the girl's faces. "Are you serious?"

"Yes," Natalia said. "Becca saved my life. I didn't think I would make it across."

"Let's get you girls home." Rafe reached for his cell phone. "No signal out here. We'll have to drive back into town. Let's hurry."

"Please hurry, Reverend Rafe. We're afraid the men who took us are looking for us."

"Get in the back seat and lay down. No one will know you're with us until we get back to town or can get a signal on our cells."

The girls slid into the back seat and laid down.

"Rafe, I need to relieve myself. Please stand guard while I take a few steps into the woods."

"Okay, but hurry. Be careful of poison ivy."

CHAPTER TWENTY-NINE

"Okay, tell us what happened? Don't leave anything out," Steph requested as she turned halfway around in her seat. "Are you girls thirsty?"

They nodded.

"There's water in the small cooler on the floor."

Becca opened the cooler. "Oh, thank you." She handed a bottle to Natalia.

They both drank almost the entire bottle before Becca began their story of their abduction, interspersed with Natalia's comments.

"Make sure you remember every detail when we get back to town," suggested Rafe.

About half way through their story, Steph tried her cell phone. "I think I got a signal. It's ringing through to Mitch's phone."

"Mitch, here."

"Mitch... we got a surprise for you."

"Huh, I hope it's good news."

"We found the girls along the roadside. We're bringing them in now."

Mitch's eyes filled with tears. "Praise the Lord. Let me talk to

Natalia."

Steph handed the phone to Natalia. "Hi… Daddy." She sniffed into the phone.

"Are you all right?"

"Yes, Daddy, I'm okay… *now*. I love you."

"I love you too, Pumpkin. May I talk to Becca?"

Becca grabbed the phone from her. "Hi, Mitch. I'm fine too. Just hungry and tired."

"Your mom will be so happy to see you."

"Me, too. We got lots to tell you." Becca handed the phone back to Steph. Tears rolled down her cheeks as she realized they were safe now.

"Mitch, where do you want us to take the girls?"

"Take them to the hospital. Azalea and I will meet you there. I'll get a private room, so we can stay incognito until we interview the girls."

"On our way."

The hospital emergency room awaited their arrival. Mitch and Azalea stood outside anxious to hold the children in their arms again.

Rafe's car stopped in front of the ER entrance. The orderlies had wheel chairs ready in case the girls needed a ride into the hospital. The girls glanced at the wheelchairs and shook their heads.

Azalea broke from Mitch and ran forward to gather the girls in her arms. All three hugged each other. Even though deep sobs racked her insides, Azalea held herself together and bit her lip to control her anxiety.

Mitch knew Azalea would lose it if he showed his emotions. He clamped his lips tight as he gathered all three in his arms, and they all clung to each other.

"We are so glad you're safe," Mitch offered through emotional sniffs. "We need to have you checked out by the doctors and nurses to make sure you're all right. Let's go into a private room."

"Oh, Daddy, I'm so happy Reverend Rafe and Steph found us. Those men were not nice."

"We'll talk about it later, but right now I want to make sure you both are okay."

"We already told Reverend Rafe and Steph what happened to us," squeaked Becca in a low voice.

Mitch's eyes turned toward Rafe and Steph. "Thank you again so much for finding the girls."

"It was no problem. We believe the Lord led us right to them."

"Oh, really." Mitch squinted his eyes while his mind spun in bewilderment.

What did Rafe mean by that comment?

"I'll tell you about it later," he patted Mitch on the back. "I need to get Steph home. She's having bladder issues," he whispered.

Mitch smirked and shook his head. "You're acting like a doting father already."

"I know, and I'm lovin' it."

The girls were ushered into the hospital and into a private room off the ER. The doctor examined each one and gave them the okay to go home. They were in good health except for being a little malnourished for the few days they went without food and water.

Azalea sniffed the air like a dog. "You both need a bath. Let's get you home and in the tub."

"Ahhh, Mom, do we really smell that bad?" Becca lifted her underarms and pulled them down to her side. "I guess so."

"I'll take Natalia home and get her in the tub," said Mitch.

"Nooo…I wanna stay with Becca," Natalia whined.

Mitch grinned. "I guessed as much. I want to stop by the LEC and inform Steve the girls are all right. It's best to keep their rescue under wraps for right now. If the kidnappers are left in the dark, maybe we'll get a chance to capture them yet."

"The girls are safe, Mitch. Let Steve handle the rest."

He glanced at his watch. "The drop off was scheduled for noon. If they don't know we found the girls, they'll still try to go to the drop off site."

Azalea crossed her arms while she tapped her foot and frowned at Mitch. His face turned red as he realized he put business before the family…again.

He raised his hands in a give-up gesture. "I'll learn, dear. I'll let Steve handle the press, but there's a lot to do in the next several hours."

Azalea smiled. "Thank you. I knew you would make the right decision."

"Not without your help." His breath was warm and moist against her face. She let out a small moan as he kissed her. "I love you for keeping my life on track."

"I'll gather some clean clothes for Nat from your house, so don't worry about her."

"Thanks."

"Do what you need to do, but hurry back."

The girls laid down in the back seat while Azalea covered them with blankets. She stopped at Mitch's house and grabbed some clothes for Natalia.

Azalea drove into her garage before she allowed the girls to uncover themselves. In the house they bathed and changed their clothes. Azalea busied herself making grilled cheese sandwiches when Mitch arrived.

Sadness developed in Azalea's eyes. "They're sticking together like glue afraid to leave each other's side." Azalea held up the spatula and raised her eyebrows, "Grilled cheese?" He shook his head.

"I don't want to waste one more hour than necessary to try and capture these kidnappers," he informed Azalea. "Do you want to sit in on their interrogation?"

"Yes, of course. The girls told me a little of what happened, but they weren't making a lot of sense. I think you need to get them to put everything in chronological order."

"Huh... Steve'll get the entire story out of them."

"If they can remember. Becca told me those men gave them pills to make them sleep. I wonder what else happened that they won't remember."

"According to the doctor's exam they weren't physically abused or sexually assaulted—just deprived of food and water. Did you see the sores on their wrists and ankles from being tied up?"

"I know. I poured peroxide on their wounds like the doctor said to do."

"As far as I can see right now, it was a kidnapping to obtain money from us."

"Still it was very traumatic for both girls, especially their swim across the river." Her eyes held a glimmer as she turned to Mitch. "What about the drop off?"

"We've been able to position several officers nearby in case they do try to go to the drop off location. I should say... if they're stupid enough to go even after they realize the girls escaped yesterday. You got to admit they weren't too bright leaving the girls alone."

"I agree. Did you notify Susan and Jake of their rescue?"

Mitch scratched his head. "I'm hesitating to notify either one. Your statement earlier about their being involved in the kidnapping to extort money from us stuck in my head. They could be considered suspects."

"I was being facetious when I mentioned it. It would be pretty hard to believe Jake would be involved in kidnapping his own daughter. Susan, on the other hand..."

Mitch shook his finger. "Azalea, Susan's been through a lot. Yes, she's manipulative, but she's said many times she wants to change and be a mother to Natalia."

"I'll believe it when I see it." She turned away. "I guess...we should give her the benefit of doubt. Who else would know you had money to pay the ransom?"

"Everyone knows my salary as a sheriff. It's public knowledge and not worth the effort to kidnap my daughter and ask for a large ransom...but very few people know about my inheritance from my parents."

"You gave a list to Sally. Are you sure you got everyone?" She started counting on her fingers. "Steph, Rafe, Jake, Susan, your financial advisor, you tax accountant, the employees at the real estate closers...and the list can go on and on if you stop to think of how many people would have access to your financial records...including your bank. If you want to get real particular, you can count me and my family."

"Now you're getting way off track...but sometimes getting way off track will bring out evidence we never thought about. You're thinking out of the box, and it's good up to a certain point. Pretty much every cent I invested was going toward the ransom if it was the only way to get the girls back."

"I appreciate what you're saying, but somewhere, somehow, someone knew about your inheritance and wanted the money badly enough to kidnap Natalia and Becca. I think...and this is just my thought...they went after Natalia and got Becca in the mix."

"Now you're throwing things out there. Everything is food for thought. After we interview the girls, Steve and I will talk and involve the BCA. Either the kidnappers are not anywhere around, or they're looking for the girls thinking they're still out in the woods. We want to cover all our bases."

CHAPTER THIRTY

After the girls ate, Mitch drove them to the LEC to have their statements recorded. They entered through the back-entrance garage where the deputies loaded prisoners to be transported and where none of the press or volunteers would see them.

"I think it's best to talk to the girls together," suggested Steve before he entered the interrogation room. "What one may forget, the other might remember."

Mitch nodded his agreement. "We need to get information as soon as possible to get our deputies and the BCA's help to apprehend these men."

Steve sat with the girls in the interrogation room while Mitch and Azalea watched from the video room.

"Now girls I need you to give me a step-by-step synopsis of what took place. We'll start before those men grabbed you."

The girls glanced at each other and started to giggle.

Steve frowned. "What's so funny?"

Becca stopped giggling long enough. "We don't know what you mean by syn...syn...nopsis."

He grinned. "I'm sorry. Give me details. We'll start with you,

Becca."

"We thought the city park would be best place to find flowering twigs and plants because it was the farthest park from the school."

"Did you see anyone in particular following you?"

Becca bent her head and scrunched up her face. "No, I didn't notice anyone. Did you, Nat?"

Natalia started to bite her nails. "Not really."

Becca shrugged and rolled her eyes at Natalia.

"We sat on a bench to eat a snack," she continued. "A white van pulled up close to us. It just stayed there and made me nervous because no one got out. I started to gather our stuff together. All of a sudden, the van backed up, and two men jumped out wearing ski masks. I yelled at Nat to run."

"Yeah, that's right. I wanted to pick up my bag, and Becca wanted to run. I reached for my backpack, and… like… the man grabbed me."

"What about you, Becca?"

"I tried to run away, but the bigger man tackled me. I fell face down and tried to fight with him. I bit him on his hand. He hollered, called me an ugly name, and then he hit me. I don't remember much until he dragged me into the van and tied me up."

"He hit you… where? The jaw? Your eye? Your stomach?" He fired one after the other.

"In my face."

"Did you mention this to the doctor? How is your face now? It looks fine to me."

"My jaw was sore at first, but it's better. My lips were bleeding when they put those dirty socks in our mouths. We tried to scream, didn't we, Nat?"

Nat nodded.

"We couldn't see where they took us," Nat added.

"Why not?"

Becca piped up, "There were no windows in the van except in

the front and we couldn't see over the seats, but we did know we were around the river because we could hear the water. They dragged us into a dirty cabin and locked us in the bedroom."

"Yeah, they tied us to chairs. I couldn't even use the bathroom for a long time."

"They came in and took the socks out of our mouths and made us swallow some pills. It made us sleepy. I felt funny."

"Funny. In what way?"

Becca tried to recreate her experience. "You know…dizzy, seeing double…and we slept a lot. Nat a lot more than me. I pretended to sleep whenever they came in the room, so they wouldn't give me pills."

"Can you describe the men?"

Becca and Natalia looked at each other. Their lips quivered, and they shook their heads.

Azalea wanted to run from the video room and gather the girls in her arms, but she knew it would hurt Steve's interrogation. Mitch watched stone faced with his knuckles curled tight into his hands. Anguish for the girls showed on both their faces.

"Nope…we never saw their faces," began Becca, "…except when the Sheriff's Posse people stopped by. Nat's mom was with one of them. They were outside, and I was able to slide my chair and open the door a little while they talked to them. I could only see the backs of their heads, but they had their ski masks crunched up on their heads. I knew it was Nat's mom because she talked real loud."

"Would you be able to recognize them from the back?"

Becca shrugged her shoulders. "I don't know."

"Anything you can tell us about any of the men? Were there only two?"

"All we saw were the two. The taller one limped. The shorter one I heard the other man call him Rodney, but I never saw his face."

Steve's eyes turned toward the two-way glass in the video room. Recognition entered Mitch's brain. He knew Steve recognized the name also. Azalea's eyes grew large.

"Mitch, Rodney is one of the men who tried to rob me on Valentine's Day. The other one I hit with my car." She touched the side of her head. "His name was Mick or Max."

"Yep. I bet it was the guy who calls himself Mac Jones."

"Yes, that's it."

Sally knocked on the video room door and popped her head around the door.

"Sorry to bother you, Sheriff, but the doctor from the hospital is on the phone. He wants to talk to you about the girls."

"Okay, I'll be right there." He turned to Azalea. "Will you be okay in here?"

She gave him a forced smile and a tense nod. "I'll be fine."

In a few minutes he was back shaking his head. "The doctor tested their urine samples and the girls tested positive for trace amounts of Rohypnol."

"What kind of drug is it?"

"On the street it's called the date rape drug. It knocks a person out almost straightaway and causes partial amnesia. They didn't want the girls to remember them or anything else about where they were being held. I'm surprised the doctor was still able to find traces in their blood. From what Becca said they hadn't any pills for almost twenty-four hours."

"Is this a prescription?"

"It's illegal in the states, but most likely smuggled in from Canada or Mexico."

"So, what you're saying is the girls might not remember everything that happened to them while they were held hostage."

"Yep. Unfortunately, it could be the truth. What did I miss?"

"Becca told Steve how she was able to slip her hands out of the cable ties and hobble out to the kitchen after the men and a woman left in the car."

"Woman?"

"Yeah, Becca said a woman delivered a white car to the men, and they took off to buy some food. It's when Becca slipped her hands out of her bonds and was able to get out to the kitchen to find a knife and cut the ties from her feet. She cut Nat's bonds, and they escaped through the bedroom window."

Steve continued to write in a notebook. Becca and Natalia yawned and waited for him to continue with the questions.

"Let's continue with what happened after you escaped."

"We ran as fast as we could. We found a deer trail that led us to the river. I knew we had to cross."

"How did you know to cross the river?"

Becca scrunched her eyebrows together and let out a sigh. "Because I remember crossing a bridge when the men were driving."

"Oh, that's something good you remembered," said Steve. "So, you crossed the river."

Natalia shook her head. "We sure did. I didn't want to cross… like… I can't swim that good. Becca said I had to."

"Nat, I didn't say you had to. I said we needed to get to the other side to get back to town."

"But I almost didn't make it. I got soooo cold."

"A lady saved us. She was walking along the river when she saw us swimming. She took us to her cabin and gave us food and dried our clothes."

Steve kept his face stolid, but his insides told him there was something special about this lady.

"What's her name? Why didn't she bring you to town?"

Natalia and Becca locked eyes and shrugged their shoulders. Becca spoke, "We told her we had been kidnapped and asked her to call our parents. She didn't have a phone. She said her name was Grace, and she used the cabin to get away. I didn't see a car in the driveway. She said she would help us in the morning. She gave us soup, and we fell asleep in front of the fireplace."

"How come she didn't help you this morning?"

"When I woke up it was just getting light out. A note laid near the bowl of muffins and juice." Becca pulled out the note she took from the cabin and handed it to Steve. "Here's the note."

Steve opened the folded paper, then with a confused look decided to go in another direction.

"Why do you think she left you all alone?"

"I don't know. She was a nice lady. She told us we would be found in the morning."

"Do you remember where the cabin is located?"

"I think so. It has a long driveway into the woods and curves a lot."

"Do you think you could find it if we took you in the same direction again?"

Again, Natalia's and Becca's eyes locked as if they carried a little secret between them.

Becca thought for a moment. "We can try."

"Let's take a ride and see if we can find this place. Give me a few minutes to talk to your parents."

Steve left the room and entered the small video room. He handed the note to Mitch. Mitch glanced at it.

"It's blank."

Steve scratched the top of his balding head. "Why would Becca carry around a note from a lady named Grace with nothing on it?"

Azalea interjected, "Also, who is the woman who picked those men up in a car and took them to town? I wonder if there's any connection with this Grace and the other woman."

"I don't feel like I'm getting the entire story from the girls," admitted Steve.

"I agree." Mitch concurred. "There are some loopholes missing. Now we know who we're looking for we need to put out an APB for those two men and track them down.

CHAPTER THIRTY-ONE

The girls and Azalea rode in Mitch's squad car while Steve followed in his unmarked squad.

"Rafe and Steph pinpointed on the map where they picked the girls up," stated Mitch after they started down the winding road close to the river. "It's at the very end of the county." Becca sat in the front seat and Azalea and Natalia in the back. "I'll drive slow so if either of you recognize any landmarks or anything while you were walking this morning, tell me to stop."

"Oh… okay," yawned Becca.

"I know you're both wore out, but we need to find those men and also find this Grace you talked about."

"Papa, we liked Grace," Natalia made a long face. "She was nice to us, but she did dress a little weird."

"What do you mean by weird?" Azalea peeked at Natalia out of the corner of her eye.

"She wore long skirts and had a big jacket on. You know, like the cowboys wear in the western movies when it's cold. She also wore high boots, but they weren't cowboy boots."

Azalea put her arm around Natalia and lifted her chin to look her in the eye. "Aren't you the fashion maxxinista." She gave her a quirky smile. "I guess I wouldn't call her clothes weird. Maybe a little unusual for this part of the country. What else can you tell us about Grace?"

Natalia put her finger on her cheek as though she was in deep contemplation. "She had long curly gold hair…and beautiful eyes that…like…lit up when she smiled. When I watched her from the fireplace, she had a glow around her."

Becca turned in her seat. "You never mentioned it to me."

"Didn't you see it?"

"No." She turned around and crossed her arms. She remained quiet while she stared out the window.

Mitch noticed her quietness, "What's on your mind, Becca?"

"I don't know. I'm confused. How come I didn't notice what Nat did about Grace?"

"Not everyone sees a person the same. Sometimes we see something in one person that's special. It sounds to me like this Grace was special to Natalia."

"Yeah, maybe."

"Mitch, stop!" Becca hollered.

His foot hit the brakes and pulled to the side of the road. Steve pulled up behind.

"What is it?"

"The rock over there. I remember the rock. We leaned against the back of it to rest so no one could see us. It wasn't long until Reverend Rafe and Steph found us."

"Okay. Do you know which direction you were coming from when you rested by the rock?"

Becca twisted her neck in both directions. "I think we came from that direction." Her finger pointed ahead of them.

"Then we already passed where Rafe and Steph picked you up."

"Yeah, I think so," said Becca.

"So, the cabin is still ahead of us."

"Yes... yes, it is," her voice excited. "We walked until we got tired, then stopped and started again. I don't know how long we walked, but it wasn't long."

He stepped out of the car and ambled back to talk to Steve.

"Becca says they stopped by this rock to rest and Rafe found them soon after... sooo the cabin where they spent the night must be ahead."

"I hope we find it soon. I've been on the phone with the sheriffs in the neighboring counties and the BCA. They're stopping every white car in the territory. Too bad Becca couldn't see the make of the car."

"We're lucky she had the tenacity to open the bedroom door and see what she did."

Steve shook his head. "They're mighty good kids, Mitch... and brave, too."

Mitch nodded. "Don't I know it." He pointed to the road. "We're going to keep traveling and see if we can find the cabin. Do you still want to follow?"

"You bet I do. I want to meet this Grace character."

The small convoy started a slow crawl down the road toward the county line—slower this time so the girls could keep their eyes fixed on the landscape.

"All these driveways look alike," commented Azalea. "They're all overgrown by trees and many only have a minimum use road to follow with their cars."

"I guess the cabin owners like it that way. Back to nature they call it."

"The driveway from Grace's cabin had tracks and tall grass in between."

"That's another clue, Becca. See... if you think hard enough, things will come back to you."

Becca's lips switched to a small smile.

The road curved, and Becca's eyes opened wide.

"I think this is the road to Grace's cabin. I recognize the tall trees by the end of the road. We hid behind them before we decided which direction to take."

Mitch turned to drive down the minimum maintenance road. Steve followed. There was no sign of any activity or anyone living in the cabin.

Mitch stopped his vehicle and stepped out. The girls followed. "Is this the right place?"

Both nodded and ran toward the cabin.

"Girls, get back here. We need to be careful how we approach. Let me and Steve go first," said Mitch, as he loosened the latch on his gun holster. Keeping his eyes and ears alert he walked up to the door and knocked. Steve stood alongside the door with his gun ready to draw.

No one answered. Birds flitted back and forth among the trees singing among themselves, and the squirrels chattered from the trees above them. They knew the birds and animals would sense tension in the air if there was trouble brewing. Everything seemed normal.

Mitch tried the door and found it unlocked. His eyes darted to Steve and motioned for him to enter the house. Steve would scout it out while he guarded the front entrance. The cabin opened into a small living area which included the kitchen and living room with fireplace and one bedroom with an attached bathroom.

Steve moved deftly through the house and gave the all clear. Mitch waved his arm for Azalea and the girls to come forward.

"Is this the place?"

Becca and Natalia moved their eyes around the small cabin.

"Sure is," replied Becca. "Grace made us soup last night and put the rest in the refrigerator. She had muffins and orange juice on the table when we woke up by the fireplace."

Steve walked over to the fireplace. He reached in and felt the ash. "You said there was a fire burning in here last night?"

"Yeah," both girls answered together.

Steve locked eyes with Mitch and then Azalea. "The ash is cold."

"Becca, are you sure we're at the right place?" Azalea probed.

"Yes, Mom." She walked over to the fireplace. "We slept in front of a real fire last night." She moved toward the table. "We ate off this table. Grace put the food in the refrigerator." She opened the refrigerator. Empty. Her eyes popped, and she turned with a puzzled expression. "I don't get it."

Becca's motions became frantic as she opened one cabinet door after another. "These are the glasses we drank from last night." She grabbed the soup bowls. "We ate from these."

She ran to the bedroom and into the bathroom. Azalea followed. Becca opened the storage cabinet and found the face cloths used to wash their faces lay in a neat pile.

She put her arms out in defeat and stamped her foot. "I know this is the right place."

Steve wiped his finger across the dresser. "Looks like this place hasn't been lived in all winter. Notice the dust on all the furniture."

Natalia's eyes formed tears. "But we know we stayed here last night. We remember everything about this cabin."

Becca walked to the bathroom and turned the faucet in the sink. No water.

She turned with her mouth agape, "I used the toilet and washed my face in the sink. So did Natalia. I don't get it."

"Either do I," echoed Mitch.

Azalea decided to check the place out herself to find some evidence to prove the girls stayed there. She lifted the bedspread and found no sheets on the bed.

It's a for sure sign no one is living here.

She knelt on the floor and checked under the bed. She noticed a ribbon under the bed and reached for it.

"Does this look familiar?"

Natalia's face beamed. "Grace tied her hair back with the ribbon."

A sigh of relief washed over the three adults. Azalea handed the ribbon to Mitch.

They got to believe the girls now.

"How do we explain this in our report?" Steve shook his head.

Azalea gave a slow smile as a warm glow engulfed her body. "I think we may have had a miracle happen here last night and this morning. I believe Grace was an angel we've prayed for to help save the girls. I also believe the light Rafe and Steph said they witnessed was the angel Grace guiding them to find the girls. Just like the shepherds were led from their flocks at night by a star to find the baby Jesus, an angel offered a light to help save our children."

Mitch's and Steve's jaws dropped. The girls' eyes popped, and they held up their hands in a high five motion to each other.

CHAPTER THIRTY-TWO

On the way back to town Azalea sat in the front seat next to Mitch, quietly contemplating receiving two miracles within twenty-four hours: First, Rafe and Steph following a light to lead them to the girls; second, the girls rescued by what Azalea believed to be an angel.

The girls sat in the back seat and talked with renewed vigor, excited to believe an angel named Grace saved them.

When they arrived back at the LEC, Mitch told the girls to lay down in the back seat. He drove to the back garage again to continue to keep their rescue secret.

"Girls, we need to keep all of this quiet until we catch the men who abducted you. Do you understand what I'm asking?"

With somber faces they replied, "Yes, we understand."

"No talking to any friends or relatives."

"Not even Grandma?" Becca inquired.

"You need to do what Mitch is asking," cautioned Azalea. "He's doing it so they can catch the criminals who kidnapped you."

"Yes, sir."

"There's still a lot of questions, and we need more answers.

Timing is of the upmost importance. We need to find the place where you were held. Do you think you could help us find it?"

"I don't know. It was across the river is all I remember," said Becca.

"Think hard, Becca. We can capture the men if they are still there."

Azalea lifted her eyebrows as she questioned the pressure he put on the girls. "You know them by name and description. It should be easy to put out an APB on them."

"I know, but it would be easier if we could find the cabin today… before it gets dark. I'll finish up a few things and drop you and Becca off at your house."

"No, Daddy. I want to stay with Becca tonight."

Mitch raised his eyebrows and gave Azalea a questioning look. "Sure, you can stay with Becca."

"If you don't mind, I'd like to land on your couch tonight. I don't want any of you out of my sight until we catch everyone involved."

Azalea's face turned a slight shade of pink. "Oh… okay."

I don't know if I can handle Mitch on my couch. So near, yet unable to touch him and give comfort him as a wife.

Mitch walked back to his office while Azalea and the girls remained in one of the conference rooms. Steve followed him and plopped his body in the chair opposite Mitch's desk.

"Steve, I want to talk to the Sheriff's Posse member who was with Susan when they performed the cabin checks. I need the information ASAP and don't want Susan to know about it." He pulled on his ear. His eyes grew cold. "Did she volunteer today and get an area assigned to her?"

"She stopped by earlier, but there was no Posse volunteer to go with her."

"Get on it right now. I want to talk to him."

"Yep, sure thing." Steve left the room and strode out to the volunteer tent. Tom Bertrum and several Sheriff's Posse members still manned the station. Most of the volunteers returned from the hunt and went home. Sunny and her group pulled up while Steve perused through the roster of assignments to see if Susan was still out.

With her hair pulled back in a ponytail, Sunny had tendrils escaping in sweaty profusion around her face. He thought she was beautiful and gave her a shy smile.

"Any news?"

He held his jaw tight, shook his head, but sent her a guarded look as his eyes motioned toward the LEC building. She raised her eyebrows, smiled and nodded. She turned and headed straight for the building but kept her pace slow, so no one would catch on.

Once in the building she caught Sally's vision and without making a sound put her hands out in a where-are-they gesture. Sally pointed to the hallway toward the conference rooms. Sunny ran down the hallway checking each room. When she opened the door and her eyes caught sight of the girls, she ran and leaned over to engulf them in a bear hug.

"I'm so glad you're both okay. Can you tell me all about it?"

"Yes…yes." They acted ecstatic to receive more attention. Azalea welcomed sharing the good news with her sister and gave Sunny a grateful smile. The girls detailed the story again.

An elderly gentleman in a Sheriff's Posse uniform knocked on Mitch's door, "Sheriff, did you want to see me?"

"Yes, Mr. Rollins, please come in and sit. I need to press you for some information that is very confidential in nature. I know you are a Sheriff's Posse volunteer and not actually a deputy, but the same rules of confidentiality apply."

Confusion showed in his eyes. "Yes, sir, I'm aware. I will do anything I can to help."

"I understand you were assigned a certain area yesterday to check on cabins on the other side of the river along with another volunteer, my ex-wife, Susan Johnson."

"Yes, sir, that's true."

"Okay, did you see any strangers?"

He bent his head and put his hand on his forehead as if he was forcing his brain to work. "Yes, we did see several people. Some of the people are year-round residents, and I recognized them as customers at the hardware store where I work."

"Okay… Did you see any strangers?… Two men in particular? One short and the other tall with a limp."

He thought again for a moment. "Yep, kinda strange those two. Wouldn't let us near the cabin. Said they were here from the cities getting the cabin ready for the opening of fishing."

"What…or how did Susan…my ex-wife react? Did she show signs of recognition to either of them?"

"She got kinda loud while we were there; but, no, she didn't say anything about recognizing them."

"Can you take us to the cabin? We think it's where the girls were being held. I want to get there before it gets dark."

He leaned forward, his eyes excited. "Were? Did you find them?"

"Yes… but no one knows. We're trying to catch the kidnappers before they leave the area."

"Oh, my." His face turned red as his hand hit his head. "I should have said something to Tom Bertrum once we returned. They said they were fixing up the place, but it sure didn't look like they spent any time working on it. I'm sure I can find it again."

He picked up the phone. "Sally, notify the four closest squads to meet here ASAP."

Mr. Rollins jaw dropped. His voice rose as he jumped up, "I get to be part of the capture!"

"You sure do, Mr. Rollins. Let's hope we catch them."

"By golly, I sure do hope so. It's a terrible thing to kidnap young girls."

CHAPTER THIRTY-THREE

The four squads converged at the LEC. The volunteers returning from their assignments and the TV station crews and press portrayed an expected curiosity as several of the training deputies dressed in their SWAT gear, loaded up in their squads, and waited for the sheriff to lead them to their destination.

Even though River Falls did not officially need a SWAT team, several months earlier Mitch asked four deputies to take specialized tactical training with the special ops forces in the Twin Cities. The department ordered some of the essential gear hoping never to use it. Now it would come in handy.

Before he left, Mitch stopped at the conference room.

"Azalea, I need to take care of something. I'll be back soon and will take you and the girls home…unless you want a deputy to drive you back and stay with you."

Azalea gave him a perplexed look but did not question him. "I'd rather wait for you."

Mr. Rollins, hands shaking, sat stolid in the back seat with his eyes fixed on the road. Mitch and Steve led the squad of law enforcement vehicles. Steve held a copy of the map given to Rollins and Susan yesterday, so he had an idea where they were headed.

"Now when we get close to the cabin, you stay close to the vehicle, Mr. Rollins. We hope there's no gunfire, but if there is, we want you to be safe."

"Safe be darned. I'm a Viet Nam vet. I've been with the Sheriff's Posse for almost twenty years and the most action we've seen was last year when we helped at the high rise and now this. I'm good with a shot gun and pistol."

Mitch smirked to himself. "Thank you, Mr. Rollins. We'll let you know if we need additional help."

Rollins eyes grew wide as they approached a long driveway. "That's it. The one with a white car parked by the door. Only yesterday there was no vehicle in sight. They said their car was being repaired."

Mitch picked up the department's two-way radio. "Okay, this is the place." He took out his binoculars. The trunk of the car stood open. "Looks like they're preparing to run. Those dressed in SWAT gear surround the building. We'll wait until you're in place. One squad stay on the road to keep the press away—just in case. The other squad follow me as close to the cabin as possible. We'll be ready in case they try to run. We want these men alive to stand trial."

While the four SWAT team members wove among the trees, Steve grabbed the loud speaker from the trunk.

The SWAT team leader used his walkie-talkie to notify Mitch they were in place. Mitch and two of the squads turned on their sirens and drove toward the cabin. They swung the vehicles sideways for protection from any possible gun fire.

Steve handed the loud speaker to Mitch. "Be my guest."

"It'll be a pleasure," Mitch stood firm and ready for action.

"Mr. Rollins, maybe you better get behind the squad… just in case there's some shooting," suggested Steve. Rollins jumped out eager to be part of the capture.

"You… in the cabin," he hollered into the loud speaker. "Come out with your hands up. We got you surrounded."

A high-pitched voice came from the cabin. "We're coming out. Don't shoot."

The door of the cabin opened, but no one walked out. Several deputies, not on the SWAT team, started with guns drawn toward the door. Glass shattered, as a rifle fired from inside the house. The bullet bounced off one of the squad cars and ricocheted to hit one of the deputies in the arm.

Since Mitch said take them alive, the two deputies dropped to the ground and held their guns ready to return fire. The SWAT team fired their rifles and shot the tires of the suspect's car.

"Get back behind cover," Mitch shouted to the deputies. "Bad judgement," he muttered to himself.

The two deputies crawled back behind their squad. One deputy held his arm. Blood started to ooze out of the wounded deputy's shoulder. Rollins grabbed the first-aid kit from the trunk and ducked and wove his way over to the deputy to apply pressure to the wound and bandage it.

He hollered back to Mitch. "It's only a flesh wound. The bullet went clean through. He'll live."

"He's just lucky. What a stupid thing to do when we didn't know if they had weapons or not."

Steve shrugged. "We seldom see any action. Even though they've received training, they don't always realize someone else will shoot at them."

Mitch ordered the deputies in the woods to fire tear gas in through the windows to flush out the men. Once the bombs were fired and the smoke filled the cabin, Mac and Rodney rushed out coughing and sputtering and dropped to their knees.

They gave themselves up without any more resistance.

"You are under arrest for the kidnapping and abduction of two minor girls and holding them hostage."

"There's no one in there. Go look for yourselves." Mac sneered as a deputy handcuffed him. "We were just helpin' ourselves to a few things 'cause we found the door open."

Mitch's laughter rang out. "No, of course not. We know they're not in there. They're home safe."

Silence followed. Mac and Rodney would have a hard time talking themselves out of a prison sentence.

The team went in with gas masks and aired out the cabin before anyone else could enter to gather evidence.

"There's an arsenal of guns in there. They could have held us off for quite a while," offered one of the swat team. "Maybe they broke in to steal those guns."

Mitch looked down into the trunk of the car.

"No, I think they were getting ready to escape. If they wanted the guns, they should have put them in the trunk first thing. Run the serial numbers to see if they've been stolen."

He walked through the front door once the team gave the all clear.

Mitch crept into the back bedroom. One chair with the cut cable ties on the floor stood close to the bed. The other chair remained by the broken window with a blanket laid over the edge. Everything exactly as Becca and Natalia described.

We got them. Thank you, Lord, for your help.

Mitch's skin tingled, not the good kind, but the kind when bugs crawled under your skin and you want to itch and scratch, but they remain invisible except for the prickly burning inside you.

"Get some pictures of the cabin and gather as much evidence as you can," he hissed to Steve. He wanted to hit those thugs in the face. "I need to leave before I punch something." Mitch slammed the door leaving Steve and his crew to manage the investigation.

CHAPTER THIRTY-FOUR

The ambulance arrived to take the wounded deputy to the hospital. The TV cameramen and reporters stood at the end of the driveway and shouted for information from Mitch. He ignored them for now. He needed to calm down and gather his thoughts together in order to make a statement once he returned to the LEC.

He walked up to Rollins and shook his hand. "Thank you for your help with the wounded deputy."

"You're welcome. I was a medic in Viet Nam, and today brought back memories. I reacted as if I were on the battlefield. I still got it." He pulled back his arm in a victory salute. "Yes!"

Mitch smiled and patted him on the back. "Your help was much appreciated."

He and Rollins hitched a ride back to town with the deputy whose partner received a ride in the ambulance. The other squads carried the two prisoners. Mitch left his squad for Steve and the several deputies who stayed behind to gather evidence.

They arrived at the LEC to more reporters. With slow purpose, Mitch exited the squad and stood on the steps by the front entrance.

"Thank you all for your support over the past few days," he shouted out to them. "We're questioning some people right now. We hope to have a report in the morning. In the meantime, if you will allow the sheriff's department to take care of our business, it would be appreciated."

Mitch turned and walked in the main entrance and strode toward the conference room where he left Azalea and the girls. Much to his surprise they were all gathered around Sally's desk along with Sunny. Azalea turned when she heard the door slam.

"Mitch!" She ran into his arms. "Oh, Darling, we were so worried about you. Why didn't you tell us you found where they kept the girls?"

He snuggled into her softness and breathed her scent. "Because I didn't want to worry you," he whispered in her ear.

"Well, we were worried," she leaned into him further as if she never wanted to let go. Then she pulled back. "We all listened by Sally's desk to the police scanner, so we could hear everything. We were so scared when we heard someone had been shot."

"It's part of the job. We put our lives on the line every day. Today several of the deputies took a risk and one got himself injured." He looked toward the girls, who were still awake even after their ordeal throughout the day.

Natalia made her way to Mitch. "Daddy, did you get the bad men?"

"We sure did, honey. I believe you are safe now." She raised her arms for Mitch to pick her up.

"Thank you, Daddy. Maybe now I can sleep and not have bad dreams."

Tears stung Mitch's eyes. "Oh, Nat, I'm so sorry for everything you went through. I'll take you and Becca home. I need to come back to question the two men."

"Mitch, Nat needs you today. Is it necessary to question them right now?"

"Yes, Azalea. We need to find the mastermind behind this abduction. I believe they're just the fall guys. I'll be by the house as soon as it's over. Steve's out there right now gathering evidence and taking pictures. He's going to be too busy to interrogate them, so it's up to me to start the process. They're claiming they had nothing to do with the kidnapping." He stopped with his explanation as the girls' ears perked up. "I'll explain when I'm done here. Please understand."

Azalea nodded in acquiesce.

Sunny, in the meanwhile, meandered back to the drop-off garage for prisoners and looked through the small glass window. Her mouth dropped open as she recognized the two prisoners. She had seen them twice—once when Azalea was robbed, and again last night at the Corner Bar.

She hurried back to the front. "Mitch... excuse me, Sheriff, I recognize those men."

"Sure, you do," piped in Azalea. "They're the ones who tried to rob me."

"Yes...but I saw them last night when some of us went to Corner Bar for a hamburger after we got back from walking the woods searching for the girls. We all camped out at Mom's overnight, but they were there eating hamburgers and drinking beer."

"Interesting." Mitch's nostrils flared. "What time?"

"Around dark. We got back as the sun set and decided to get something to eat. I called Mom to see if we could stay with her. Those men were flirting with the other waitress—the one that used to work at the high rise, Callie Weber."

"Callie Weber, are you sure?"

"Of course, Azalea knew she worked there. She asked me and Steve to do some surveillance after hours at the bar because of Susan." Sunny giggled as she remembered Steve's getup. "You should have seen Steve with a toupee and glasses."

"She wasn't even a suspect. How could she know about my money unless..." Mitch snapped his fingers, "Susan, of course."

Azalea eavesdropped on their conversation. "I mentioned Callie to you once before. You kinda blew it off."

"Yes, but... oh, never mind. Another clog in the clock."

Azalea turned to Sunny. "Do you want to come home with us tonight?"

"No, thanks. I think I'll bunk at Mom's." Sunny's eyes rested on Mitch's tired frame. "Can I divulge to Mom the girls are safe? I'm sure it'll make her sleep better."

Mitch scratched his head and smirked. "At this point, you can tell her, but please emphasize everything is still confidential. I know it may be hard for her to not get on the phone and call all her friends, but we need to protect the privacy of the girls right now."

"Understand. I'm sure Mom will, too. Don't be surprised if she wants to come and see the girls tonight."

Mitch raised his hand to his head and massaged his temples. "Please, if possible, keep her away. I love her like my own mother, but I don't think we can deal with too many more people tonight."

"What about the volunteers I brought with me?"

Sunny looked at Mitch for some solution.

"Please tell them the National Guard volunteers will be here tomorrow, and they can go back home." Mitch ran his fingers through his hair. "That reminds me... I need to call the Governor and inform him we found the girls, and he can cancel the National Guard. Uff da! Too much to do at one time."

"I'll see you all later."

It surprised Azalea when Sunny, who was not prone to show affection, reached out to give her a hug. Azalea returned the hug while her eyes traveled to Mitch with a wink.

He cocked an inquisitive glance.

Sunny turned to Sally, "Thanks, Sally, for letting us listen in with you."

Sally's face turned pink as she gave a short wave to Sunny. She knew she broke protocol when she allowed civilians to listen in to the private police scanner.

After Sunny left, Mitch wanted to gather his family together and take them to Azalea's house. The girls kept glancing at each other, whispering, and poking each other in the ribs.

Mitch gave them a sideways glance and drew his eyebrows together, "Something on your mind, Natalia?"

"We got to tell you something," Becca feebly whispered, while Natalia kept shaking her head.

Mitch took the girls into his office, pulled his chair from around his desk, and sat down. Azalea shrugged her shoulders with her hands out giving Mitch the I-don't-know sign as she stood in the doorway.

"They've been a little secretive since we got back here," she volunteered.

Natalia started to form tears in her eyes. "Daddy, we both saw something but kept it secret from everyone."

He gently laid his hand on Natalia's shoulders. "Okay, do you want to tell me now?"

"I don't want to, but I know I got to." She turned to look at Becca. "I'm sorry, Becca, I made you keep the secret."

"It's okay, Nat. We need to tell Mitch and Mom now before we get into any more trouble."

"Daddy, the lady who brought the car out to the men and left with them…"

"Yes, you mentioned it before."

"Well, she had long brown hair."

Mitch remained calm as if he was interrogating a suspect instead of his daughter. "Okay, can you tell me how you know this when you told us they all wore ski masks?"

"The men wore the ski masks when the lady delivered the car, but we saw the lady with the long brown hair."

Mitch's hand hit his forehead as he thought he put two and two together to make four. "Callie Weber."

"It could have been a wig," piped in Becca.

Mitch's concentration waivered. He moved behind his desk and picked up the phone. "Steve… what's the status of your evidence gathering?" Mitch listened. "Yeah… the girls gave me additional information. I'm having Callie Weber picked up for questioning."

"Daddy," Natalia's tears started. Mitch wanted to protect his daughter from any more stress.

"Pumpkin, you go home with Azalea. I can't drive you home right now. I'll see you a little later."

"But…"

He shook his head. "No more, Nat. You and Becca had enough trauma for one day."

CHAPTER THIRTY-FIVE

Another deputy dropped the girls and Azalea off at her house.
"How about pizza? I can put a frozen one in the oven, and it'll be ready in twenty minutes."
"I'm not hungry right now, Mom."
"Me either."
"I'll put one in the oven anyway."
"Whatever," Becca whispered in a low voice.
"Becca. Natalia. Is there something you want to talk about? I believe you should be talked out by now."
"No, Mom. We're disappointed Mitch wouldn't listen to us and let us finish telling the story."
"Do you want to tell me?"
Becca shook her head. "We need to talk to Mitch."
"He'll be here in a little while. He wanted to interrogate those men."
"Call us when the pizza is ready."
Exhausted from the day's activities Becca and Natalia went upstairs. Azalea called them down a short time later, and they ate their pizza in silence.

"We're tired."

"Too big a day. Go dress for bed, and I'll tuck you in.

After Azalea helped them to pray, she kissed them goodnight, and left the small light burning in the room.

Downstairs she poured herself a glass of wine and mulled over the day's events.

The girls are holding back something. Even though they said the lady had long brown hair, I don't understand why Callie would be involved. Yes, Callie was seen with the kidnappers at the bar, but does it make her a kidnapper, too. Of course, nothing normal has happened with this entire abduction.

Mitch arrived at the back door several hours later. His azure eyes no longer held the brightness she was used to seeing, but instead showed the tortured dullness from the day's activities. A pain squeezed within Azalea's heart as she thought of everything bad that could have happened but did not evolve. He poured himself a glass of wine and sat next to her.

"I couldn't get a confession out of the men even though there's enough evidence against them." He shook his head in resignation. "The biggest problem is the girls never saw their faces. Even when Becca said she opened the bedroom door the men still wore the stocking masks. The only thing they remembered was the lady with the long brown hair."

"Did you bring in Callie Weber for questioning?"

"Yep. She denied everything. She was so vehement about her innocence. Her husband showed up and vouched for her whereabouts on the day the girls escaped. She was with him doing yard work until she had to go to work at five. According to the girls the car was delivered in the middle of the afternoon. So, we let her go. We're back to square one if we can't figure out who the woman was. Oh, by the way, Callie put in a complaint that someone stole her drivers' license several days ago. Whoever did it could have used it to purchase the car for those two men. I'm surprised they didn't try to steal another car."

"Daddy," Natalia stood at the top of the stairs.

"I thought you girls were sleeping." Azalea gave them a surprised wide-eyed look. Becca stood behind Natalia rubbing her eyes.

"We need to talk to you," Natalia's meekness gave her the same innocence Mitch remembered vividly when Susan walked out on them. Mitch wanted to run to her and keep her safe. However, his tired body could not move.

He waved at them. "Okay, come on down." Mitch and Azalea moved apart and sat on opposite ends of the couch, while the two girls took up the middle.

"All right, girls, what's up?" Azalea gave them a befuddled look.

"Daddy, you wouldn't listen to us earlier—like—we wanted to tell you something."

"You jumped to conclusions," interjected Becca.

"What are you talking about?"

"Daddy...the woman we saw. We wanted to explain more."

He put his glass of wine on the coffee table and placed his arm around Natalia and hugged her to him. Natalia leaned into him for comfort.

"Daddy, we know...or we think we know...who the lady was that brought the car to the men just before we escaped."

Natalia crossed her feet and twisted her hands together. The tears started. "Becca was able to get the door open... *sob sob*, when we heard them say they were going to town to get some food. *Sob, sob.* The lady had long dark hair."

"Yes, you told me all that before."

"It was a wig," piped Becca.

Tears continued to course down Natalia's cheeks.

"Becca, how do you know this for sure? Will you finish the story for us?"

"I saw her first and tried to close the door, so Natalia wouldn't see her when they stepped outside."

"Okay, now you girls got me curious. Who... did... you... see?"

Becca's eyes stung as she rubbed them. Her voice became mute. "Ahhh..."

"*It was my mother*," bawled Natalia, as she flung herself into her dad's arms and wiped her tears on his shirt. He held her tight.

Azalea's hand flew to her mouth and felt her heart sink. She and Mitch exchanged shocked glances over Natalia's head.

"Are you sure?" Mitch's eyes focused on Becca for affirmation.

Becca nodded. "We only saw her from the side. She wore a long dark-haired wig and tried to hide her face. She bent over and when she stood up, she threw her hair back. I saw the side of her face. I looked at Natalia and realized she saw her, too."

"Are you going...to arrest...her?" blubbered Natalia, as she pulled away from her dad's embrace. He held her at arm's length.

"We'll get a search warrant for Susan's apartment and bring her in for questioning."

"You girls were very brave to come talk to us. What an eye-opening experience for all of us. Now it's time for bed."

Becca and Natalia started back up the stairs. Becca halted and turned around, a pained expression showed in her eyes.

"We're sorry, Mitch. We were afraid to tell you what we saw, but we didn't want to cause any more trouble for anyone else."

"No, I'm the one who's sorry. I know you were scared to talk to me. I shouldn't have jumped to conclusions."

"I didn't want it to be my mom," admitted Natalia. "Why did she do it, Daddy?"

Mitch shook his head. "I only wish I knew."

With drooping shoulders, the girls wrapped their arms around one another and climbed up the stairs.

He turned toward Azalea. "I don't think Susan's aware yet we have her accomplices. She expected the money to be delivered today. Since they didn't show up with the money, I'm sure she's out searching for them. She more than likely saw Steve and his crew at the cabin, so she knows we found their hideout."

"Aren't you afraid she'll run?"

"Not without knowing if they picked up the money or not. Half a million dollars is too much to just walk away from. I don't know where she was today. She stopped by the volunteer tent, but Tom didn't give her an assignment. I'll have one of our unmarked squads do surveillance outside her apartment tonight until we can get the search warrant... just in case."

"Can't you pick her up tonight?"

"We can, but we need more to go on."

"Isn't the girls' testimony enough?"

"Tomorrow we'll interrogate Rodney and Mac again. It surprised me they never asked for an attorney after we read them their Miranda Rights. They'll think twice after they spend a night in jail. They never asked for a phone call either. Anyway, if they tried to call her, we would know it right away."

Frustration built up inside Mitch. In his old life he would have scolded the girls about interrogating the wrong suspect when the department could have been concentrating on a confession from Mac and Rodney. However, he knew the girls had been through enough the past week. He blamed himself for not listening to everything the girls wanted to tell him.

He bowed his head. "God, give me peace tonight and the right words to explain to the girls once we interrogate Susan. It's going to break Natalia's heart again."

CHAPTER THIRTY-SIX

Azalea moved back into the comfort of Mitch's shoulder. He wrapped his arm around her, so she could snuggle in closer. They remained silent as they sipped their wine. Azalea tried to take in what the girls revealed.

How could Susan be involved in kidnapping her own daughter? Was Jake involved in any of this? Why would Susan involve herself? I knew when she showed up wearing designer labels and professional highlights in her hair that she had wealthy parents. Could the girls be mistaken? After all they were given drugs that could distort their memory. This whole scenario can't be true.

"I wish something nice would happen soon, so we can forge ahead and forget this terrible ordeal."

"Yeah, I know what you mean." He refilled his glass and drank the contents, feeling its calming effects.

He pulled her toward him. His mouth met hers in an intense kiss. She tasted the sweetness of the wine on his lips.

"You better get me some blankets and a pillow, so I can get some sleep. Otherwise, we're going to end up in your bedroom."

Azalea was feeling the headiness of her second glass of wine.

"Well, I wouldn't mind that in the least." She gave him a provocative smile and planted a kiss on his neck.

"Ohhh..." The tenseness removed from his body, he laid her on the couch and kissed the soft fullness of her lips. He pulled away and sat up straight. "We need to get married as soon as possible. I don't want to wait until after Steph's baby is born. She'll look beautifully pregnant in our wedding pictures, or we could just take headshots."

Being in a playful mood she wrapped her arms around him.

"I agree. I want us to be together as one like God intended for a husband and wife. Let's plan for a wedding in June instead of end of July."

"As long as you make it the first part of June."

"I'll check my list of weddings for that month and pick one with the fewest bookings. I don't want to spend most of my wedding week making flowers for other brides. What about a honeymoon?"

"Where would you like to go?"

"Surprise me. Make it a short one as I'll probably have more weddings the following week."

"Mrs. DeVries—that name sounds so nice on you."

"You know we never discussed my taking your last name. If it's not a big deal for you, I'd like to keep the name Rose because of the flower shop, but you can still call me Mrs. DeVries."

"You're the independent type, huh."

"I learned it by trial and error after Jake and I split. I like my independence, but I know I need to depend on God and...I need you in my life from now on."

He yawned. "I think the wine relaxed me enough, so I can sleep. Are the girls okay?"

"Let's go up and check on them while I get you a pillow and blanket."

They tiptoed to Becca's bedroom. Mitch gently kissed each girl on their forehead. He stood by the door and gave them his first genuine smile since the girls disappeared before he slipped out of the room. He took the blanket and pillow from Azalea and made his way downstairs to the couch.

Hearing the doorbell at six in the morning brought Mitch out of a sound sleep. He jumped up wearing only his underwear and t-shirt—at first not realizing where he was. Then it sank in.

He heard Azalea's door slam and rapid footsteps down the stairs. Azalea checked the peephole in the front door and turned toward Mitch.

"Quick, get dressed!" she hissed and rolled her eyes. "It's my mother!"

He hurried to get at least his pants up and zippered. She mouthed the words *thank you* before she unlocked the door.

"Azalea, you're a big girl. You don't need to worry about your... Ah, Mrs. Rose, how wonderful to see you...so early in the morning." He was being facetious, but Bernadette ignored his remark.

"Where're the girls?"

Azalea frowned. "Upstairs sleeping...and thanks for waking us up."

She stopped dead in her tracks. "I'm sorry. I figured with everything happening you would be up," she gave a stern look toward Mitch and finished in a snarky voice, "and...alone."

"Mother," Azalea scolded. "Mitch reminded me I'm a big girl now. If I wanted him to sleep over, it's my right and my house. Anyway, he slept on the couch to watch over us."

Bernadette's face turned almost as red as her Carnation Red lipstick. "I apologize. You're right. You are old enough to make your own decisions. I couldn't sleep so I got up early to make my special caramel rolls for everyone. Do you mind if I bring them in for your breakfast?"

Azalea licked her lips as her voice changed to anticipation. "Really! You made your special caramel rolls. By all means, bring 'em on."

She left to retrieve them from the car. Mitch finished dressing.

"I better get home, shower and change. Big day ahead. By the way, what's so special about her caramel rolls?"

"They only have two gazillion calories and are the best in the world."

"Well, here they are." She walked in out of breath and handed the rolls still warm from the oven to Azalea. "Since the girls aren't up, I'll head over to the flower shop and have everything ready for your employees."

"Thanks, Mom." Azalea wrapped her arms around Bernadette. "You're the greatest."

"Is someone…" Becca paused at the top of the stairs. "Nana!" Her eyes grew wide as she bolted down to give her grandma a hug.

Natalia walked out of the bedroom rubbing her eyes. She stood shyly at the top of the stairs.

"Come on down and let me give you a hug, too" motioned a smiling Bernadette. Natalia beamed and rushed down the stairs.

Bernadette grabbed both girls in a bear hug. "Can I call you Nana like Becca does?"

"Of course, we'll be family in just a few months."

"Ah, Mom… we need to talk about that."

Bernadette's face crumbled. "You're not calling off the wedding?"

"No… no." Her eyes met Mitch's, and she ambled over to his side and placed an arm around his waist.

"We decided to get married earlier than planned. How about a June wedding?"

Bernadette's jaw dropped. The girls jumped for joy and clapped their hands in a high five.

"I figured everyone would be excited. I want to have one of

those caramel rolls before I head back to work."

Azalea set the rolls on the island and started the coffee maker. "Mom, again thank you for the rolls."

Mitch grabbed one out of the pan and bit into it. "Umm... yum." He smacked his lips and rolled his eyes. "These are indeed the best caramel rolls." He motioned to the girls. "Come on, dig in."

His phone rang, and he ran to retrieve it from the other room. "Mitch here."

"Yep."

"Did you get a search warrant?"

"You did what?" His voice garbled as he bit into a roll. "I stayed at Azalea's last night, but I'm heading home to shower and change. I'll be there within the hour."

"What am I munching on? Only the best caramel rolls in the world." He threw the last bite into his mouth. "See you in a bit."

He reached for his jacket as Azalea handed him a cup of coffee. He took a few sips. "Gotta go. The men want to sing and are asking for their attorney." Self-conscious of his actions, Mitch kissed Azalea with his sticky lips, but she did not mind as she returned the kiss by putting her hands on each side of his face.

"I want a kiss every morning before you leave for work after we're married."

"Deal." He smiled and whispered in her ear. "Just don't kiss me like that in the morning, or I won't be able to go to work."

She giggled as he walked out the door. She turned to find three sets of eyes staring at her.

"What?" Azalea held out her arms.

"Oh, nothing," Bernadette replied. "Now let's take a few minutes to talk about your wedding."

CHAPTER THIRTY-SEVEN

The deputy managing the front desk knocked on Mitch's door. "Sheriff, we have your ex-wife in the interrogation room. Detective Bishop is waiting for you."

"Okay. Thanks."

He put down the statements the two men wrote earlier in the morning with a court-appointed attorney present for each of them. He rubbed his temples and felt a stress headache rise to the top of his head. The frustration and disappointment of the past few days showed in his face along with dark circles under his eyes.

Steve did not look much different. Both of them put in many hours on search and rescue, and now they needed to provide evidence to convict the people involved in the kidnapping.

Mitch dragged his body from the chair to meet Steve by the interrogation room.

"FYI...when we searched Susan's apartment, we found luggage in her apartment already packed and stuffed in the closet."

Mitch leaned against the wall and closed his eyes in a pinched, tension-filled expression. "I guess it really doesn't surprise me. With a deputy outside her apartment building last night, she wouldn't get very far if she tried to run."

Steve stood with his hand on the doorknob. "Ready to do this?"

"Yeah, I guess so. Let's get it over with."

Steve held the door open, so Mitch could enter. Both stared stone-faced at Susan DeVries who sat at the table with her hands folded and her head bowed.

She jerked her head up and curled her lips in a smug expression. She started to rise. "Mitch, why was I dragged from my apartment and forced to sit in this room?" Her voice held the sound of sweet innocence. "We need to get out there and find the girls."

"Sit down, Susan." Mitch growled as his lips tightened in a fine line. He and Steve took a seat across the table from his ex. Something cold slithered inside him as he wondered how he could have married this woman.

"I asked Detective Bishop to be here with me to ask you a few questions."

"Why was my apartment being searched? Were you looking for drugs?" She attempted to goad him. "I certainly wouldn't keep them in the apartment. You know I'm on parole."

Mitch pulled on his ear. "Susan, this is hard on me, and it's going to get harder on you. I have no one to blame but myself for letting you back into our lives. Before we begin, Detective Bishop, please read Susan her rights."

While Steve read the Miranda Rights to Susan, her eyes bored into Mitch as if she was desperate to read his mind.

"Do you understand your rights?"

"Yes, of course." Her eyes broke contact and wavered back and forth. A quick flash of anger crossed her face, but then her face went still as stone.

Mitch wanted to see her reaction. "I want to tell you first of all—we found the girls." He waited. "Maybe you already knew." He waited. Nothing. "They escaped their kidnappers and were found wandering through the woods."

All of a sudden as if on cue. "Oh, thank heavens." She let out a dispassionate sigh. "When can I see Natalia?"

He held up a hand. "Please allow me to continue." He grimaced, and his body shuddered. "We also have evidence you were involved in the kidnapping. Your apartment was searched this morning, and in the trash container outside the building a wig was found which matches the description of a woman seen delivering a car to the men who kidnapped the girls. What do you have to say?"

"What can I say? It's a big building and the wig could belong to anyone in the apartment complex." She leaned back in the chair and shook her head, as if by doing that every strand of hair would fall into place. "I want an attorney present before I say anything. You have no evidence to hold me. The wig could have been planted there to incriminate me."

Steve piped up, "It's on its way to the lab right now. The forensics team at the BCA will take whatever DNA they can find on it. It's all the evidence we need besides our eye witnesses."

"Eye witnesses?" Her eyes shot open, as she tilted her head.

Mitch knew she was playing with him and Steve. He'd seen this same scenario before where the accused is caught and there's no way out.

Mitch put both hands on the table. "Okay, Susan. You can call an attorney. But before I walk out of this room, I have one question to ask you. Why?"

"Why? I don't have the faintest idea what you're talking about." She sat straighter and put on a blank expression.

"If what we believe is true and the evidence proves it, you will never see Natalia again."

His hands tightened into fists as he stood up and walked out of the room.

"It was a rough interview," Steve admitted as he followed Mitch to his office. "She knows all the tricks."

"Rough! It hasn't begun yet. Soon as her lawyer gets here, I know she'll dummy up just like she did now."

"We need to break these other two into admitting she was behind the kidnapping."

"Both their lawyers know we got them dead-on. I'm sure they'll ask for a plea bargain in order to get a lighter sentence. It's all in the timing."

Sally stuck her head in the door. "Sheriff, the volunteers and reporters are congregating outside. Don't you think you should say something? The mayor is out there, too."

"Yes, we can't put this off any longer. As soon as Azalea arrives, we'll talk to the reporters. I'll go and give the word to the volunteers and thank them."

He grabbed his jacket from behind the door. Steve accompanied him. They walked out the door in unison toward the volunteer tent.

He picked up the bull horn from the table. "I want to thank you all for coming out today. We want to inform all of you the girls are now safe, and we're questioning several men. I'll have more news within a few hours, but you can all go home. Again, thank you all for your support and kindness throughout the past week." His voice choked. "It's so wonderful to be part of a small community where everyone comes together to help one another out."

Woot! Woot! The crowd cheered and clapped as Mitch put down the bull horn. The reporters surrounded him and Steve as they attempted to walk back into the Law Enforcement building.

"Can you give us more information on when the girls were found? Can you tell us who you are holding in custody?"

Mitch shook his head. "Sorry, I can't give you any more information. Everything is still under investigation. All I can say is the girls are safe. We hope to give you more information soon."

Jake Leddering showed up during the last part of Mitch's speech. He turned to face an angry Jake.

"Why didn't anyone call me and tell me the girls were safe?"

"Jake, can you come into the building. We can talk about it there."

"I want to know now." His phone rang. He reached in his pocket and his eyebrows crunched together. "Why would my attorney be calling me?" He pointed to Mitch with his index finger. "I'll meet you inside."

Mitch and Steve scurried back into the building. "Wonder what that call is about?"

"You don't think Susan had the attorney call Jake. When Sunny and I did surveillance in the bar where Susan works, Jake was a steady customer. They were getting a little chummy."

Mitch pulled on his ear. "This is getting weird."

Azalea drove up in her car with the two girls. She saw the volunteers mulling around the tent and noticed Jake on the phone. She knew she was going to be in trouble with him for not calling about the girls' rescue. She wanted to get into the building to use Mitch for protection before Jake stopped her.

"We need to make a fast entry into the building, girls. Are you ready?"

"Yes," both echoed.

They almost made it up the few steps when Jake shouted. "Azalea! Becca!" He stuck his phone in his jacket. "Wait." He jogged up to them.

He wrapped his arms around Becca. "I'm so glad you're okay. You'll have to tell me the whole story."

"Hello, Jake." Azalea moved toward Becca.

"Okay, what's going on? How come no one called me about finding the girls? I've been sick to my stomach worrying about Becca… and so has my mom."

"I'm sorry, Jake, but we needed to keep it confidential about the girls. Mitch was afraid the kidnappers would run, and they were just about to when they were arrested. You need to talk to Mitch and Detective Bishop. I didn't even know they were going after the kidnappers until it was over with."

"I just got a call from my attorney that Susan Johnson has been arrested. This is ridiculous. What other trumped up charge is Mitch thinking of next? Is he going to arrest me, too, for talking to Susan?"

"Jake, stop it! You're making a scene out here. Please go inside and talk to Mitch."

"I most certainly will."

Azalea rolled her eyes and looked up to the heavens.

Lord, I think I've put up with enough of Jake's antics. Please give me patience with this man.

They entered the building together. Mitch and Steve huddled in his office going over a game plan while they waited for Jake. Sally knew something was going to explode, so right after she ushered them back to Mitch's office she returned with the girls and escorted them to one of the conference rooms.

"What's going on?" Jake demanded. "I received a call from my attorney saying he was hired by Susan to defend her against her arrest here."

"Jake, first of all, Susan has not been officially arrested—just detained. We are holding her until we can verify evidence found in and around her apartment to implicate her in the kidnapping of her child and holding her and Becca hostage."

"Oh, my…" he sat down in the vacant chair next to Steve. "I thought it had something to do with drugs." He shook his head. "I don't believe it."

Mitch and Steve communicated to each other with a slight movement of their eyes. Mitch gave Steve the go ahead to talk to Jake.

"I'm sorry, Mr. Leddering, we can't discuss this any further with you until we have all the evidence in place. We do know there was a female involved in the kidnapping. We have several eye witnesses who place her with the two men we arrested yesterday."

"Can I see her?"

Azalea piped up, "Are you serious? Jake, this is your daughter we're discussing here. You would take Susan's side over your own daughter?"

"No...I...I," he stuttered. "I don't know what to say. I'm stunned."

"You'll have to go through the proper channels to see Susan. You're not her attorney, so you need to fill out paperwork to see her."

"I see," he uttered still in a daze. "Okay, I'll let you guys do your work."

He walked out of the office and headed toward the exit door. Down the hallway he heard "Jake, help me!"

Susan was being escorted by a female jailor to the detention area. She broke loose and ran toward Jake.

"Prisoner loose," shouted the female jailor. Everyone nearby ran toward the door while Susan ran into Jake's arms and clung to him.

"Jake, they think I kidnapped my own daughter," she sobbed.

CHAPTER THIRTY-EIGHT

Mitch, Steve and Azalea heard the jailor shout and all three sprinted out of the office to intercept the escapee. They found her clinging to Jake where she lost all control and began trembling and emitting strangled sobs from her lungs. Several officers stood around them ready to grab Susan and place handcuffs on her. Mitch shook his head, and they backed off.

Mitch wanted to throttle her for her dramatic antics. "Okay, Susan, enough of your shenanigans. Your attorney will be here soon, and Jake can do nothing to help you."

She backed away and wiped her eyes with the back of her hand. The jailor took her by the arm and with two other deputies escorted Susan toward the detention area. As they passed the conference room two young girls stood watch through a partially opened door. Susan made eye contact without a flicker of emotion on her face as they walked by. The girls made a quick retreat and closed the door.

"It's not what it looks like," Jake held out his hands. "I know what you're thinking, but I'm not involved with her. She wanted me, but I couldn't." His face squished up in distaste.

"Oh, Jake," admonished Azalea. "Mitch's ex-wife...really?"

"I told her I couldn't get involved with an ex-con. It'd ruin my business and my reputation. She kept coming on to me."

"And you kept going to the bar... so what else could she think?"

"Azalea, I'm not involved with her. I liked the attention I got when I was at the bar even though she flirted with other men."

Steve's ears perked up. "What other men? Any you can identify?"

"Sure. She flirted with pretty much every man in the bar. Even those two men who attempted to rob Azalea and are out on bail."

"So, she did know those men," Mitch's face turned grim and lit a fire in his eyes.

Mitch and Steve sat with the girls again and suggested they repeat their story in case they missed any small incident which they could use as evidence. In the meanwhile, Rodney's and Mac's attorneys met with them again.

After an hour of questioning the girls, Mitch and Steve emerged with the two in tow.

"I think the girls are tired of answering questions." Steve smiled politely at the two.

Azalea turned to Mitch. "Can I take them back to the house or do you need them here?"

"I'd like to do a line-up to see if they can identify the two even if they kept their ski masks on during the entire time."

"Except for when they were outside with the Sheriff's Posse member and Susan," added Azalea.

"Huh... when did this information turn up?" Steve turned toward Azalea.

"Didn't the girls say anything in your interrogation?"

Mitch and Steve turned toward Becca. Mitch leaned over and put his hands on Becca's shoulders. "At any time... and I emphasize the word any time... did you see the faces of the men?"

"No, like Mom said… when they were outside with the Sheriff Posse guy and Natalia's mom, they had their ski masks rolled up. I saw the backs of their head. When they left, I shut the door and pushed my chair back, so they wouldn't know I saw them."

"Wow! It might help us out with a line-up. Why don't you girls take a break, and we'll get a line-up together. We'll see if you can pick them out of a group of men. They won't see you, but you can see them."

"Sheriff," Sally called Mitch on the intercom. "A fax just came in from the BCA on the wig."

Mitch, tired of sitting at his desk, jumped up and sprinted out to Sally's desk. After the discovery of the wig, Steve requested one of the deputies to drive to the BCA in Minneapolis with the wig and request an immediate analysis. In normal time it would take weeks to get an analysis back, but Steve put in a call to Agent Schmidt.

"Thanks. It was fast work on their part. Please locate Detective Bishop and tell him the report is in."

"Yes, sir."

A few minutes later Steve walked into Mitch's office.

"The line-up is almost ready. I have several of our undercover officers plus a couple other prisoners along with Rodney and Mac."

"Sounds good." He threw the report down on his desk toward Steve. "I hoped Susan was innocent, and she was being set up. The report says the sample from her hair and the wig match. Dumb of Susan to dump the wig in the apartment trash bin."

"Yeah. Usually the bins are picked up daily, but we got there before the garbage trucks. Don't start to get soft now. We're going to have to charge her with kidnapping. We still need more evidence to wrap everything up…like an admission from Mac and Rodney."

"Let's see what happens with the girls in the line-up. If they identify them, their lawyers will probably suggest they give up their accomplice."

"Okay, Becca and Natalia." Steve started his normal routine speech. "The window is a two-way mirror. You can see them, but they can't see you."

"Okay." There was a bright look of eagerness on Becca's face. "I'm not afraid."

Since they did not have an official line-up stage like the bigger cities, they cleared the interrogation room of the table and chairs, so the girls could see the men, but they couldn't see them.

Six men stepped into the room. The jailor told them to stand against the far wall. Steve communicated to the jailor through his phone. "Please have each of the men step forward toward the mirror."

Each took four to five steps toward the mirror. Mac was the only one with a limp.

"The one with the limp," whispered Becca.

"You don't have to whisper," snickered Steve. "They can't hear you."

"All right. The tall one with the limp. The other guy called him Mac."

"Yeah, he limped and complained 'cause his leg hurt," offered Natalia.

"Do you recognize the other man?"

"I'm not sure. I only saw him from the back."

"Please have the men turn around and walk back to the far wall."

Becca pointed to a short stocky man with thinning hair. "That's him. His shoulders slouched. Is his name Rocky…or Rodney?"

"Yep. Thank you, girls. You've just identified the men we knew kidnapped you."

"Really! We did good?"

Mitch placed his arm around each girl, "You did good."

Steve stepped into Mitch's office later that day. "Mac and Rodney have officially been charged with kidnapping."

"Our job is almost done on this case. By the way, the cabin has been yellow-taped and the owner notified the cabin was considered a crime scene. I don't want to repeat the words he said about the situation."

The deputy at the front desk dialed the intercom to Mitch's office. "Sir, the two defense attorneys for the accused kidnappers want to talk to you."

"Send them back." Mitch rubbed his hands in anticipation, and hoped the attorneys took the time to convince their clients to name the person who hired them. Both attorneys had been court-appointed earlier when Mac and Rodney tried to rob Azalea on Valentine's Day.

Steve stood to leave. "I need to make a few phone calls," he used as an excuse.

Mr. Fitch, an older experienced attorney, represented many of the inmates. Mr. Appleby was new in town, and Mitch knew it was one of his first big cases as a court-appointed attorney.

"Mr. Fitch. Mr. Appleby." Mitch greeted them with a nod. "Please sit." He spread his hand toward the two chairs across from his desk.

Each attorney sat and opened their briefcases.

Mr. Appleby began, "We've been notified by the county attorney that our clients' cases will be officially charged in court as soon as possible."

"The sooner the better for all involved," stated Mitch as he crossed his arms and waited for the attorneys to give their pitch.

Mr. Fitch cleared his throat. "We're looking at a deal for our clients. We know you're close to the situation with your daughter involved. We prefer to deal with the county attorney for any sort of deal."

Mitch's voice grated raw and he leaned toward the two, "The correct word is kidnapped...because that is what happened."

Mr. Appleby flinched, "Okay, we'll use the word...kidnapped."

"Of course, there'll be two trials. One for attempted robbery and the other for kidnapping."

"Ah...hum... We want to ask for leniency for our clients if they turn over state's evidence and give the name of the person who hired them."

"Gentlemen, how thorough did you read the report? The county attorney may allow some concessions because the girls were not assaulted or beaten. However, they were starved for several days, drugged, given only a minimum amount of water, and tied up."

Mr. Appleby's Adam's apple bulged as he swallowed. "Ah... I realize..."

"Yes, we've read the report," Mr. Fitch interrupted. "I've got other cases to deal with and want to get this over as soon as possible. I've talked to my client and so has Appleby, and they're willing to talk. Both realize there's no way out of this one."

"Well, let's get the county attorney's office on the line and set up a time to meet. The person we think is involved can be held for forty-eight hours without charges, so I am in agreement to get this done now."

His heartbeat quickened as he dialed the county attorney's number.

Maybe we can get this solved today, and I can go home and feel at peace.

CHAPTER THIRTY-NINE

After meeting with Sam Harris, the county attorney, and Attorneys Fitch and Appleby, concessions were agreed upon for their testimonies. Affidavits signed by Rodney and Mac indicated Susan as the person who hired them to kidnap Natalia and Becca.

"What a day!" Mitch drew his hand across his forehead.

"I can't believe the BCA put everything aside to get the DNA test done on the wig," said Steve.

"Yeah, pays to know people at the BCA."

"You mean Norman Schmidt."

"He's been great helping us out many times. I think he still feels bad over what happened to Azalea."

"I remember. It wasn't that long ago. I guess it's déjà vu the BCA was so willing to help out."

"I'm glad this day is over."

"Well, not so fast. We need to make it official and book Susan on suspicion of kidnapping."

"I know. I wish the whole situation would go away, and I wouldn't need to face her again."

"Is there a soft spot in your heart for her yet?"

Mitch answered in an emphatic, "No! Maybe at one time, but there's nothing there anymore."

"Do you want me to handle the booking?"

"I think because she's my ex it would be wise. I want to talk to her one last time in the interrogation room to see if she'll admit to me why she did it."

A deputy knocked on Mitch's door and stuck his head in.

"Excuse me, Sheriff, I want to show you what we found close to the proposed drop off site for the money."

He turned, took a few steps, and returned with a rifle in a case.

"What on earth!" exclaimed Mitch.

Steve pulled a pair of gloves out of his pocket and picked up the rifle.

"Where exactly did you find this?"

The deputy glanced at Mitch. "You told us to watch the drop off site. Since no one showed up all day, my partner and I decided to walk around the area. I remembered a spot when I was a kid where you could look down on that site. We found this rifle behind a rock. If you would have made that drop off, someone would have waited for you and used this rifle."

Mitch's face blanched. He sat unmoved at his desk. The memory returned to him where Azalea mentioned that if something happened to him, Susan would get custody of Natalia.

Was this Susan's idea of getting custody?

―※―

They waited for Susan's attorney to arrive. They briefed him on the evidence they collected against Susan. However, they left out the information about the rifle until they could trace the serial number.

Steve notified the female jailor to bring Susan to the interrogation room. The attorney spent fifteen minutes with her. He stepped out of the room and walked back to Mitch's office.

Mitch, body taunt, drummed his fingers on the table, while Steve fidgeting with his pen doodled on the front of the file.

"Okay, Sheriff, I've talked to Susan. You can interview her now."

The three walked to the interrogation room. With no makeup and her hair limp, the orange jail suit made her face look washed out and not the vibrant woman they previously knew. This time she remained handcuffed. The female jailor stood by the door. When they entered, the jailor went to stand in the hall.

"Susan," Mitch began with reluctance, "we asked your attorney here because you refused to talk when we initially questioned you. Now we have sufficient evidence to hold you for kidnapping."

"Please explain to my client what evidence you have against her," her attorney demanded, even though he knew the answer.

Mitch looked toward Steve. "Detective Bishop will go over what we have."

"We have evidence from her two accomplices that Susan hired them to kidnap the girls for twenty-five thousand dollars each."

"My client claims she was set up. The two men wanted to get even with her because she wouldn't party with them. They also wanted to get even with Ms. Rose for hitting one of them with her car."

"Ohh…" Steve eyes widened as he held his lips tight before he burst out laughing. "Well, we have signed statements from each of them." He threw the file down on the table. "Plus, we have two other witnesses. Both girls recognized Susan delivering a car to the two accomplices even though she wore a wig to disguise herself. We also have the salesman at the car dealership in Douglas County where the vehicle was purchased identify her. Of course, she wore the wig when she purchased the car and used a stolen drivers' license from a fellow employee."

Her attorney gave Susan a long, hard cold look. "Susan, do you have anything to say?"

She pinched her lips together and shook her head.

Steve continued, "We also have the wig identified by the two girls as the wig worn by the woman delivering the car to the two accomplices. It was sent to the BCA for DNA identification. There were several strands of hair stuck in the wig and we removed several strands from the brush in her apartment for comparison. As a favor the BCA did a quick turnaround and found the hairs to be a match."

"Okay." He held up his hands. "I've advised my client of her rights, but it's up to her if she wants to give you a statement. The proof is on the prosecution. All I need to do is prove my client was nowhere near the scene when the children were kidnapped."

She sat in the chair and fairly snorted. A hysterical laugh burst out of her. "I wouldn't hurt my own daughter. I'm not a crazy woman."

The attorney groaned and crossed his arms. "I would like my client to take a mental evaluation test. I don't believe she's competent to stand trial."

Both Mitch and Steve rolled their eyes. "You can request anything you want, but it's not going to make a difference. She is still being booked for kidnapping," Mitch snapped.

The attorney put his hand on Susan's. "I'll get a psychiatrist here in the morning. Don't you worry."

"Before they take you away to booking, I have one question to ask you as Natalia's father. Why?"

"Why? Why?" She lifted the side of her mouth in a sneer. "You ask me why?" She showed her teeth. "Because I hate you."

Those words shot daggers into his body, but for his own good he needed to forgive her. He learned enough from Reverend Rafe to realize forgiveness was essential to move on with Azalea, Becca, and Natalia.

"I forgive you, Susan. I just hope someday you can forgive yourself for giving up a wonderful little girl. I only hope she can forgive you in time."

Susan closed her eyes and threw her head back. When she opened them, her orbs blazed demon-like into his. They shot darts of hate toward Mitch and she growled. "You're lucky they're still alive. I could have easily killed them... and you."

Mitch could feel the muscles tighten in his jaw from his clenched teeth. He hissed, "Are you giving up your right to remain silent? If so, we can continue this conversation."

"Grrrr... get out of my sight." She ran toward him with her nails outstretched ready to scratch his eyes. Steve stepped in front of her and knocked her off balance. She fell to the floor.

Her attorney sprang to her side to pick her up.

Steve stood between Mitch and Susan. "Mitch, I don't think it's a good idea for you to stay in here right now."

He turned on his heels, walked out, and slammed the door. He went to the video room where he could watch her through the window.

Why did she do a complete personality change? First, she says she wouldn't hurt her daughter. Then turns around and says she could have had them killed. I think she does need a psychiatric evaluation.

CHAPTER FORTY

Mitch arrived at Azalea's late in the evening.
"I saved dinner for you." She hugged him and laid her head on his chest.

"What a trying day." He dropped his utility belt on the kitchen table and folded his arms around her. The scent of warm vanilla filled his nostrils. His body relaxed. "We booked Susan on kidnapping charges." He nestled his face into her hair. "Um… you smell like cookies."

"Been baking and reading Psalms at the same time trying to find some comfort from all this."

"I told Susan I forgave her. She laughed at me."

Azalea pulled back. "She what?"

"Susan's attorney wants her evaluated by a psychiatrist. He believes she has some sort of personality disorder. She said in one breath she would never hurt Natalia. Then her eyes turned almost satanic, and she went into a rage and hissed about how easy it would be to kill them."

He failed to mention finding of the rifle behind the rocks.

"Oh, no!" Azalea covered her mouth in shock. "I know I need

to forgive, but the thought of our children being killed for money is beyond imagination."

"Tomorrow is Sunday. I know it'll be tough on the girls, but we need to sit down and tell them about Susan. Monday we'll schedule a press conference. All three are scheduled before the judge on Monday to plead. I'm sure Susan's attorney will ask for an extension until she can be evaluated."

"I'll be by your side on Monday. We need to stand as a family."

Reverend Rafe stood at the back of the church and welcomed his parishioners. Natalia and Becca ran up to him for a group hug. "I'm so glad you could make it to the service. My sermon will be complete with you both in attendance."

"Reverend Rafe," Becca smiled, "we want to thank God for Grace." His eyes twinkled as he smiled.

"Service is about to start. Steph's up front feeling a little tired this morning."

"We need to talk to both of you after the service about our wedding," announced Azalea. "We're moving the date up."

He winked at Mitch. "I've been waiting for you two to make that decision. Glad to hear it." He shook Mitch's hand. "Congratulations on getting her to the altar."

The praise team began to sing the first song while they continued to stand in the doorway with Rafe.

"I better get up front. See you after church."

Azalea loved to worship with song, and the Praise Team always picked such wonderful music. The four walked to the front of the church toward their favorite pew. Members in the congregation broke out in smiles as they passed, and some near the aisle stood to shake Mitch's hand and pat him on the back. When they entered the pew the song "Whom Shall I Fear, God of Angel Armies" by Chris Tomlin was being sung. Azalea raised her arms in worship.

Yes, Lord, I know who goes before me and stands behind me. Dear Lord, You are the God of angel armies keeping watch over us and always by our side.

Tears misted in Azalea's eyes. She knew the praise team gave worship in song to Grace who saved their girls and kept them safe. Rafe thought it a fitting song, as he, too, raised his voice in praise along with the entire congregation. Mitch, moved by the song, for the first time raised his arms in worship.

Rafe cleared his throat to give himself a moment to reflect on the emotions of the congregation. "I want to welcome each and every one of you here today, especially Azalea Rose and her daughter Becca and Mitch DeVries and his daughter Natalia. You all know what transpired this past week. So many of you volunteered to help search for the girls."

"I don't know the whole story, but I'm sure we'll find out within a short time. I do want to tell you about Angels among us. Open your Bibles to Hebrews Chapter Thirteen Verse Two." He paused while the congregation opened their Bibles. "The verse reads, 'Do not forget to entertain strangers, for by so doing some people have entertained angels without knowing it.'"

"That's exactly what happened to our two little girls sitting in front. After they escaped their captors an Angel who called herself Grace rescued both girls from the river and brought them to a cabin where they spent the night. In the morning the girls woke up with no one in the cabin, but there was sustenance for them to eat. They started on their journey home through the woods. Not knowing which direction to take, they trusted God to lead them. My wife and I were among the volunteers searching the county. We saw a bright light in the middle of the road and followed it like the Star of Bethlehem. With nothing in the sky to produce that sort of light, it soon disappeared. All of sudden we heard two tiny voices. The girls stepped out of the woods and ran toward us."

The members of the congregation murmured, many intakes of

breath and wide-eyes, but they remained silent and hooked on his every word.

"I can't tell you much more except to say God had His hand in their rescue. We are so grateful. Whether Grace was a real human being or an angel, it doesn't matter. To the girls she was their guardian angel. We praise God for all the little miracles in our lives. Every day some sort of little miracle can happen, and you don't recognize it as a miracle. We seem to only recognize the big miracles, but there are little ones if we just look around and keep our eyes open."

"Miracles are shoulder-taps from God, whispers…or even shouts…to remind us we're not alone. Miracles give birth to hope, a living hope."

CHAPTER FORTY-ONE

Six Weeks Later—the Middle of June

The pianist started to play the music for the wedding march. Mitch and Azalea wanted an intimate wedding with a few close friends and relatives in attendance.

Mitch's family was small with just one brother, his wife and two children, so there were more friends than family on his side. Azalea's family was larger, and they seemed to take up the majority in attendance. Azalea invited her staff: Karol, Barbara, Lexi, and Buttercup and their husbands as she considered them family. A few minutes before the ceremony started, Jennifer Williams walked in with her partner, Sydney Hines.

Azalea stood frozen in the small room in the back of the church. Her bouquet shook in her hands.

Becca and Natalia, in identical dresses, already started down the aisle spreading rose petals around them. Sunny, wearing a sleeveless sky-blue street length dress, turned and waved for them to hurry up. She followed the girls strolling at a slower than normal pace. Steve met her halfway and held out his arm.

Azalea's teeth started to chatter, and Steph turned to comfort Azalea.

"Come on now, Zalia. You know you've been waiting for this moment since Christmas. What can I do to calm you?"

"Noth...ing..." she chattered. "I...am...fine." They walked to the beginning of the aisle. The girls and Sunny stood in the front waiting for Steph and Azalea.

Mitch stood next to his brother, the best man. Rafe tapped his foot as he waited to perform the ceremony.

Her heart melted at the sight of Mitch's steady gaze. She kept her focus on him and knew him as her love, her future life.

An eight-month pregnant Steph took a few steps in her walk down the aisle when she felt a kick and grabbed her stomach.

"Are you okay?" Azalea whispered.

"Yeah, I'm fine. The little one kicked...hard."

Azalea giggled as she patted Steph's stomach. "Just don't go into labor during the ceremony."

Steph turned and rolled her eyes at the thought. She started down the aisle holding the flowers in an attempt to camouflage her pregnancy. It did not help...much.

Azalea spent the previous week agonizing over the flower arrangements and bridesmaids' bouquets. This was her wedding, and she wanted traditional but with a flair. She accomplished it with the girls wearing multicolored rose halo hairpieces and carried pink sweetheart roses. Sunny's and Steph's bouquets were deep pink roses draped with various greens.

Azalea decided to carry cream-colored roses with pink tips and streams of pink genestra stems to accent her ecru colored off-the-shoulder calf-length dress. It was an order-from-the-catalog dress, but it fit Azalea to perfection.

Her heart beat so fast she thought she could hear it above the music as she strolled to the music. Once she arrived at the front of the church Mitch stepped next to her to assist her up the last step. All fears and nervousness left as soon as he touched her. He smiled, and his nostrils flared.

He's nervous, too. Whew! I'm glad I'm not the only one.

Reverend Rafe began, "We are gathered here to witness the marriage of Azalea Jasmine Rose and Mitchell Arthur DeVries."

It's all Azalea heard as her head spun. She heard Rafe talking but was not taking much in until he asked Azalea to read her vows. She spent the last several weeks trying to think of the right words to say to Mitch, but nothing seemed appropriate. She threw away all her attempts and decided to wing it.

"Mitch, I don't remember the day or the time when I finally admitted to myself that I loved you more than life itself, but I do remember waking up in the hospital bed and hearing your words of love. At that moment I knew I had loved you for a long time. You have proven it over and over again that we can make a life together which includes God in our family, and I will be so proud to be your wife. I promise to love you in sickness and health, and to forever be by your side as your partner. I promise to be a good mother to Natalia and love her as my own."

"Azalea, you've been the love of my life for a long time. At Christmas time I thought I lost you forever. My life would not be the same without you by my side. I take you and Becca as my family. I've waited a long time to find you. God brought you back to me. You are my wonderful miracle, and I will love you and take care of you as long as I have breath within me."

Rafe cleared his throat. Watching his best friends tying the knot made him close to speechless. "Do you, Mitchell Arthur DeVries, take Azalea Jasmine Rose as your lawful wedded wife?"

"I do."

Rafe cleared his voice again as his eyes turned briefly to his wife who stood close by and remembered their wedding day. He could see her eyes squeeze together as she clutched her baby bump while she held two bouquets.

"Do you Azalea Jasmine Rose take Mitchell Arthur DeVries as your lawful wedded husband?"

Azalea smirked, "Of course, I do."

"I now pronounce you husband and wife. What God has joined together let no one put asunder."

Azalea's radiant face turned up to meet Mitch's eyes. Mitch did not hesitate to wrap his arms around her. With a soft, "*at last*", he settled his mouth on hers. She returned the kiss until Rafe cleared his throat again.

He whispered, "I think you two need to get a room."

Mitch and Azalea chuckled as their foreheads touched. The minister had a sense of humor.

The pianist played as the couple started down the aisle with eyes only for each other.

The attendants followed with Rafe close behind. He wanted to check on his wife to make sure she felt okay before they attended the reception at the River View Hotel.

"I'm fine, Rafe. Don't worry about me. I've been getting these little twinges all day with the baby kicking. A whole month left before the baby comes."

Forty guests arrived at the hotel. Chrys and her husband, Taylor, played the hosts. They enlisted the help of their two unruly boys to greet the guests and escort each one to their table.

A local radio host also doubled as DJ on the side started the music as soon as the guests finished their meal. He started out with slow ballads, so the wedding couple and the attendants could get in a dancing mood.

Sunny pestered Steve into trying a waltz while the girls got Bernadette and Tom out on the floor.

Halfway into the night the DJ put on the Chicken Dance, and they all gathered in a circle snapping their fingers and wriggling their butts to the music. Afterwards he put on some old-time rock-and-roll music.

"I'm bushed," admitted Azalea, while she fanned her face with her hand. "Those dances are for the younger generation."

"Depends on who you consider the younger generation. Did you see your mom and Tom out there trying to outdo the grandkids?"

They stopped to enjoy the crowd.

The DJ started a slow dance and most of the young people left the floor. Mitch reached for Azalea's arm. "Now is the time when I can hold you close until we get to our honeymoon."

"You've kept our honeymoon a secret. I didn't even know what to pack."

"Since your mom is staying with the girls, I didn't want to leave them too long, so I booked us at the Grand Hotel on Mackinaw Island in Michigan."

"I remember going there as a child. I'm excited to go back."

Rafe and Steph waltzed close by them.

"Doing well, Steph, considering Rafe has to hold you at arm's length."

"Ha. Ha. Very funny," she chided back. "Wait until this happens to you."

Both their eyes twinkled with humor as they looked at each other, then laughed as they turned toward Steph and Rafe. "We never discussed adding to our family," said an amused Azalea.

"I never got a chance to dance with the bride," said Rafe. "Do you mind switching partners?"

Mitch and Azalea separated ready to switch. All of sudden, a gush of water flooded the floor. Steph's eyes crackled with emotion as she looked at Rafe and held her baby bump. "My water broke."

"Oh, my gosh! Steph, you're going into labor," exclaimed Azalea.

Rafe's expression was priceless as he stared at the floor. "Oh, my. Oh, my. What do we do?"

Azalea laughed. "Rafe, hold it together. First of all, you better take Steph home and start counting the minutes between contractions. Remember your baby classes. Don't lose it now."

"I've never been a father before. I guess I'm panicking here."

He helped his wife off the dance floor.

"Mitch." Azalea's face turned toward him with a worried frown. "I'm going to make sure Steph gets to the car okay. Would you find someone to take care of the floor?"

"Sure, you go ahead. I'm no good at this baby business."

Azalea met them at the front door. Rafe pranced around nervously. "Would you stay with Steph while I get the car?"

"Of course."

"I'm already having contractions," said Steph after Rafe left them. "Started this morning, but I blew it off as nervous energy. I can feel now they're a lot harder. Ouch…oooh." She grabbed her stomach. "And more uncomfortable."

"Relax, Steph. You need to go home, grab your overnight bag, and head to the hospital. Maybe they can stop the contractions at the hospital, but since your water broke… I don't know. The baby may be here sooner than you think."

Rafe pulled up to the curb. Azalea waved. "We'll stop by after the reception is over. I'm excited for you two."

She turned to go back into the hotel.

The baby's a month early. Not a good sign. I didn't want to worry Steph.

CHAPTER FORTY-TWO

The DJ quit playing at ten and the wedding party started to wind down. Since Steph and Rafe caused the most excitement for the evening, the remainder of the reception appeared dull compared to going into labor.

Bernadette sidled over to Mitch and Azalea. "I think Tom and I will take the girls back to my house for tonight. You two need your privacy. I'm sure you're not going to leave for your honeymoon until you check on Steph and Rafe."

"Certainly not." Her eyes pleaded with Mitch. "We can't leave until we know Steph and the baby are okay."

"You're right. It's one thing I love about you—always concerned about others. Let's head over to the hospital and give them support."

"Thanks, Mom." She reached her arms around her mother. "When are you and Tom going make an official announcement?" Bernadette blushed as Tom overheard Azalea and walked over to put his arm around Bernadette's waist.

"As soon as Bernie gives the word. I'm ready right now."

"Bernie? No one has ever called you anything but Bernadette."

Bernadette leaned into Tom's arms. "I kinda like the nickname. It makes me feel special." Her Carnation Red smile widened as she turned her head toward Tom.

"I'm happy for both of you. With all the commotion the past several months, I've not had much time to get to know you, Tom. I hope to change that when we return."

"Me, too."

⁂

Azalea still despised the antiseptic smell of the hospital and the memories of her hospital stay over the holidays. By the time they arrived at Steph's room, the smell started to dissipate.

Steph was in her last stages of labor with contractions coming minutes apart. "They said I'm almost dilated and the baby *is* coming. There's nothing they can do to stop labor now. I'm worried the baby's too early."

Azalea held one hand and Rafe the other as another contraction wracked her body. "AH!" She clenched her teeth, tightened her grip on their hands, and bore down. "I want to push."

"No, not yet," hovered Rafe. He reached for a cool washcloth and wiped Steph's face.

Azalea tried to make light of the pain and groaned. "My hand will never be the same again after that grip. Hope I can still make flower arrangements." The three smiled at the humor. "Seriously, Steph, I know you and Rafe pray all the time. The baby will be fine. Becca came two weeks early and look at her."

The maternity nurse walked in the room dressed in a surgical gown. "Let's check your dilation. If everyone would leave the room until I'm finished with the exam, it would be appreciated."

The exam only took a few minutes. The nurse opened the door and let the three back in.

"I think it's time to take you into delivery. An incubator is ready to receive your baby, because it's a month early." Rafe's face paled. "Reverend, if you're going into the delivery room, you'll need to get surgical scrubs on."

"Okay," he squeaked. His face turned from pale to a slight shade of green. "Let's go," he said in a less than enthusiastic voice and with his hand on his stomach.

"Rafe, everything is going to be fine." Mitch patted him on the back. "You look a little green around the gills. Steph is going to need you in there."

Gulp. "Yes, I know. I'll get my act together."

"We'll be in the waiting room across the hall. We don't want to miss this big moment with you guys," said Mitch.

Still dressed in their wedding clothes, Mitch and Azalea waited for Steph to deliver the baby. After pacing the floor for fifteen minutes, Mitch left and returned with two coffees.

"It may be a while." He sat down and put an arm around his new wife. "What a way to spend our honeymoon night."

Azalea smirked and almost blew coffee out her nose. "At least we're together… and right now alone."

He gathered her up so she lay halfway across his chest and his eyes bore into hers. He passed taunting little kisses starting at her eyes, down her face, and ending up in an explosion of passion on her lips.

Her breathing stopped during the kiss. When it ended, she inhaled a long breath and sighed. "Ummm. You keep doing that to me Mr. DeVries, we might end up with an addition to the family."

"I wouldn't mind in the least. You're right. We never did talk about children. If it happens, it would be wonderful to have a child or children together."

"Good thing we're moving into a big house. We can fill it to the brim. Also, Steph and Rafe's baby needs a playmate."

"The house should be ready to move in within a few weeks. The basic remodeling is almost done. The girls will have their own room, and we'll have our suite for privacy."

"Sounds like heaven. I hope my house sells soon. Jake brought some people over yesterday."

"It will. Don't worry. If nothing else, we can rent it out."

Several hours later Rafe ran out of the delivery room and removed his mask. "It's a girl!" he shouted with a big smile on his face. "She's the cutest little thing, and she weighed in at six pounds on the nose. The doctor said if Steph carried it to full term it would have been over eight pounds." Rafe beamed with pride. "She's red and screaming already, but she's ours. The doctor says she's a perfect little girl." His eyes looked up. "God be praised."

"God is good all the time," replied Azalea.

Mitch followed with, "All the time God is good."

Tears welled up in Azalea's eyes. "I'm so happy for you and Steph. It's a dream come true for both of you. God has truly blessed you."

"Yes, He is good. Thank you. The baby will need to spend some time in the incubator to make sure she's breathing okay. We won't be able to take her home until they make sure her lungs are developed enough."

When Steph returned to the room, she reached for Rafe, and they clung to each other. Mitch and Azalea stood close to the bed and without speaking admired the couple's love for one another.

"She's so beautiful, isn't she?" commented Steph, as the nurse wheeled the incubator with the baby into the room. She started to plug everything into the wall for the baby. "Do you think we could hold her for a few minutes while you hook everything up?"

"Sure, I don't see any harm. The baby is breathing well on her own, but this is just a precaution." She opened the incubator and lifted the baby. Steph beamed with pride as the nurse placed the baby in her arms. She rocked her back and forth and made little cooing sounds. "Do you want to hold her, Rafe?"

He took the baby from Steph and placed his hand on the baby's chest. "Lord, God, thank you for this wonderful little bundle. We give her to You, Lord. Someday she will praise You like we praise You."

"Have you picked a name yet?" inquired Azalea.

"Yes, we did." Rafe handed the baby back to Steph. She opened the blanket, so Mitch and Azalea could get a close look at the black-haired little girl with dark chocolate eyes. She let out a yell when the blanket was removed. "She's our little angel," his eyes twinkled.

Steph's eyes held Azalea's as they waited to find out the name.

"We decided since she's our little angel, we will name her Grace. After all Nat and Becca were saved by Grace, and we're sure she was an angel sent to watch over the girls. We hope she'll watch over our little Grace."

THE END

NOTE TO THE READER

Thank you for reading *Saved by Grace, Book Three,* in the *River Falls Mystery Series*. Even though River Falls, Minnesota, is a figment of my imagination, it is also an accumulation of the small towns where I lived or visited in my past. All small towns have their eccentricities in their traditions, as well as the families who live in them.

If you haven't read *Secrets in the High Rise, Book One*, or *No Reasonable Doubt, Book Two*, I urge you to get a copy to tie the entire series together.

It's now at this point that I admit many of the miracles in all three books are true actual miracles which took place at some point in time and told to me either in person or from someone I know. I changed the names to protect those who wanted privacy.

I started writing because of my inability to find many books where the main characters weren't all in their teens or early twenties. My books are considered cozy mysteries and were created for the adult reader who appreciates a mystery, romance, or thriller, along with a little bit of humor.

Most of my characters are not young, but experienced in life, and have their share of baggage. Even though my books are mysteries, they are filled with love and compassion, forgiveness, and miracles.

Should there be a fourth book in the series? I could go on with the series as there are still characters in the books who need completion in their lives. If you would like to learn more about River Falls, I would consider writing another in the series, but right now I'm moving on to another series called "*Hill Country Dreams*".

I apologize in advance if you find any errors in the book, such as grammar and punctuation. The book has been reviewed and edited many times, and it's human error if we missed anything.

Please view my website (https://jarost-author.com) for future books and their launching dates. Hopefully, my readers will leave a positive review and feedback on Amazon. I can also be reached on my Facebook page at J. A. Rost and email at booksbyjarost@outlook.com.

God bless y'all,
J. A. Rost

ABOUT THE AUTHOR

I was born and raised in the small town of Alexandria, Minnesota. My interest in writing began in junior high school. I initially gave up my love of writing to raise a family and continue in other careers, but my imagination could not be stopped. I now reside in the Hill Country of Texas with my spouse and two dogs, Lightning and Storm, but continue to spend part of the summer in Minnesota promoting my books and visiting relatives and friends.

I enjoy writing for various magazines and online websites with my short stories, fiction and non-fiction. Even though I often write under different pen names, I decided to become an Indie author in 2017 and publish the River Falls Mystery Series.

The first book of my new series *Hill Country Dreams* is scheduled to be released in 2019. Hannah Kuhlman is a police officer in the Austin suburbs who secretly witnesses her boss socializing with several members of the Mexican Mafia. Fearing she is being watched, she takes a leave from work. While running from danger she falls and wakes up with a Texan Ranger hovering over her. Hannah learns she has time traveled back to the year 1895. She is taken to the small town of Fredericksburg where she meets her great-great Oma and Opa. She learns the life and death struggles of the early pioneers and a better understanding of her German heritage. When Indians kidnap several women, including Hannah and her future Oma, things look bleak. Where is her Texas Ranger and Opa when they're needed? Will Hannah be able to return to present time after she loves someone from the past?

Made in the USA
San Bernardino, CA
25 May 2020